The Barrier

Book One–Discoveries

By G. S. Gates

To Owen

From Gary

Eloquent Books
New York, New York

Copyright 2006 by G.S.Gates.
All rights reserved.
No part of this book may be reproduced or transmitted in any form
or by any means, graphic, electronic, or mechanical, including photocopying,
recording, taping, or by any information storage retrieval system, without the
permission, in writing, from the publisher.
This is a fictional book based on fictional characters and events.

℃

Eloquent Books
New York, New York

Eloquent Books
An imprint of AEG Publishing Group
845 Third Avenue, 6th Floor - 6016
New York, NY 10022
www.EloquentBooks.com

ISBN: 978-1-60693-854-6
SKU: 1-60693-854-1

Printed in the United States of America
Book design by Wendy Arakawa

DEDICATION

To all those who have encouraged and waited so long.
Thank You.

Chapter 1

Melina Wilson ducked and fell to the right in a rolling dive to avoid the hissing laser bolt as it came hurtling towards her. As she did so, her left leg came up and the beam of protons changed colour from green to red as it hit her boot.

"Damn," she thought, as she twisted around to get a better position to fire her own weapon. Lying prone, she lifted her laser and fired, all in one movement. The beam hit the emblem of the Evil Empire, dead centre of her assailant's chest. The figure dressed in white dissolved in an explosion of white light.

"Hah!" Mel exclaimed. "Take that, you bully, for attacking poor defenceless heroines." Scrambling to her feet, she dived full length behind a pile of packing cases, noting as she did so that she felt heavier than before.

"Computer," Mel's voice sounded unnaturally loud in the confines of her helmet. "Has the gravity been increased?"

"Gravity has been increased to one point two five Gs," the computer replied in its low, steady tones.

"Why?"

"You have sustained damage to you're left foot. You're mobility has been compromised."

"Rubbish. It was just a glancing blow." Mel's voice took on a petulant note.

"In a true combat situation, your leg would have been stunned for some time. Do you wish to override?"

Mel snorted. Do you wish to override? Do you wish to cheat, it meant.

"No. But, I think you're wrong."

"I am not programmed to make mistakes," came the soft reply.

Mel sighed. Computers were supposed to be unemotional, but that definitely sounded smug.

She shook herself mentally and went back to concentrating on the task at hand. She looked cautiously around the pile of cases to see what was happening.

This simulation was of a small spaceport on a desert planet. Some thirty metres in front of her was an Evil Empire combat shuttle. On a ramp leading up to an airlock were six more storm troopers, all holding laser rifles. Behind them was another figure dressed all in black, and towering over the others by at least a metre.

Mel's heart began to beat faster. She recognised the taller figure. This was the leader of the Evil Empire; the ultimate object of the game was to kill the leader, thus freeing the known universe. This was the first time she had got this far.

But how to win? Pick off his bodyguards, one by one? No, she was already injured. One more hit would put her out of the game altogether. Do or die, she decided. Rush the shuttle: kill the leader before the bodyguard could react. Decision made, she acted upon it.

Jumping out from behind her cover, she started her run at the shuttle, firing wildly as she went. The extra gravity slowed her down, but two troopers fell to her erratic aim before the others turned their guns her way. Their shooting proved to be less erratic, and three bolts of white lightning hit her. The gravity jumped to three Gs and Mel's body hit the ground with a thump that knocked the air from her body.

A bleep sounded in her helmet. "You have been disintegrated. Programme terminated. Do you wish to save?"

Mel groaned softly and let her head fall back onto the floor as the simulation dissolved around her, leaving just a bare, metal room. "Yes," she groaned. "Save, damn you, Melina four."

As she lay on the floor getting her breath back, Mel heard the sound of slow clapping behind her. Pushing herself up into a sitting position, she pulled off her helmet and shook free her long, dark hair. Looking round, she saw the slim figure of Myan Sexton standing in the doorway clapping slowly, and smiling.

She walked forward and stood over her friend. Looking down, she said, "Well done, Mel. You've reached the last level, but I don't think a suicide attack is the way to win this game."

"You've a better idea?" Mel replied grumpily.

Myan tapped the side of her head with an elegantly long finger. "Use your head, girlfriend. Outthink them. Your problem has always been that you act first and think later."

Mel wriggled as she stripped out of her games overalls. "A

surprise frontal attack can often work."

Myan gave a short, derisive laugh. "Not against six well armed bodyguards."

Mel smiled back at her friend, her frustration disappearing as it often did around Myan. They had been friends for most of their lives, from pre-school to college. They tended to balance each other out: Mel forthright, impatient, and direct, and Myan thoughtful, diplomatic, and forgiving. Even their appearances complimented each other: Mel tall and dark, Myan blond and petite.

Mel scrunched up the overalls and threw them into the recycler.

"So, have you come to pit yourself against the Evil Empire?"

Myan held up her hands in mock horror. "No. I leave that sort of game to the boys and macho girls, like you." She giggled as Mel pulled a face at being labeled macho. "I wanted to know if you and Aaron would like to join Tony and me at the theatre tonight. There's a retrospective of Tom Stoppard plays being performed."

Mel sniffed and stretched her self to her full five foot eleven inches. "There is no 'me and Aaron.' Two dates with him was more than enough. If I wasn't bored to death by him banging on about the 'simple beauty' of mathematics, then I was trying to fight him off. He was like an octopus with tentacles everywhere. No, he's been dumped, literally as well as figuratively."

Myan groaned. "Not another boyfriend beaten up."

"I do not beat up boyfriends. It's just that some of them

don't recognise the word no, and then I feel I have to practice some of those judo throws we were taught in class."

"Well, you could come on your own. I'm sure Tony wouldn't mind."

"I'm sure he would," Mel said, smiling. "Thanks, but no thanks. I've still got my sculpture to finish for the end of term exhibition, and I'm supposed to be having dinner with my father. The first time for months, I might add."

"Well, politicians are very busy at the moment," Myan said, diplomatic to the end.

Mel smiled and took her arm, leading her out of the simulation booth. They both waved at fellow classmates pulling on games overalls, getting ready to run their own programmes.

Turning to Myan, Mel sighed. "I know that my father's busy; the debate on the Barrier takes up a lot of his time. As vice-president, it's his responsibility to see all the debates go smoothly and every Warden gets a chance to have his or her say. It's just sometimes I wish he was a medical technician, or something that had more regular hours." Her face took on a more wistful look. "I remember, when I was younger, he would always come and look in on me. Now I don't see him for days, sometimes."

"Well," Myan said, squeezing her arm, "you're a big girl now. Maybe he's just trying to give you some space."

"Maybe he is. Have fun at the theatre, and, of course, have even more fun afterwards."

Mel's jibe that Myan and Tony's relationship had entered a closer phase was rewarded by a red flush spreading across Myan's face as they separated to go their different ways.

Shouldering her bag, she went through the glass entrance of the university building into the permanent twilight that was London. Waiting for her was one of the government's official cars, as there was every night.

The car purred almost silently through the London streets, its electric motor singing quietly. Mel sat in the back appreciating the good side of being the only daughter of the Vice-President of the Republic of London.

There was no doubt she was well protected. When the Barrier around London had been first energised, some two hundred and fifty years ago, there had been incidents of terrorism and attacks from those left outside. These had stopped after a radius of ten miles around London had been forcibly cleared, and all had been quiet for some two hundred years. Then, ten years ago, the president and Mel's father had suggested that the Republic might remove the Barrier and rejoin the rest of England.

A hot debate took place and, shortly after, the Isolationist movement sprang up. At first, they contented themselves with lobbying Wardens and holding demonstrations. But then a group of more radical members had tried to kidnap Mel. An alert security officer saved her, and the would-be kidnappers had all been killed in the attempt. Since then, she had always been guarded.

Mel had rebelled against this cosseting only once. At the age of twelve, following a lecture on the Barrier at school, she had been dared to go with some friends and touch the Barrier. Giving her escort the slip, she had gone to Newgate to see the Barrier. All she could remember of the trip now was that, when she had touched the Barrier, her hair had stood on end and her skin tingled. That and, when they had returned, she found her home in an uproar, with her father ready to mobilise the whole of London to find her.

The look of relief, and then anger, and then relief again on his face, and the way that he held her so tightly, had made her realise how badly she had frightened him. She never tried to lose her protection again.

Mel settled into her restricted lifestyle and, at the age of sixteen, entered the university to study art. This was one of the rare bones of contention between her and her father; she felt that maybe he had wanted her to follow him into politics, but Mel had wanted to follow in the footsteps of her dead mother. Probably, she thought later, to feel closer to a woman she never had the chance to know.

Her mother had died at the age of thirty-two, when the direct guidance system had failed in the Holborn Road and an automated delivery truck had knocked her off the bike she was riding.

She had been killed instantly.

Mel was only six, and suddenly motherless in a world where the death of one so young was almost unheard of. But she was the daughter of an unusual man, who spent the next twelve years being both father and mother to his only child.

When she reached her teenage years, she had started to wonder about what her mother had been like, and began to extensively research her life. Discovering that she had been an artist, Mel had decided to see if she was also artistically inclined, and enrolled in a five-year art course at the University of London.

She was now at the end of her fourth year and, at almost twenty years of age, had grown both physically and mentally. She was popular enough with her fellow students, although, apart from Myan, she had few close friends.

Male relationships were even fewer. She had a certain celebrity, being the daughter of the vice-president; people trying to get close to him would try first to get close to her, and after a couple of boys she dated proved to be more interested in being seen with her than being with her, she became a bit cynical about relationships.

This bothered her very little, as she knew there was plenty of time, and at this time in her life she was more interested in her growing career. Her efforts in class were not going unappreciated. Her class tutor had complimented her on her painting of the Barrier, remarking that she had a good eye for detail. She was also preparing a sculpture for the end of term exhibition. It was to be a nude work and the model was going to be herself.

Mel had no intention of warning her father about the sculpture. He would see it when it was unveiled at the end of term. Simply titled, "Self Portrait in Nude by Melina Conner Wilson," she hoped the sculpture would throw her father out of this melancholy mood he had been in the last few weeks.

Arriving home at the apartment she shared with her father in the Parliament block, she ate a light snack from the food dispenser and, after putting the plate and utensils into the recycler, Mel made straight for the room she had converted into a studio.

Activating the palm lock on the door and locking it behind her, she went to the drawer where she kept the bug-detecting device she had sweet-talked a young Protector into getting for her. She still thought of Richard occasionally, even though he had been promoted and reassigned over a year ago. After all, he had been her first and, so far, only, lover. It was inevitable, really; when Second Lieutenant Richard Downing had been assigned to her and her father, he was by far the youngest and best looking.

He was tall, blonde, and well built, and they had been lovers for over half a year. He had told her that every room in the apartment was bugged, for her and her father's own protection, of course. So to keep her privacy in the studio, she had talked Richard into getting her the de-bugging device.

She smiled fondly to herself as she thought of Richard and how he thought that he had seduced her, when in fact it was Mel who had done all the seduction. He had not really stood a chance against Mel when she had decided it was time to lose her virginity. Mel had been sorry when he had chosen to take his promotion to the Presidential Guard; she soon realised that she had not actually loved him, but she missed him just the same.

Passing the detector around the room, it stayed quiet, as it had done for the last month. It appeared that security was getting fed up, at last, with losing bugs and cameras every time they installed them in her studio.

Setting up the full-length mirror she had replicated, she stripped off her university coverall and posed naked in front of the mirror. Turning sideways, she looked from her breasts to the breasts on the sculpture with a critical eye. It was surprising, Mel thought, the over-inflated sense one had of one's self. The breasts on the sculpture were far too big and out of proportion with the rest of the body. Still naked, she picked up her sonic chisel and began to remodel the offending glands.

It was some hours later that the insistent bleeping of the intercom finally broke her concentration. Mel glanced up at the wall clock, its red glowing figures showing that over four hours had passed since she had started work. The trouble with modern technology was that sometimes it did too much. As the natural light outside had died, the artificial light inside had compensated. Mel had not noticed the difference.

Stretching like a cat, Mel went over to the com-unit; remembering just in time her state of undress, she selected sound only.

"Yes!" She instantly regretted the sharp sound in her voice but, like most artists, she hated being interrupted when she was working.

"And a good evening to you as well, my dear," came the reply. The voice was deep, resonant and laced with good humour. "I wondered if I might have the pleasure of your company at dinner. Or were you planning an all night session, working on your creation? Which I might point out that I have yet to see."

"Daddy!" Mel felt suitably guilty, but still slightly irked that her work had been halted. "Let me get a shower and I'll be right out."

Washing off the accumulated dust as quickly as possible, she wrapped a towel around her hair and, getting a colourful caftan from the replicator, she joined her father in the main room.

He stood with his back to her, looking out the large picture window, which showed panoramic views of the Thames at Westminster. He turned, smiling as Mel came up behind him and she reached up on tiptoe to kiss him on the cheek.

Although almost five foot eleven inches herself, he was taller still. It had been said that one of Melville Wilson's most noticeable attributes was his imposing presence. Six foot three inches tall, and wide of shoulder, he was forty-five years old, with just enough grey in his hair to make him look distinguished. He also carried the aura of a person whom people immediately trusted. Recent polls had shown that he was more popular than the president.

Mel picked up the meals from the dispenser and brought them to the dinning table. They sat down and Melville picked up a fork, saying, "Well, when do I get to see this creation of yours?"

"You will just have to wait for the exhibition like everyone else," Mel replied with a teasing smile on her face.

Her father shook his head slowly. "The older you get, the more you look like your mother," he said softly.

They ate in silence for a few moments. Mel could feel her father studying her. He laid down his fork and spoke. "We have never talked a lot about your mother, have we?"

Mel looked up, surprise and not a little hope written on her face. Her father had always been reluctant to talk about her mother; she knew that, even now, he still missed her. "Well, I've researched her public life quite a lot. I know how talented she was as an artist; a lot of her work is on display at the new Tate." She paused and stirred her food with her fork, "But you knew her best. What was she really like?"

The question came out almost as a plea. For many years now, Mel had been asking herself a lot of "what if" questions. What if her mother had not died; would she have liked her? How different would her upbringing have been? Would she have thrown herself into her art the way she had? What changes would there have been in her life?

Melville got up and fetched coffee from the dispenser. He sat back down, and looked at Mel over his steepled fingers. He stayed silent for a moment, collecting his thoughts before he spoke.

"Well, as I said, you are beginning to look more like her every day. She was the sweetest, kindest person I ever knew. She also had boundless energy and an impulsive streak that could be hell to live with. Once she latched onto an idea or started a project, it was the devil's own job to get her off it. She would work all night in her studio, take two hours sleep, and emerge the next day bright eyed and bushy tailed to do another marathon session in her studio. You're not quite as bad as that, but I bet you could be if I let you."

He took a sip of coffee and leaned back in his chair, a slight smile on his face as he thought back. "Practically the only time she did slow down was when she had you. Even then, she went about the birth in her own fashion: one day into labour, the next day you were born, the day after that she was back at work."

Mel sat engrossed as her father talked about her mother in such an uninhibited manner. She knew from her own researches that Joanna Martin was reputed to be the most beautiful woman of her generation.

CHAPTER 1

Many had vied for her attentions, but it was Melville Wilson, then a rising star in politics, who had won her heart. By London's standard, they were young when they had married at twenty-five. With an increased life expectancy, thirty-five was the average age for couples to marry. Mel had been born two years later.

After Mel's birth, Joanna Wilson had produced some of her best work. It was almost as if she had known time was short.

After the accident, Melville had thrown himself into his work, Mel had not felt neglected. She and her father had spent a lot of time together, and he had tried to be both mother and father. This had left Mel with a very masculine outlook on life, although a succession of nannies had helped.

Since those tragic days, Melville had risen through the ranks with his childhood friend, Terrence Charterhouse, to become Vice-President of London to Charterhouse's President. Now they were working on London's greatest challenge: the removal of the Barrier.

When the Barrier had been energised almost two hundred and fifty years ago, the population in London had numbered around a million. Within a hundred years, that number had doubled, and experts were predicting that within another fifty years, room would run out behind the Barrier.

The first government of London quickly passed a law restricting couples to only two children but, even so, there was still an acute housing shortage. As always, necessity, being the mother of invention, brought an answer.

As buildings could not expand outwards, they had to go

upwards. Whole areas of London were razed and, in the spaces, giant, square buildings were constructed. At the centre of these squares, they built factories and offices. Those who worked in these complexes were allocated living space in the surrounding buildings, cutting out the need for travel.

As a person aged and then retired, they would move into accommodations around the medical centres, close to the doctors and nurses. Members of the government and civil servants lived in units surrounding the parliament building, one of the few original London buildings to escape being demolished. Other apartment blocks surrounded other surviving monuments such as Buckingham Palace, St. Paul's cathedral, and the British Museum. The security forces and general technical staff occupied these blocks.

But space was finite. Medicine improved and people's life expectancy had increased to over a hundred and thirty years. Two events in the last hundred years had eased the problem slightly. One was the development of the food replicator, which took a base product made from an aquatic plant grown in the Thames and rearranged its molecules into tasty, recognisable food, full of necessary proteins. This had freed up the whole Northside of the Thames for living accommodations, as there was no longer any need for agricultural land.

Secondly, a hundred years ago, another law was passed restricting couples to only one child. But more recently, experts were becoming worried that the gene pool was decreasing, and were predicting that the ratio of abnormal births would increase. And the ratio was already too high.

CHAPTER 1

So the current government began to look at extending the Barrier outwards. The reason for the Barrier had become outdated. Its original purpose, to protect London from an increasingly hostile country, appeared to be no longer necessary. There had been no attacks from the outside for over a hundred and fifty years; there had not even been any contact with the outside world for over fifty.

The event that had necessitated the construction of the Barrier had been the so-called Third World War. This was thought to have started in the Middle East, after Syria, in desperate economic trouble and with its people rebelling, had attacked Israel with nuclear weapons. They had hoped the rest of the Arab states would back them against the old Zionist enemy and distract its people at home with a good old-fashioned Holy war.

It sadly misjudged the Israelis. They were not about to let the others in the Middle East gang up on them. They retaliated, not only against Syria, but also against all their old enemies. The United Nations tried to step in and stop the war, but proved to be too weak and divided.

A full-scale nuclear war ensued.

It lasted only seven days but, in the end, turned the whole of the Middle East into a radioactive wasteland.

Although the West would have suffered a nuclear winter, actual destruction would have been avoided if radical Moslems had not organised every independence and terrorist group in the world to act when Syria attacked Israel. A new breed of nuclear bombs, no larger than a suitcase, was developed, and then planted in every major city in Europe, Asia, Africa, and the Americas.

Billions died instantly, millions more from radiation poisoning. Law and order broke down all over the world.

The computers controlling America and Russia's vast armoury of nuclear weapons decided that their countries were under attack and, when they received no counter-orders, the leading military and civilian personnel having been killed by the city bombs, they launched an all-out attack. The weapons did the job they were designed for. They devastated the enemy. The childish boast of, "if I can't have it, neither will you" came oh so true.

Britain got away fairly lightly at first. Devices were placed in all major cities, but only three exploded. Manchester, Coventry, and Middlesborough were all destroyed. The areas around them turned into radiation hot spots.

The reduction in America and Russia's nuclear armouries had meant that their missiles were pointed at each other. But, of course, the skies darkened and a twenty-year winter set in.

With millions dead or dying, the emergency services soon failed. The government transferred it seat of power to the Lake District and tried to keep control. Thousands of refugees from the destroyed cities headed north and south.

Faced with a sudden influx of people seeking safety, Scotland and Wales closed their borders and declared full independence. Soon after, London invoked an ancient charter granted to them by William the Conqueror, and declared independence as well.

At first, this declaration had little affect on the thousands of refugees streaming into London from the north, until a scientist called David Baser developed a practical energy force field. Station posts were placed around London and, less than two months after the war ended; they were energised to envelop a large area of London.

The force field, or Barrier, as it became known, was a masterful feat of engineering. It was shaped like a dome with an apex of a thousand feet; from the inside, it blurred the vision like a heat haze. From the outside, it shimmered and was almost opaque. It allowed the entrance of air and rain, but anything larger trying to enter was met with an increasing electric shock.

There were three entrances set into the Barrier. One in the north, one in the south, and a third in the roof of the dome. For a short while, helicopters used this entrance, until fuel for these vehicles ran out.

The new government of the Republic of London soon realised that, while they had something others did not, they would always be under threat. So they traded with other surviving cities, swapping their Barrier technology for supplies, building materials, and key personnel. Having a head start on the new technology, London prospered where others failed. In all, Newcastle, Birmingham, Liverpool, Shrewsbury, and York erected barriers and declared independence. Within fifty years, only London, Birmingham, and Newcastle's barriers had not failed. A rumour had swept the city some years ago that Newcastle's barrier had fallen.

This left the rest of the country to fend for itself. Top military and police personnel were the first to be invited behind the Barrier, to handle security. They assisted with weeding out the uneducated, the elderly, the sick, and the indolent. These undesirables were ejected and replaced with people who could prove that they would be useful to the new order that was emerging. Once these new citizens and their families were settled in the New London, and while the rest of England and Wales reverted to the Middle Ages, the fortified city moved into a new technological era.

Meanwhile, the rest of the world had its own problems. Before communications had failed completely, it had been learnt that Europe had broken down into a collection of republics and principalities, mostly fighting amongst themselves.

Large parts of the U.S.A. had been rendered uninhabitable by the war. The more remote areas, like Alaska and the mountainous states on the Canadian border, declared independence, and little more was heard from them.

Very little was known about South America, Africa, and Asia, as contact was lost almost immediately after the war. With the loss of oil from the Middle East, sea and air travel soon ground to a halt. Satellite communications were knocked out in the war between the super-powers and, overnight, the world became a more isolated place.

What news did come through came mostly from the occasional trading missions that were allowed to sail up the Thames estuary. But over the last one hundred years, these had stopped when Londoners declined to go outside the Barrier to meet with them. Over time, London had become more and more insular.

But as time passed, the population of London had grown too large for the confines of the Barrier.

CHAPTER 1

London had to expand or explode.

Terrence Charterhouse and Melville Wilson had devised a strategy for shutting the Barrier off and for London to rejoin the outside world. But strong resistance was being met; over two hundred and fifty years of isolation had left a lot of people with acute cases of agoraphobia. The thought of no Barrier to surround and protect them left many terrified.

All this was incidental to Mel. She knew the history of London well; it was her mother's history that interested her.

Her father spoke at some length, giving Mel insight into who her mother was. At times, she felt he was talking to himself. Finally, he stopped and said, "I think that's enough of the past for now. It's late and I've got a busy day tomorrow." He stood up and stretched his tall frame. "I'm going over to the eastside to talk to a meeting of Wardens about the Expansion. And you have classes!"

"Really Daddy," Mel protested jokingly. "I'm not a child, you know. I can take a few late nights now and again."

Melville went over and laid his hand gently on the top of her head, ruffling her hair. "I know, I know." His voice took on a wistful note." "You've grown up so fast. Where did all those years go?" He bent and kissed the top of her head. "But even when you're forty or fifty years old and with a child of your own, you'll still be my little girl. So bed! Okay?"

Mel held up her hands in mock surrender and rose out of her chair. "Okay, okay. I'll go quietly, if only to stop my father becoming a nag. Goodnight."

She kissed his cheek and disappeared into her bedroom before he could realise that he had been left with clearing the dinner things away. As he collected the used dishes and took them to the recycler, Melville shook his head and thought again, How like her mother.

By the time that Mel got up the next morning, her father had already gone. He left a message on her terminal saying that he expected to be in meetings all day and not to expect him home too early.

As the government drew closer to a decision about the Barrier, this had been happening more and more. Mel was determined that they were going to take a break in one of the vacation centres when this Barrier business was all over.

Vacation centres were located in all of the medical blocks, the idea being that you spent time away from where you lived and worked, met new people, and spent your time as you pleased, swimming, playing various sports, or just relaxing in the saunas or artificial sunrooms.

Mel called up her schedule for the day and met with a pleasant surprise. The whole of the morning's classes had been cancelled. This meant that she was free to do as she pleased.

She decided to go to the north entrance and see if she could improve on her painting of the Barrier. Throwing her nightclothes into the recycler and getting a light blue one-piece suit from the replicator, she took the lift down to the ground floor of her apartment building.

Removing her bicycle from its storage point, Mel set off north to the Barrier gate. She knew without checking that the car that normally took her to classes would be following her. She wondered briefly who the driver was this morning. They seemed to be changed more often now since Richard had been reassigned. The thought occurred to her that if her father had known about her affair with Richard, he was maybe pulling strings to stop her getting close to any more of her protectors.

Mel shook her head, dispelling the unworthy thought. Her father had always wanted to discuss everything with her. She fondly remembered the time she tried to talk to him about her periods. For an orator of Melville's experience, his explanation had left her more confused than ever. Knowing when he was beaten, Melville had a doctor explain it.

It was a four-mile ride to the north entrance from the apartment block surrounding Parliament, and it was a nominally fine day. This meant that it wasn't raining. All you ever got living under the Barrier was very fine drizzle, no matter how hard it rained. The rain hit the Barrier and dispersed to become drizzle. This property of the Barrier affected sunshine as well; it never reached full intensity.

Sometimes, when the weather outside was really fine, the entrance in the top of the Barrier would be opened and the small park below it would be bathed in pure sunshine for a few hours. Such was people's mistrust of anything from the outside that they would gather on the edges and watch the more adventurous stand in the middle. Nobody stayed there for too long.

There was very little ground traffic as Mel rode through the streets. A flitter buzzed overhead on some security mission or other, but there was very little to disturb a pleasant, early morning ride. Mel reached the northern edge of the city slightly breathless but exhilarated.

The area around the entrance was deserted as usual. It was only opened now for security patrols to go out and check the perimeter. Her father remarked recently that this had been cut back from once every six months to once a month.

Mel set up her lightweight telescopic easel and fixed her canvas to it. She decided that she was going to repaint the two white pillars that were so prominent in this section of the Barrier. Richard had told her that this was where the force field could be deactivated. Between these two posts shimmered the Barrier.

As always, Mel moved closer to the Barrier until she could feel her hair begin to stand on end, and the sensation of a thousand needles pricking at her skin.

Touching the Barrier had quickly become a rite of passage for London children. Only once had she actually touched the Barrier. The resultant shock had thrown her six feet backwards and given her a large bruise on her backside. She had not repeated the experiment.

Mel returned to her easel and soon became absorbed in her work. She paid no attention to the passing hours until finally she felt, rather than saw, a presence next to her. The car's driver was trying to get her attention. Mel sighed dramatically, as if this was the umpteenth interruption that morning. "Yes!" she snapped, making no attempt to look up.

"You have an important message on the com-unit in the car, Miss Wilson."

Mel felt her irritation rise. If this was just her father saying that he was going to be home later than he had thought, she

CHAPTER 1

would be most annoyed. She laid down her brush and palette, and stalked to the car. Sliding into the back seat, she activated the com-unit. After a moment's wait, a picture formed on the screen, not of her father, but of the president.

"Uncle Terry! How nice to hear from you. This is unexpected." The words gushed from her mouth. Ever since she could remember she'd had a crush on the man she knew as Uncle Terry.

The same age as her father, he had boyish good looks, his hair almost untouched by grey. He stood as tall as Melville Wilson, with a more slender build. His expression at the moment was pensive, and Mel suddenly felt uneasy; he stared at her silently for a moment.

"Lina." The use of her pet name came easily, but he hesitated as if he didn't know how to continue. Haltingly, he carried on. "Lina, I have some terrible news." He stopped again, shuffling uncomfortably in his seat.

Mel felt a growing coldness creep over her. "What . . . What is it? Is it Daddy?" Instinctively, she knew the answer.

The president's face seemed to lose all its colour. He open and shut his mouth twice before answering. "There's been an incident. Melville was going across town to meet some wardens, when the train he was travelling on . . . exploded. There were no survivors."

Silence descended as Mel's unresponsive brain tried to take in the president's news. Questions flooded her head. There were things she wanted to ask, but she couldn't form the words. How? When . . . Why?

It was a few moments before she realised that the president

was still talking.

"Just sit tight, Lina. Your driver has instructions to bring you straight to the Palace. I'll be there waiting for you. Hold on and I'll see you soon."

The screen went black and Mel sank back into the seat feeling dazed, her thoughts disjointed. She struggled to absorb what she had just been told, her mind racing, thoughts criss-crossing her mind, surfacing in random order.

Daddy dead. An explosion on a train. Unheard of. What about her painting? Her father would never see her sculpture now. What about her bike?

Mel opened a window to speak to the driver. He was wheeling her bike over to her easel.

"Michael. My . . . my bike."

The driver looked at her, his expression sympathetic. "There's another car coming to pick up your equipment. I'm to take you straight to the Palace."

Mel nodded mutely. The car began to move silently along the road and, as the journey progressed, the news of her father's death began to sink in further.

Mel desperately tried to bring to mind a picture of her father but failed. This is ridiculous, she thought, I can't remember what he looks like. Panic began to build inside her; she could feel huge sobs starting low in her body and threatening to take control. With a superhuman effort, she clamped down hard and regained some of her composure.

They were at the Palace within ten minutes. The gates were open, and they swept through. Mel could see the tall figure of the president waiting for her on the marbled steps.

He opened the car door for her, helped her out, and led her up the steps and into the entrance hall. With his arm round her waist, he guided her into one of the reception rooms and sat her in one of the plush leather chairs; taking a seat opposite her, he leaned forward and took both her hands in his. Mel lifted her head to look into his sad eyes. "Lina . . . How are you?" Charterhouse shook his head and smiled a sad smile. "That's a stupid question," he muttered. He fell silent.

"Uncle Terry," Mel's eyes picked with unshed tears, "what happened?"

The president stood up and began to pace the room. Mel's eyes followed his pacing form, waiting for an answer. When none came, she asked again, her voice cracking under the strain.

He stopped pacing and stood in front of the empty fireplace, his hands clasped behind him. He looked in down at Mel and took a deep ragged breath. "Melville was on his way to a meeting of Wardens in the eastern section when there was an explosion on the train he was travelling in. The whole carriage was destroyed, killing everyone inside."

"But what caused the explosion?" The confused, pained look in Mel's eyes made Charterhouse sigh and look away.

He resumed pacing again. "The investigation is still going on. But there is very little on an electric train to explode like this. So we must presume sabotage."

Mel looked up, her expression even more shocked.

"Sabotage! But who would do such a thing?"

Terrence Charterhouse sighed and shrugged his shoulders.

"I just don't know, Lina. I just don't know." He sat down and took her hands in his once more. "If Melville has been murdered, we will find his killers. I promise you that."

Mel stood up and pulled away from his grasp. She felt an irrational need to run away, escape from something that she couldn't quite pin down.

"Thank you, Uncle Terry." The quaver in her voice matched the tremor in her body. "I know that you will do all that you can. I think I should go home now."

"No! No! You must stay here at least tonight. I've had a guest room prepared for you."

Mel began to object, but he put his hands on her shoulders, squeezed them, and smiled down at her. "Please. It would make ME feel a lot better."

"Thanks." Mel gave him a quick hug. "Maybe I shouldn't be alone tonight. But only tonight, okay?"

Charterhouse pulled on an old-fashioned bell cord hanging down the side of the fireplace. A light rap on the door announced the arrival of a presidential aide, a middle aged, matronly woman.

"Ah, Laura. Please show Miss Wilson to her room and see that she has everything she needs." He turned back to Mel. "Lina, try to get some rest and I'll see you at supper. I hope to have a preliminary report by then."

Mel nodded silently and followed the aide upstairs to a guest bedroom. Once inside, she was left alone with her thoughts. All the feelings she had been fighting down came up to overwhelm her. She fell on the bed and tears coursed down her cheeks until she fell into a restless sleep.

When Laura woke her, night had fallen. She cleaned herself up and joined the president for supper. He had very little new to report, except that the security services had confirmed that the explosion was not natural. She picked at her food and he talked about her father and his memories of him until the aide returned to take Mel to her room.

The president's words did not sink in and, by the time she got into bed, it seemed that her brain had shut down and her whole body had gone numb. She lay awake staring at the ceiling, not really thinking about anything, until she dropped into a fitful, dream-ridden sleep.

The next morning, when Mel awoke, there was a moment when she thought it had all been a bad dream. But the unusual surroundings and the all too vivid memories of the day before served to convince her it was all true. Melville Wilson, her father, was dead.

Tears threatened to well up again, but Mel held them back. She couldn't spend the rest of her life numb with grief; she had decisions to make. The first thing, she decided, was to get home. That meant the apartment in Westminster. Then she could decide what she was going to do next. She found a fresh set of clothes at the foot of the bed, the jumpsuit she had been wearing yesterday was gone. As she sat, dressed, studying her reflection in a mirror, she could see little outward sign of change. Her eyes were a bit red, and there were signs of bags beginning to appear under them. But she felt the change inside.

Mel had very little memory of when her mother had died.

All she could remember was that something seemed to be missing. As if she had lost her comfort blanket, the death left a hole that could be filled by a favourite toy or, in her case, by her father.

This time, she had only herself.

Shaking herself out of her reverie, she picked up a hairbrush and began to comb the tangles out of her hair. Applying some make-up to hide the blotchiness around her eyes, she checked her reflection in the mirror again. The fresh clothes were of sombre colours, not shades she would normally have chosen, but they were right for her mood, and the occasion.

She sat for a moment on the end of the bed, collecting her thoughts and finding the courage to face this new world she had been thrust into. Finally, she rose and crossed to the com-unit on the writing desk. As she activated it, a picture of the aide, Laura, appeared on it and spoke before she could say anything.

"Good morning, Miss Wilson. Would you care for some breakfast?"

For a moment, Mel considered skipping breakfast, but a picture of her father came to mind, berating her for missing meals while working on her sculpture. So she ordered coffee and toast, and asked to see the president as soon as possible.

Laura gave a professional smile and answered. "The president is in Parliament at the moment. But he left instructions that you were to be taken there as soon as you were ready."

"I'll be ready as soon as I've eaten."

Mel disposed of the toast without realising it, but the coffee served to wake her up more fully. Going downstairs, she found a car waiting for her.

At Parliament, she was met by the president's personal secretary and ushered into his private office. That aide informed her that the president was in the Chamber debating yesterday's incident, and would join her as soon as he could.

After showing her how to operate the closed circuit television screens, he left her on her own. Mel studied the screens, which spread across one wall of the office. They each showed different parts of the House, and she increased the volume on the one showing the Chamber. It appeared to be full; all sixty members had turned out for this occasion. As she watched, Wardens were standing up and delivering their condolences and expressing their outrage at the loss of the vice-president.

After the Barrier had been energised, the old multi-party system had been dropped because most of the six hundred-odd MPs had come from outside London. When democracy was re-established, areas in the new Republic of London had been designated Wards, and one person was elected Warden for each area. This gave them the honorary title of Member of Parliament, but the official title remained Warden.

Wardens stood to be re-elected every five years, not on a party-decided policy, but on their own merits. The individual may lean towards conservatism, liberalism, or even socialism, but it was up to the electorate of his or her area to make its choice.

The Wardens elected the president and the vice-president every five years, and the president picked his cabinet from the House.

Finally, a Member asked the president to report on yesterday's incident. Charterhouse stood and told them mostly what he had told Mel last night. Investigations were still going on and as soon as he had any solid facts, he would present them to the House. The session came to an end and the Chamber began to empty.

Shortly afterwards, Terrence Charterhouse entered his office and, after kissing Mel on the cheek, sat down behind his desk. He looked at Mel for a moment before speaking. "Lina, I don't believe I said last night how sorry I am that this has happened. Melville was my friend for many years. I'm going to miss him terribly."

"I know, Uncle Terry, I know." There was a moment's silence between them before Mel continued. "I heard what you told the House. So nothing new has come to light, then."

The president looked a little sheepish. "That's not exactly true. I wouldn't want this advertised, but I told the House a little white lie." He reached into a drawer and pulled out a data pad, which he handed to Mel. "These are the preliminary findings; they reached me late last night."

Mel activated the pad and began to scroll through the pages of information. After a few moments of trying to understand the mass of unintelligible data, she looked up at the president, a deep frown on her face.

He smiled in response and took the pad from her hands. "I know how you feel." He re-ran the information for himself. "It doesn't mean a lot to me either. But the most important piece of data in here is that the explosive used was of a type called Semtex." He paused as if he expected Mel to say something. When she didn't, he continued. "Semtex is an explosive that has not been seen in London for over two hundred years."

"Then, where did it come from?" Mel wondered where this was leading.

"It could indicate—and remember this only conjecture—that the person, or persons who sabotaged Melville's train came from the outside."

"From the outside! But there hasn't been any contact with the outside for such a long time. Why now?"

The president shrugged his shoulders tiredly. "I don't know, I just don't know."

The intercom on his desk buzzed, and Charterhouse listened for a moment. With a curt, "Send him in," he lifted his finger from the unit. Turning back to Mel, he smiled warmly. "I imagine that at the moment you feel very frustrated. So the least I can do is let you see how the investigation is going for yourself."

The door opened and the president's secretary ushered in a man dressed in the uniform of the Protector forces. The black of his uniform was broken only by the silver of his rank insignia: Captain.

He stepped smartly up to the desk and saluted. "You asked to see me, sir."

Mel studied the captain as he stood at attention in front of the presidential desk. He appeared to be around thirty years old, was over six feet tall, and of a slim build. His hair was as short as only the military forces can get it. From his profile, Mel could see that he had a strong jaw line. She wondered what his eyes looked like; she had read somewhere that ancient races had thought that the eyes were the windows to the soul.

The president looked up and signalled the captain to relax. "Yes, Captain, thank you for coming." He lifted a hand in the direction of Mel. "This is Miss Melina Wilson; Melina, this is Captain Cord Taylor."

Mel held out a hand, and the officer took it with a strong, sure grip. She looked into his eyes; she liked what she saw. They were hazel in colour and seemed to be open and honest. For some reason, she already felt safer with him around.

"Miss Wilson," he spoke softly, "my deepest condolences on your loss. I knew and respected your father. He will be greatly missed."

"Thank you." She gave what she hoped was a gracious smile and, reluctantly, removed her hand from his.

The president's voice broke in on the mood. "Captain Taylor is leading the investigation into the . . . incident. He will escort you to the Protector force's labs, where they will explain what they have discovered so far. I wish I could come with you, but there is too much to do here. The vote on the future of the Barrier will go ahead, and I must see if I can rally support for your father's last wish."

"I understand, Uncle Terry. You already have done so much."

Charterhouse got up and came around his desk to give Mel a light hug and a kiss on her cheek. When you have finished at the labs, Captain Taylor will see that you get to where ever you wish to go. Would you like to stay here for a few more days?"

"That's very kind, but no." Mel felt she should be at home with familiar things around her. "I have to go home some time, better sooner than later."

The captain escorted her through a maze of corridors and out into the midday sunshine of London. There was a military vehicle waiting for them but, as the captain opened a door for her, Mel said, "My uncle said that the labs are located in the Westminster medical block." The officer nodded his head in agreement. "Then, it's such a nice day, why don't we walk."

"Of course, Miss Wilson," the captain replied.

As they walked under the archway of Parliament's living quarters and made their way to the medical centre, Mel looked up at the figure of the captain walking beside her.

"Captain, I think I would prefer it if you dropped the Miss Wilson routine. It makes me feel old. My friends call me Melina, or Mel for short."

He smiled back at her. "It would be my pleasure, Mel. But you must call me Cord."

A small shiver went down her spine as he spoke her name. Must be getting colder, she thought. They kept their silence for the rest of the walk.

On reaching the entrance of the medical block, Cord underwent a small change in his manner. He glared at the corporal on duty at the security barrier when the corporal's version of standing at attention did not meet his expectations. However, his manner allowed them access with the minimum of checks or fuss.

Once inside, an earnest young man around Mel's age met them. He showed them into an anteroom and offered them refreshments that they declined. They sat down to wait.

The wait was not long, as the next person to enter was Dr. Jonathon Marks. The first thing that struck Mel about the doctor was his appearance. A small man who looked like he was heading fast towards his first century, he had an alarming shock of white hair that seemed to explode from each side of his head, leaving a wide swathe of bald scalp down the centre.

To Mel, he reminded her of pictures she had seen of the pre-Barrier scientist, Albert Einstein. She wouldn't have been surprised if he had talked in clipped, German tones, like in old video shows.

In this she was to be disappointed; when he did speak, it was in a soft voice with an accent indistinguishable from her own. "Miss Wilson." He came over and took one of her hands in both of his. "My deepest condolences. It is an outrage, the death of your father. I knew him, you know. Many years ago, it was he who recommended me for this job." He shook his head sadly, all the while pumping Mel's hand and arm up and down.

Mel finally managed to extract her hand from his. Just in time, she thought, before permanent ligament damage was done. The doctor, now with both hands free, began to wave them around like a character in a melodramatic play.

"My staff and I will do all we can to track down the evil people who did this. Such a tragedy. Such a fine man." He looked at Mel again, and shook his head. "I knew him, you know. Such a fine man."

Mel couldn't help but smile, even in the face of her loss. Her spirits felt lifted by this small, energetic man. He gave the impression of an absent-minded professor, but her father had told her of this man. He was known privately, to his staff, as Sherlock, because of his uncanny ability to leap to the correct conclusions with only the bare minimum of evidence. It had been said that, if you fed him real chicken for dinner, rather than replicated, within half an hour he could tell where it had been killed and how long ago. Give him longer and he could tell you how many eggs it had laid in its lifetime.

The captain was getting impatient; he coughed loudly and broke into the doctor's tirade against murderers and their like. "Thank you, Doctor," he said in a firm voice. "Is there anything new in the investigation?"

Dr. Marks theatrically slapped the palm of his hand against his head. "You must stop me if I ramble on too much. I tend to get carried away, you know." He took Mel's arm and tucked it under his. Patting her hand, he said. "Come with me, my dear, and I will show you what progress we have made."

They left the anteroom and went down the corridor to another room, above the door of which was a rough, hand painted sign which read 221B Baker Street. The doctor noted Mel's smile at this. "One of my young assistant's strange sense of humour." Mel heard a note of pride in his voice and could quite imagine that he secretly revelled in his nickname.

The room they entered was, Mel presumed, Dr. Marks' private office. If you looked carefully, you could just make out the shape of a desk under an avalanche of data pads, computer disks, and even paper.

After the president's neat and well ordered office, this one looked like an explosion had taken place and nobody had bothered to tidy up afterwards. All about the room were data pads and pieces of equipment. Mel looked around for somewhere to sit, but all the chairs seemed to be covered with assorted goods.

The doctor motioned her to the only clear chair in the room, the one behind his desk. Cord cleared a corner of the desk and perched himself there.

The old scientist hunted for a while through the collection of data pads on the desk, picking one up, turning it on, and muttering to himself before throwing it back onto the desk again. Finally, he found what he was looking for, and studied it for a few moments before handing it to Mel.

"This is the data that was collected at the site of the explosion. The chemical compounds that were present in the residue of the explosive leads us to believe that the type used was of a kind known as Semtex. As no stocks are known to exist in London . . . " He paused in his report and looked at Cord, who continued for the doctor.

"We've made extensive enquiries and used the most sophisticated sensors available to us and we can find no trace of the stuff in London."

"Then," the doctor cut in smoothly, "we must assume that it came in from the outside."

Mel dropped the pad back onto the desk; again, it was full of numbers and figures that she didn't understand. "But, I thought that the Barrier was impenetrable."

Cord stiffened slightly and cleared his throat before answering. "Well, that's not exactly true. There are a few ways into London from the outside. The old tube trains tunnels were a favourite way of gaining entrance in the early days, but they were soon blocked up." He stood and began to pace the room. "Another way in was where the Barrier crossed the Thames. A steel mesh was installed to stop that; it was last inspected ten years ago. We're checking to see if it's been breached. Finally, there are the sewers. Not a nice way to come in, but there are hundreds of choices for the would-be interloper. We patrol the sewers still in use, and have blocked up the ones that are of no use to modern London, but it's estimated that there could be hundreds that we don't even know about. So, I could not say, in all honesty, that the Barrier is impenetrable."

"So it would seem," Mel said, looking thoughtful as she digested this latest information.

Cord gave a shrug of his shoulders. "Nowhere is completely safe, Mel. Especially against a one-man suicide squad."

"A one-man suicide squad!"

"Yes, my dear." The doctor's face creased into an expressive frown. "This is the latest information we have. We checked all the victims' ID implants; they are practically indestructible. One body had no implant. No one has been reported missing from London, so we must assume that he came from the outside."

Mel sat back in her chair and picked up the data pad again. "What about fingerprints?"

"We have not used fingerprints for over a hundred and fifty years, so that avenue of investigation was of no use to us." Dr. Marks shook his head. "There were very little remains of the unknown body, so it is our belief that he was carrying the bomb when it exploded."

"Hence," the captain continued, "why we think it was a suicide bomber. Not expected to return to wherever he came from."

For the first time since her father's death, Mel felt emotion other than grief. She felt frustrated. "So, that's it then. File it and forget it. Case closed." Mel could not keep the bitterness she felt out of her voice.

"No, Mel. That's not it." Cord looked down at her, his voice still soft, but with a determined edge. "There are quite a few questions unanswered. Did he come from some sort of organisation on the outside? Did he have help inside London? How did he get in? And most importantly," he paused for effect, "are there any more of them, waiting to attack again?"

Mel raised one eyebrow at him. "What about the Isolationists? I know they haven't tried anything like this for twelve years, but . . ."

Cord smiled; he had done his research. "You mean your attempted kidnapping. After that, they disappeared for quite a while. But since your father and the president have been pushing for the Barrier to be turned off, there have been one or two incidents."

"I had no idea that feelings were running so high." Mel was somewhat surprised that her father had told her nothing of this.

"I'm afraid that I must agree with Captain Taylor." Dr. Marks nodded his head rapidly as he spoke. "A lot of people in London suffer from a form of agoraphobia. Not so much a straight forward fear of open spaces, but of all the space outside the Barrier. Having no Barrier to protect them from the outside terrifies some people. And people who are terrified will do anything to protect themselves."

He went over to one of the chairs and began to sort through the pile of data pads there. "Ah! Here," he said, handing the pad to Mel. "These are the latest statistics from the medical centres. As you can see, in the last ten years, stress related, agoraphobic illnesses have doubled. Researchers are of the opinion that they are all related to the increasing discussions about removing the Barrier."

"But, murder," Mel said, horrified. "Blowing up trains, killing people . . . ?"

Cord held up a hand to stop her. "I said it's another question to be answered. My gut feeling is that the unknown body is the most important find so far. It's my fear that there are more like him waiting to come in, or worse, already inside London."

The old scientist nodded his head in agreement. "It is so sadly true, I'm afraid. So much killing. So sad."

Mel dropped the pad she had been holding. She was feeling depressed; she had thought that this visit would answer all her questions. Instead, it had posed a whole lot more.

"So, what now? If this attack came from the outside, what can we do about it?" Mel was beginning to lose hope of ever finding her father's killers.

Cord sighed. "What can I say, Mel? We will find and block wherever they got into London. We will check and reinforce all entrances. Your father's death will be taken as a warning that security was getting lax and, finally, we will make a ten-mile sweep around the Barrier and clear the land of any hostiles."

Mel stood up and came round the desk. Suddenly, she felt tired and wanted to go home and hide herself away. "I know you'll do whatever you can, Cord," she held out her hand to the doctor. "Thank you, Dr. Marks, for your time."

The doctor saw them to the reception area before taking his leave of them. As they left the building, stepping into the fast approaching twilight, Mel gave a long drawn-out sigh. When Cord opened the door of the car for her, she slid in silently. When the car drew to a stop outside her apartment block, Mel looked at the captain sitting next to her.

"Thank you for all your help, Cord. You'll keep me informed of any new developments?"

He smiled back and nodded. "Of course."

She smiled wanly back and made her way to her home without seeing anybody, which was a relief. Mel had had enough of people's sympathy today. People meant well, she supposed, but it became very tiring.

Everything inside looked the same. She sat down at the table she had shared with her father such a short time ago. Now, looking at the empty seat opposite her, she felt the pricking of tears beginning to form in her eyes.

Mel took a deep breath and stood up. Making her way to the replicator, she ordered a light salad, but as she sat down again, the com-unit began to bleep softly. He looked at it for a moment, debating with herself whether to ignore it or not. She realised she would have to answer it; the house computer knew she was home so would not engage the answering service, and the apartment was very quiet and lonely.

Mel pushed the receive button and a picture of the president appeared.

"Lina, how are you?"

Mel straightened herself up and began to say she was fine, but her voice betrayed her. "I'm . . . hanging on," was her answer in the end.

The concerned look on the president's face deepened. "Hmm, I wish you would come and stay at the Palace with me, at least until the funeral is over. We are planning a memorial service at St. Paul's tomorrow; it will be transmitted live to all of London. I thought we could have a quiet funeral the next day. You, me, and whomever else you think should come. Okay?"

"That's fine, Uncle Terry. Whatever you think is best." Mel felt relief at not having to handle the arrangements. Letting Uncle Terry's staff take care of things was for the best. They had the expertise.

"That's decided, then." The president gave a broad smile. "A car will pick you up at 1 p.m. tomorrow; you can give your list to my aides then. What you need now is a good night's sleep, so I've asked my personal doctor to call on you this evening. He will look you over and provide a sedative."

Mel started to protest, but the president cut her off. "I would feel a lot better if I knew you were all right. The next two days are going to be rough; you will need all the strength you can muster. Dr. Poole will bring a nurse with him; she will stay the night."

Mel sighed and just nodded. She felt too washed out to argue.

Charterhouse smiled again and said. "I'll see you tomorrow, then. Please get some sleep. Goodnight."

The link went dead, and Mel went back to picking at her meal. Dr. Poole arrived half an hour later, gave her a brief examination, and fixed a sedative pad to her arm. The nurse saw her to bed and stayed by her side until she fell into a deep, dreamless sleep.

CHAPTER 2

When Mel awoke the next morning, she felt better. There was still an ache deep inside her, but it was duller and deeper down. She lay in her bed staring at the ceiling of her bedroom, a place of great familiarity. As a young child, she would stare at the ceiling and imagine she could see the face of her mother watching over her. Now, she looked for her father, and took comfort as the decoration on the ceiling formed into the face of her father.

Tears began to flow down her cheeks as, for an instant, the faces of both her parents appeared. She lifted a hand towards them and they vanished. Pulling herself together, she realised that she could hear noises from the kitchen area and, even better, she could smell coffee.

When she entered the dining area, Mel found the nurse who accompanied the doctor last night scanning the video dailies. Before she switched off, Mel caught sight of the lead story: her father's obituary. The nurse, a pretty woman who appeared to be not much older than Mel herself, smiled and said. "Good morning. Would you like some coffee?"

Mel nodded her thanks and sat down at the table. The nurse sat opposite her and passed her a cup of black coffee.

Mel sipped her coffee and studied the woman. She figured that they were about the same age; she had a pleasant, open face which Mel could not resist taking a liking to. Her blond hair was cut short, and she wore a simple, light blue coat. Mel held out a hand saying. "I'm sorry I don't remember if Dr. Poole introduced us last night. I'm Mel Wilson."

"Abigail Hopkins. Call me Abbi."

They sat in silence for a while, drinking their coffee, until Abbi spoke again. "The president called while you were still asleep. I updated him on your condition and he asked me to remind you to make up a list for tomorrow."

Mel sighed, but set to work on compiling a list; they were mostly names of Wardens that her father had worked closely with, except for the only other relative that Mel knew of, her father's brother, Granville.

Both sets of Mel's grandparents had died in the Great Plague of forty years ago, and Mel had never met her uncle. Her father wouldn't talk about him much; all she knew was that he worked in the news and entertainment industry. A call to the president's office set his staff looking for him; within an hour, they called back to say that he had been contacted and would be at tomorrow's funeral.

As one o'clock approached, Abbi and Mel went through Mel's handmade wardrobe and came up with a suitable choice of what to wear. Mel was pleased to find that Abbi would be with her at the funeral. Between her and Myan, she thought she

CHAPTER 2

would be able to cope better.

Having kept herself busy all morning with preparations and decisions, Mel was now sitting, waiting for the car to take her to St. Paul's. The apartment was unnaturally quiet, and Mel was once again struggling to come to terms with what had happened. It was beyond belief that only two nights ago she had sat down for dinner with her father . . . and now he was gone.

The car arrived and took them to the cathedral where the media and guests awaited her. The president opened Mel's door himself, and he took her arm to guide her up the steps of London's only remaining cathedral.

About twenty years after the Barrier had been energised, it was realised that space was going to be required for living and working areas. So a decision was made that all unnecessary buildings, no matter how historically important, would be demolished to make way for a new London, designed to make use of its finite space to the greatest extent.

At first, all churches were deemed unnecessary. Although attendance to all religions had fallen to an all-time low, there was still wide spread rebellion from all denominations at the loss of their places of worship. While the first government of London tended to operate a "do as you are told or end up outside the Barrier" policy, it soon realised that it could face real opposition if it didn't compromise. So, it appointed the current Bishop of London, the Right Reverend James Harding, Bishop of the Republic of London, jurisdiction over all religious affairs.

His instructions were simple: control the religions or find them all scrapped.

Harding called all the religious leaders together and talked them into forming a combined religion. This became known as the New Order. It was made up of various parts of all the old religions, Protestant, Catholic, Jewish, Moslem, and many other, smaller sects. They combined together all the main parts of each of their tenets in different ways until they formed a church that appeased them all.

Of course, there were those who could not accept the New Order but, in the early days of the Republic, London was a totalitarian state; those who were not for the new Republic were against it and very quickly found themselves on the outside with no way back in.

In the spirit of using every resource to its utmost, the New Order religion soon found itself the social services of New London, as well.

Mel took her place in the presidential pews, alongside Terrence Charterhouse and the rest of his cabinet. As she watched the other guests filing in and taking their places, she saw Cord with fellow officers, dressed in full ceremonial uniform.

The service took about two hours. The Bishop talked about the gift of life, and the president took to the lectern to talk about his friendship with Melville Wilson and how he would be missed. Mel sat dry-eyed, but her spirit was lifted by this demonstration of the regard others felt for her father. After the memorial service was over, there was a reception at the Palace, where Mel greeted everybody individually and took his or her condolences. Myan was there with her family, and Mel ended up consoling her, as she was in floods of tears. Finally, as the reception neared its end, Mel managed to get a word with the president.

"Uncle Terry, what about the vote on the Barrier?"

He shook his head sadly. "I'm afraid it goes badly, Lina. Those who were on the fence, so to speak, have been shocked by this attack. Word that someone from the outside was involved has made them side with the Isolationists. I can't say that I blame them too much. Who wants to rejoin a world that can perpetuate such outrages?"

"But father said that it was 'expand or suffocate'!"

Charterhouse shrugged his shoulders. "I know, and I still agree with him." He smiled and put his arm around her shoulders. "But, you are not to worry about it. My aides are working on those who are wavering and we still have a few days before the vote." He glanced at his watch. "It's getting late and you've had a full day. You go home now and get some rest. I'll see you tomorrow."

He kissed her forehead and ushered her towards the door where Abbi waited for her. Back at the apartment, Abbi fixed another sedative patch and Mel went straight to bed, sleeping soundly until the morning.

The next day, after Abbi had coerced Mel into eating a full breakfast, Myan came to visit and they spent the whole morning talking about her father. Cord Taylor called to say that he had received some new information and that he would investigate and let her know the outcome.

The funeral came and, as her father's coffin disappeared behind the curtain at the crematorium, all the emotions Mel had kept under reasonable control the last few days caught up with her and the floodgates opened.

Seated between Myan and Terrence Charterhouse, she had never felt so alone.

Accompanied only by the president, Myan, and Cord as military escort, Mel went down to the banks of the Thames and scattered her father's ashes onto the water.

With a shortage of space to build, let alone bury people, the scattering of ashes on the Thames quickly became a tradition, as the waters of the Thames went beyond the Barrier and symbolised the move into the afterlife.

Back at the apartment, there were only a few old, close friends of her father, plus her Uncle Granville and his wife. He appeared to be genuinely distressed by the death of his only brother and, when he left, he promised to keep in touch. Mel decided that, at a later date, she would have to find out what the trouble had been between them.

Finally, as the day drew to a close, there was only Mel, Terrence Charterhouse, the nurse Abbi, and Cord left.

Charterhouse looked at the captain over the rim of his glass. "Why don't you tell Lina what you have discovered, Captain?"

The tiredness Mel had felt from a long and emotional day disappeared, and she centred all her attention on the tall captain. He looked into her eyes and correctly read the expectation there.

"It's not that much, Mel. We haven't arrested anyone, or even discovered the identity of the unknown body. But . . . ," He put down his glass and took up what Mel was beginning to call his reporting stance, hands behind his back, rocking slightly on the balls of his feet. "But what has been discovered, on an airborne sweep of the outside perimeter, is a possible base for outsiders coming into London."

"A possible base?" Mel questioned. "Didn't the sweep team check it out?"

"No. They were unable to land, as they were at the limit of their range. Flitters only have a range of twenty miles, and take-off uses most of the fuel. They were ten miles out and, if they had landed and taken off again, they would have had insufficient fuel to make it back. Plus, there were only two of them and, whilst they didn't see anybody on the ground, if they had landed, they may have run into more trouble than they could have handled."

"So what happens now?"

The captain glanced at the president, who nodded to him to continue. "Now we take out a ground force and make a closer examination of the area."

There was silence as Mel digested the information that had been presented to her. Finally, she looked directly at the president. "I want to go on the ground sweep." It came out more as a statement than a request.

Both the president and the captain spoke as one. "Under no circumstances. It's much too dangerous!"

Mel stood up, her hands clenched into fists at her side, a determined look on her face. "I'm sure you both have my safety at heart. But I've sat around moping and vegetating too long. I would feel a lot better if I could do something constructive."

Charterhouse placed his drink on the table. "It's just too dangerous, Mel. We have no idea of what may be out there."

Mel turned to look at Cord. "A good question, Uncle Terry. What do you expect to find out there, Cord? An armed force waiting for you? A last ditch battle for the control of London?"

"No! Of course not," Cord answered. "The camp appears to be deserted. Its occupants are probably long gone. But," he held up his hand as he saw Mel was going to speak again. "But, there are more dangers than people with guns and bombs. This is outside the confines of London we are talking about, not a Sunday afternoon stroll in the park."

Mel started to speak again, but this time was cut off by the president. "I agree. If a force goes out to examine this site, then it will consist of experienced personnel. Not young girls who should be back in collage."

Charterhouse saw by look on Mel's face that he had gone too far. He tried to limit the damage. "Besides, Mel, what good would it do to put yourself in danger? It won't bring back your father."

"It would do ME good!" Mel's voice deepened with anger and frustration. "It would help if I could see what London is up against. Who were these people who took my father away from me and why?"

With her face reddening, all her pent-up anger and frustration came tumbling out and was directed at the closest people available. The president and Captain Cord Taylor.

"I WILL find out more about these animals, with or without your help."

With that, she turned and stalked past the nurse, who had come out of the kitchen area to see what all the noise was about, and went into her bedroom. Throwing herself onto her bed, she lay back and listened to the muted voices from the other room. As her anger drained away, the tears began to fall and, when Abbi came and tried to attach another sedative patch, she pushed her away. The time for containing her grief was over. Mel let the tears flow and she cried herself to sleep.

When she awoke late the next morning, the strongest feeling Mel had was one of embarrassment. She decided she must contact Uncle Terry as soon as possible and apologise. However, the emotional excesses of the previous day had helped. She felt a lot stronger.

Mel got straight through to the president at his office. He was smiling and pleasant as always. Mel, still embarrassed, got straight to the point. "I've called about last night, Uncle Terry. I was very rude, and I apologise."

Charterhouse smiled and gave a little nod. "No need to apologise, Lina. You've been through a torrid time just lately. However, you might offer some apologies to Captain Taylor. He was quite distressed at your annoyance and seemed to take it quite personally."

"Oh!" Mel felt her face flush. She hadn't thought of what effect her outburst might have had on Cord. "I'll contact him right away."

"Wait," Charterhouse gave a small laugh. "There's no need to call him; he will be picking you up in half an hour. Captain Taylor has given me certain assurances concerning your safety, and I have given my permission for you to accompany the ground force on their mission. Taylor will take you to Protector

Headquarters, where you will be kitted out and give some basic training."

"Oh! Thank you, Uncle Terry. I will try not to get in anybody's way."

"Don't thank me yet, Lina. You have a week of hard work coming up. Thank me afterwards, if you have the strength. I must go. DO take care."

Mel leaned back in her chair and grinned widely at the ceiling.

"YES!" she exulted.

Abbi came from the kitchen carrying a tray with breakfast on it. "I'm sorry, Mel," she asked, looking surprised. "Were you talking to me?"

"No, to all of London." Mel jumped up and grabbed Abbi by the arms, almost upsetting the tray. "Abbi, I'm going on a trip outside." Suddenly the tray caught her attention. "Is that for me? Great, I'm famished." With that, she sat down and began to eat. For the first time in days, she noticed and enjoyed what she was eating. The fact that she was going to do something constructive in the search for her father's killers had boosted her morale. Although there was still an empty place inside her that throbbed like a dull toothache, having something else to do helped enormously.

She chose a simple blue jumpsuit from the replicator and sat down to watch the news vid before Cord's arrival. To her surprise, there was no mention of a possible camp, or the trip outside. The top story was the upcoming vote on the Barrier.

The latest poll was in and for the first time, the Isolationists were winning. More people wanted the Barrier to remain.

The buzzer sounded and the doorman announced Cord's arrival. Mel met him at the door, trying to contain her excitement. He smiled at her and said, "Have you talked to the president?" Mel nodded. "Well, are you ready to start your training?"

"Absolutely."

"All Protector forces undergo at least a year's training before they can go on an outside expedition."

Cord laughed as Mel's face dropped at the thought of a year's training before going outside. She had not really thought it through, but half expected to go to the camp that afternoon and be back in time for tea.

Cord laughed again. "What did you expect? Pack a picnic lunch, jump into a ground car and go? Beyond the Barrier is a hostile environment."

Mel turned away; she was colouring up with embarrassment at being exposed as naïve. Besides, what could she say? Guilty as charged, Captain?

"Don't worry," Cord continued. "It won't take a year to get you ready. A week's intensive survival training should do it. But before we start, there is one important ground rule we must get settled. If you go on this mission, you are under my orders, the same as everybody else. Understood?"

Mel smiled and gave a mock salute. "Yes, my captain."

"Then what are you waiting for? Let's go."

After saying goodbye to Abbi and thanking her for all her help, they went out into the street. There was no plush, official transport waiting this time, just a standard, military ground car.

Cord did the driving, taking her across the river to where the old Imperial War Museum had once stood. This area had all been cleared for farm land in the early days but, once the replicator had been perfected, the land had been turned over to the Protector forces for a training area.

On arrival, the first thing they that did was get Mel's picture and retina recorded for a pass. Then, it was on to the Quartermaster's, where Mel was kitted out with a standard field uniform for a Protector trooper. This consisted of a black, simulated leather one-piece suit, boots, and a helmet with a two-way radio. Along with that, Mel was also issued with a survival kit that attached to the uniform's belt.

"Normally," Cord commented, "you would be issued with a defence stick, a knife, and a stun gun at this time. But I think we'll wait and see how training goes, first."

Cord's manner, Mel noted, had gone back to the efficient, military style again. The charming Cord was evidently off duty at the moment.

With her arms loaded down with equipment, Mel was shown to a small cubicle, where she changed while Cord stood outside. She emerged wearing the skin-tight uniform, carrying the helmet under her arm. The effect on the captain was noticeable. Spinning around like a model at a show, she asked, "Like it?"

Cord coughed and cleared his throat before answering. "Yes. I never knew those uniforms could look so good. However," he raised his hand to touch Mel's shoulder length hair, "this is not regulation. If you were really a recruit, you would have to have it cut short so your helmet fitted snugly. In your case, I think

CHAPTER 2

we'll just get a larger helmet."

They left the Quartermaster's and crossed the parade ground where various drills were going on, and into a smaller building on the other side, marked Training Headquarters, Cord then led her into a room where two sergeants sat drinking coffee.

The captain returned their salutes and said, "At ease." He waved his hand at the two men. "These gentlemen are Sergeants Williams and Masters. Sergeant Masters will be your instructor for the next week. Sergeant, this is the VIP I told you about, Melina Wilson."

Masters looked, Mel thought, like what would be referred to as a grizzled veteran. Medium height, almost as wide as he was tall, iron-grey hair, and a face etched with deep lines.

Cord glanced at his watch. "It's now 1300 hours. Sergeant Masters will escort you to the mess for some lunch, and start your training afterwards. He'll bring you to my office at 1600 hours and I'll take over from there. Okay?"

Mel nodded. Cord looked at her and smiled. "Listen to what the sergeant has to tell you. He's one of our most experienced men. He is the man who trained me." Turning back to the sergeant, he finished, "Carry on, Sergeant."

Mel followed Masters to the non-com's mess and, once they had picked up a meal from the communal replicator and sat themselves down, she looked around. The room was almost full with non-coms, and about a third of these were women.

Mel felt she had a hundred questions about the Protector forces and she had quite a few questions about Cord, as well. But she couldn't see the sergeant talking about his commanding officer's secrets, so she satisfied herself with some more neutral inquiries. "Sergeant, what exactly are we going to do this week?"

"Very simple, Miss," he answered around mouthfuls of food. "Give you the knowledge to survive on the outside, should the worst happen on a mission, which, of course, it won't." He picked up a fork and put more salad on his plate. "First, this afternoon, we will start with a look at previous missions and see how you react to them. Tomorrow, we will take a short trip outside; after gauging your reactions to that, we can plan the rest of the week. Navigation lessons, unarmed combat, weapons training, etc."

Mel was puzzled. "Why are you so interested in my reactions?"

"Agoraphobia. I hear that the doctors are saying it's becoming more common now. Well, if they had asked us, we could have told then that it's always been a problem." Masters waved his fork in front of her nose. "I've seen perfectly rational, courageous men and women turned into gibbering wrecks by a trip outside. You never know for sure who's going to be affected. So, before wasting time on training, the best thing is to take them out and see what happens."

"And the videos?"

"Real bad cases have been known to faint just watching the videos. One man who reacted badly said to me, 'I just couldn't stand all that sky.' You'll understand better when you see the videos."

After lunch, the sergeant conducted her to a small room where he ran the first video. It ran for about twenty minutes, showing shots of the area surrounding London. The view was much the same. Sparse vegetation, no buildings, although Mel thought she could see what looked like a forest in the distance. The date index on the tape showed that this was taken only last month.

"How often do these trips take place?" she asked.

"Whenever we have enough recruits to make it worthwhile. It's no good having a fighting force ready to defend London if your troops curl themselves into a ball the first time they go outside."

He took a seat beside her. "How do you feel?"

"Fine, just fine."

The sergeant removed the first tape and inserted another. The content was little different, as were the remainder of the tapes, but Mel watched each one, fascinated by the pictures of a world she had never seen but was just the other side of the Barrier.

She also saw what the sergeant had meant about the sky. Depending on the day the film was shot, it was either a brilliant blue, or a dark grey, or blue shot through with white clouds scudding about. She had never seen such variety of colour in the sky.

When the last video finished, Mel sat back and sighed. Tomorrow, she would be out there seeing that sky for herself.

Replacing the last video on the shelf, Sergeant Masters looked at his watch. "We have some time left, so I think we'll introduce you to your uniform."

They went into an adjoining room where there were displays on three of the walls. The sergeant motioned her to a seat, and went to stand by a marker board. Preparing himself for something he had obviously done many times before, he cleared his throat and began his lecture. "Right, the uniform you are wearing is standard issue for all outside expeditions. It's made from a synthetic material, which clings tightly to the body to form an armour. It is fully waterproof, and will deflect knives and gas-propelled projectiles. It does NOT, however, make you invulnerable. It will not stand up to a determined attack with a knife, laser weapons, or a point-blank shot. It is designed to give you a chance to react in the event of a surprise attack."

He crossed over to one of the displays. "This uniform, as you can see, has been cut into sections. Note the thin wires embedded in the material. Under the flap on the left thigh, there is a thermostatic switch. By turning the switch clockwise, the suit can be heated to ward off the cold. On its lowest setting, the solar batteries will last for eight hours; on its highest setting, the batteries will need recharging after two hours."

Masters looked across at Mel who nodded to show that she understood. He continued. "The solar batteries are on the right thigh, and to recharge them, you pull back the flap, like so, to expose the solar panel. They take four hours to fully recharge."

He looked again at Mel. "Now," he said. "Please demonstrate what I have just told you, on your own uniform."

Mel hesitated, taken unawares by the sudden change in the direction of the lecture, but then lifted the flap on her left thigh and felt for the small control knob there. Turning it fully clockwise, she immediately felt the suit get warmer. Then, lifting the other leg onto a chair, she lifted the flap on her other thigh;

under that, she could see the silver glint of the charging grid for the solar batteries.

"How long for the batteries to recharge, Miss Wilson?"

"Four hours. Minimum,"

"How long will they last on maximum?"

"Eight hours. Sorry, no. Two hours, "Mel gave her best smile. "Eight hours on minimum setting, Sergeant."

The sergeant gave no sign if the smile had worked one way or another.

"Moving on to the belt around your waist," he picked up the belt from the display stand. "It splits down the middle to double in length, and has a breaking strain of two hundred and fifty pounds. This can be used as a short rope, or coupled with others by the buckle." He split the belt in his hands and connected it to another belt. "As long a rope as you need."

Throwing the belts back onto the display, he moved on to the stand where a survival kit was spread out.

"This is your survival kit. In here is everything you should need to survive for forty-eight hours. It has one pack of dried rations. Not very tasty, but they'll keep you alive. They should be added to water, but can be eaten dry. One pocket-knife, with various attachments. One compass with neck strap. One high intensity, narrow beam torch. One set of flares. There are four of these; they will only go ten feet into the air before exploding, and flare for only ten seconds, but they are also high intensity. The whole kit is attached to the belt at the front. Any questions?"

Mel shook her head and he moved on to the next display.

"The third part of your kit, the boots. These are made from

the same material as your uniform, only thicker and tougher. The slot in the top is for your combat knife; there is a slot in both boots, for the left handed. Concealed in the heel," he twisted the heel on the right boot and a small metallic object fell into his hand, "is a simple Geiger counter. It has a digital display, and zero is normal background radiation; the higher the number, the more radiation. Although it has been over two hundred years since the Breakdown, some areas outside are still contaminated. Use it; it could save your life."

He paused again for questions, then move on to the last display, the helmet. He picked it up and turned it over in his hands. "This is your most important piece of equipment," he rapped his knuckles on the top. "It's very tough; the face shield tips back like so, and is made of an aluminium / glass alloy. The only thing that will cut it is a laser. It also polarises according to the strength of the sun." Masters tipped the helmet up so Mel could see inside. "Inside here is a two-way short-range radio, which begins to operate as soon as the helmet is placed on the head. Transmissions are picked up on a receiver that sits inside the ear. The microphone is positioned in front of the mouth and is voice activated. The radio also acts as a homing device, which enables search squads to locate missing personnel. A practical demonstration will take place later."

The sergeant glanced at his watch. "If there are no questions," he raised an eyebrow inquiringly, "then our time is up for today." He replaced the helmet on the stand and turned to Mel. "I'll escort you to Captain Taylor's office and see you tomorrow at 0800 hours."

CHAPTER 2

As she followed the sergeant back to the Administration block, Mel felt a bit overwhelmed by all she had learned in such a short time. She had thought she knew a lot about her environment, and had strong ideas about what was outside the Barrier. But now she was learning that she knew almost nothing.

Changing back into her jumpsuit, Mel stashed the uniform and equipment into a kit bag and slung it across her shoulders. She found Cord at his desk, and waited for him to finish some paperwork before accompanying him to the Officers' Mess for a meal. After a pleasant meal, Cord drove her back to her apartment and followed her into the lift. At her door, he leaned down and kissed her, gently at first, but as she answered him with her body, pressing closer. When Mel did push him away, they were both a bit breathless.

"Coffee?" she asked. He nodded, smiling.

Once inside, she motioned him to sit down, saying, "I'll get that coffee."

She emerged from the kitchen moments later, and then excused herself to go into the bedroom.

A short while later, she stood in the doorway and made a small cough to get Cord's attention. He turned to see Mel dressed in the body-moulding uniform, her hair long and flowing around her shoulders. He came over and put his arms around her waist, pulling her, unresisting, to him.

"Where do you think you're going? Night manoeuvres?"

Mel looked into his eyes. "I got the impression that you liked the way I look in uniform."

"Hummm. That's very true, certainly better than most of my

troopers." He passed his hands up and down the whole length of her body. "I've often wondered about these trooper uniforms. Do they come off as easily as they go on?"

Mel looked at him with a glint in her eyes. "They do go on easily, but there is some difficulty getting them off again. I may need some help."

"Well, a good captain always tries to help the men, or women, under his command."

Picking her up in his arms, he carried her into the bedroom and, laying her down on the bed, where he found that Mel was not being entirely truthful; the uniforms came off quite easily.

Their lovemaking was short and passionate at first, but a second, more gentle session, left them both sated. Mel laid her head on Cord's bare chest and, as she slipped into sleep, she realised that she had not felt so contented for days.

The next morning, Mel was up before Cord, and on the com-unit telling Myan all that had gone on the day before. Joining Cord in the shower nearly undid all the good work of the water; after breakfast, they left together in the jeep.

This time, they headed for the north entrance at Newgate. Waiting for them there was Sergeant Masters, four recruits, and a heavily armoured ground vehicle. As he climbed from the jeep, Cord returned the salutes of the sergeant and the four recruits.

"All set, sergeant?"

"Yes, sir," the sergeant answered smartly.

"Very well. Helmets on and mount up."

Mel climbed inside and found her self seated between Cord and Sergeant Masters, who was driving. Cord spoke softly over his radio and Mel watched as a section of Barrier between two posts faded away to nothing, leaving a clear view forward.

Cord tapped Masters on the shoulder and gave him thumbs up, the signal to proceed. The roar of the engine became louder as the vehicle rolled slowly forward, travelling some four hundred yards before coming to a halt. Cord turned around to face the rest of the passengers.

"Now," he said, "the sergeant will roll back the roof. Once fully back, if any of you have any problems, let me know. Sergeant."

Masters flicked a switch on the dashboard and the roof began to move slowly back. All five passengers gave a collective gasp as they looked up. As one, they began to crane their necks, looking around them. Mel was staggered by the colour of the sky. She head never seen such a blue colour; the videos had not done it justice.

A young, male recruit sitting behind her dragged Mel's attention away from the scenery; his breathing had become faster and he was making a gurgling noise.

"Problem, Hanley?" Cord looked at him intently.

"No . . . No." With an effort, he took a deep breath and began to pull himself together and, although he had lost some colour from his face, sat up straighter in his seat and in a stronger voice said, "No, Sir. No problem, sir."

The captain nodded. "Good man. Carry on, Sergeant."

Masters put the vehicle back into gear and began a large, slow circle which would bring them back to the gate. Mel returned her attention back to the landscape. The terrain was uneven and looked the same as the videos had shown. Bare and desolate.

As they swung around towards London, the Barrier that had kept the people of London isolated for over two hundred years came into view, and Mel felt her breath taken away.

She felt it was beyond description.

As she gazed at the Barrier, Mel added another item to her mental list of ambitions. She had to return and paint the Barrier from this side. The colours were so different. The morning sun slanted across it and, as they moved towards it, different shades came and went.

Mel felt a touch on her shoulder and turned to see Cord giving her a concerned look. "Okay, Mel?" he asked.

"I'm fine." She looked back towards the Barrier. "It's magnificent. The Barrier, I mean. It looks so different from this side. Almost surreal."

Cord smiled. "Surreal. I must admit that I have never thought of the Barrier that way before. It must be the artist in you. You're looking at it from a different perspective."

As they reached the gate, Mel looked at the others; they all seemed to be handling the trip quite well. Even Hanley had got some of his colour back.

Once inside, they split up. The sergeant and the recruits returned to the camp in the ground vehicle, and Mel and Cord used the jeep. Cord dropped her off at the training block and told her to wait in the room where the uniform had been displayed.

A short while later, Sergeant Masters arrived. He sat her at a desk and turned on a large video screen, which was set into one wall. The picture on the screen was split into two parts. The left-hand side had a map of Britain; so did the right side, but with distinct differences.

The sergeant began the lesson. "Today, we start navigation. We will continue with this training until I am satisfied that I could drop you anywhere in England and, with a map and a compass, you could find your way home to London."

He turned to the screen. "On the left is a map of Britain before the Breakdown. On the right is a map of what we believe is a correct assessment of the country now."

Mel shifted in her seat. The map on the right was one she had never seen before. Masters continued. "The first and most obvious difference between the two maps is that the top of the country has been lopped off of the right hand map. Scotland energised its own Barrier five years after London. We have very little information as to what has gone on there since. "Circles," he pointed with a finger on the right hand map, "indicate Barriered cities."

Using his finger again, he said. "London, Birmingham, Liverpool, and Newcastle. This map was last updated fifty years ago, so this information may be out of date. For all we know, London may be the only city left with a Barrier. Broken circles indicate the cities we know have lost their Barriers." There were five broken circles marking Carlisle, Exeter, Wrexham, Nottingham, and Norwich.

"The red circles," Mel noted that these were much larger than the empty circles, "indicate radiation hot spots. During the Breakdown, the bombs detonated in these places rendered them uninhabitable. Scientists believe that it will be a thousand years before the radiation drops back to what it was." There were three red circles on the map. One was in the Manchester area, one in the Coventry area, and the other on the coast at Middlesbrough. The red stains spread out to envelop the areas around them. The radiation cut a wide swathe through the middle of England.

The map then changed to one of London. This one was overlain with grids, which were numbered one way and lettered the other. The rest of the day was spent understanding maps, latitudes, longitudes, and how to read a compass.

It was late evening by the time Cord got Mel to her apartment. They enjoyed a late dinner, but replaced dessert with more "Night Manoeuvres."

The next day, after a re-cap on the previous day's lessons, Mel was taken, blindfolded, to the eastern side of London where she was left with only a compass. Dressed in full uniform, she was told to make her way back to the barracks by the shortest route. Sergeant Masters said it should take her about two hours. Four hours later, footsore, sweaty, and bone weary, she arrived back, to be greeted by the sergeant at the gate.

After a short break, it was back to the lecture room, where her route back was displayed on the video screen. A tracing, made by the homing device in her helmet, was overlaid onto the map of London. It resembled a mass of spaghetti, twisting first one way then another, as she lost her way and doubled back on herself. After two hours of finding out where she had gone wrong, Cord came for her and took her home.

Although Cord stayed the night, Mel could do little more than eat dinner before falling asleep over coffee. Cord put her to bed.

Day four dealt with Mel's general fitness. She faced a battery of tests and general exercise, which Sergeant Masters said she passed "adequately." He then introduced her to another instructor sergeant.

"This is Sergeant Connors. It will be her job to give you a basic grounding in self-defence. I'll return for you at the end of the day." With that, he left and Mel turned to study her new instructor. Connors was a small, waif-like woman who did not look much older than Mel herself. Short blonde hair framed a petite-featured face, and she was shorter than Mel by a good four inches. Mel followed her into the gym, wondering what sort of self-defence was taught here.

Mel sat down on a pile of mats and waited for the sergeant to start talking. She stood for a short while, reading a data pad that Masters had passed to her. "I see that you have had the standard self defence classes in school. Basic Judo and ju-jitsu. You never took the advanced classes?"

Mel shook her head.

Motioning Mel to get up and come forward onto the mat, Sergeant Connors said, "Well, let's see what you know."

They spent the next half-hour with Mel demonstrating moves like the foot sweep and the shoulder throw, until the instructor called a halt. "You seem to have grasped the fundamentals pretty well. We may have time to show you some advanced moves later. What I really want to show you in the time we have together is the fundamentals of kickboxing. Kickboxing is using your feet and hands in coordination. The feet are used primarily, because they are stronger than the arms, and your boots are a lot better weapons than your bare hands. Some moves in kickboxing take years to learn properly. In the time we have, I can only teach you moves that may prove useful, and won't injure you doing them."

She moved over to the wall where there was a full-length picture of a man dressed in a Protector uniform. "There are lots of weak points on our bodies. Moving her finger to the relevant point, she continued. "The groin is, of course, the favourite spot. Although, on this gentleman you would probably break your foot, as all uniforms come with strengthened crotch pieces. Other weak spots," her finger moved to the relevant points on the chart, "are at the top of each thigh. A good blow here will cause a dead leg; the solar plexus, not, as commonly thought, in the gut area, but here, just above. A sharp, hard blow here will wind your opponent and allow you to get an advantage." The finger moved upwards. "Off the body, the best place to strike on the face is the nose. Hundreds of nerve endings collect here and a blow hard enough can kill."

They spent the rest of the day practising various moves. Sergeant Connors demonstrated the high kick and the spin kick, and showed Mel how to get momentum into her kicks. They finished the session with the sergeant holding large pads on each hand and Mel kicking them as hard as she could.

By the end of the day, Mel was tired and slick with sweat, but had learnt a lot about self-defence and built up a great respect for her instructor. They were just finished when Cord arrived.

"If you've finished, sergeant, I would like to get Miss Wilson home."

"Yes, sir. We still have to deal with the night stick and hand weapons. But we can cover that tomorrow."

Later that evening, after dinner and as Mel and Cord sat entwined on the couch, Cord stroked the top of Mel's head and asked. "Well, your week's nearly up. How do you feel about venturing outside?"

Mel tilted her head back to look up at Cord. "I'm looking forward to it. I've learnt a lot in the last four days." She smiled impishly. "And quite a bit in the last four nights, too."

Cord's arm tightened across around her waist. "And what about afterwards? Are you going to join up?"

Mel laughed. "I don't think I'm the army type, do you? I don't think Sergeant Masters was too impressed with the amount of questions I kept asking. As far as he and the forces are concerned, things are the way they are and should not be questioned. Just accept them and obey orders." Mel wriggled in closer. "No. I'll go back to college, finish my sculpture, and become a famous artist, like my mother."

"A sculpture? May I see it?"

Mel went silent for a moment. She had decided not to show it to anyone before its end of term unveiling. As she thought of that decision, she thought of her father, and felt guilty for her present high mood. The last few days had been so busy and she had found contentment in Cord's company.

Mel stood up and looked down at Cord on the couch. He had a concerned look on his face; he had sensed her mood change and wondered if he was the cause.

Mel smiled and held out a hand to him. He took it saying, "I don't want to see the sculpture if you don't want me to. Not if it's going to upset you."

Mel shook her head. "No. It's not you. It's me. I want to show you. However," her eyes twinkled, her good humour restored. "You must realise that you are very privileged. It's not finished and I never normally show my work to anybody before I think it's ready."

Mel led him to her studio. As they entered, the lights came up automatically and, with a flourish, Mel removed the covering sheet.

Cord was almost silent as he examined the sculpture. The only sound he made was an occasional "Hmmm." Finally, Mel's patience got the better of her and she said. "Well, what do you think?"

"Well, I recognise the subject, of course. But there are some bits that are not quite right."

Mel crossed her arms and put on an air of righteous indignation. "Oh, yes, Mr. Art Critic. What parts, exactly?"

Cord pointed to the breasts on the sculpture. "Those are definitely not big enough," he stated.

Mel stood alongside the sculpture and puffed out her chest so the disputed glands strained against the material of her light blouse. "I think I've got them just about right."

"Ah. But you're looking at them from the owner's point of view. I'm looking at them for a visitor's perspective."

Mel gave up trying to keep a face of righteous indignation, and broke down into a fit of giggles. Trying to keep her composure, she said. "Well, Captain, how do you suggest we solve this argument?"

"Now that's easy. We compare the two sets in question. Stay there." Cord stood himself between Mel and the sculpture. He then proceeded to place his hands around the breasts on the sculpture, then, under Mel's amused gaze, he moved his hands towards her. Before she could stop him, he ran his finger down the release strip on her blouse and pulled the two halves apart, leaving her naked to the waist.

"Now," Cord said with a lecherous look on his face, "we compare sizes." His hands came to encircle Mel's breasts and her surprise turned to laughter as he pulled her closer and they met for a long kiss.

"I should throw you out for such outrageous behaviour."

"If that's what you want, I'll leave right now."

"No way, soldier. What I want is for you to finish what you started."

They sank down together onto the carpet and later, when they finally made it to the bedroom, it was late before they got to sleep.

The next morning, it was back to the barracks where Mel met up with both Sergeants Masters and Connors. They demonstrated the rudiments of the nightstick and the general-purpose side arm issued to all Protectors who went outside.

After a shaky start, Mel began to get a feel for the nightstick. This was made of a light alloy and extended to over four feet, if required. Sergeant Connors showed how it could become an extension of the arm and, by the end of their session together,

Mel felt happy with it hanging from her belt.

Sergeant Masters then showed her a short-range laser pistol. Mel had never seen one of these before, either in private or being worn by one of the Protector forces. When asked, Masters told her that they were only issued to outside patrols and to the Presidential Guard, who wore them concealed.

After an hour on the indoor range using the pistol at low power, Mel's best score was five out of ten targets hit; she was even less impressed than the sergeant was.

After lunch, it was back to the classroom where her training had begun. He put her through tests on all she had learnt in the past week. Then they reported to Cord's office, and Mel waited outside while the sergeant went in alone.

On the trip home, Cord remained irritatingly silent until, finally, Mel, tired of waiting for him to tell her, said, "Well? What's the verdict? Do I go on Monday or not?"

Cord laughed and looked at his watch. "Well done! You lasted almost five minutes. I didn't think you would have lasted even one before you demanded to know how you got on."

"If you don't tell me right now, you'll be sleeping on your own tonight and fondling my sculpture is as close as you're going to get."

"Whoa! You certainly know how to get your own way, don't you?" Cord looked at her and smiled. "Masters was quite impressed with you. Said that if you could learn how to obey orders, you had potential as a soldier. Coming from Masters, that is quite a compliment."

"So, I'm going, then."

CHAPTER 2

"Yes. You are going. 6 a.m. Monday. You, me, and some of our most experienced personnel will be taking a trip outside."

Mel settled back into her seat with a satisfied smile on her face. The only down side she could see was that she had forty-eight hours to kick her heels. But after the last week, she wasn't going to let forty-eight hours worry her.

However, that did not stop her from seething with excitement all weekend. She tried to keep busy, shopping with Myan, having lunch with Uncle Terry, even crossing London to visit her father's brother and meeting his family.

While she was there, she tried to find out why her father had never talked about Granville. But, all he would say was that they had a difference of opinion. But, he insisted that, now her father was gone, his family was hers.

She was still curious, but too involved in the coming trip to dwell to long on the mystery. She resolved to look further into it when she got back. By the end of the weekend, she was really keyed up; she had been unable to tell anyone about the mission and she had seen very little of Cord, as he was busy himself preparing for the trip.

By the time Cord called to collect her on Monday morning, Mel had already been up and waiting for over an hour. She was dressed in full uniform and desperately trying not to drink too much coffee. The last thing she wanted to do was ask for a toilet stop.

They met the rest of the expedition at the North Gate. Mel saw there was to be quite a procession; five ground vehicles were lined up in front of the open gate and a flitter was being towed through the gate as they arrived.

Mel watched as it took to the air, and wondered what she would have to do to persuade Cord to take her for a trip in that. With the flitter leading the way, they got underway.

Each car held five troopers and a driver. Cord drove the lead car and Sergeant Masters brought up the rear. Now wearing her helmet, Mel could hear continual chatter between the cars and the flitter over her radio. She dug deep for the discipline that kept her from asking questions every minute, and only responded to the rare comment that was directed at her.

As they moved further away from London, the landscape slowly changed. The occasional bush, or small tree, or even a pile of rubble where a building once stood came into view. This time, the tops of the vehicles stayed closed, so Mel had to make do with observing through a small, round window in the car's side.

As the cars trundled slowly over the uneven terrain, the flitter, which had made the trip in half the time, sent back a continual stream of reports, from which Mel gathered they had found no evidence of human habitation. She didn't know whether to feel relieved or disappointed.

As the convoy came close to their goal, Mel could see that what she had thought of as a forest was no more than a collection of irregularly placed trees and shrubs. They halted at the edge and Cord ordered them out of the cars. The rest of the journey would be carried out on foot.

They split into groups of four, Mel went with Cord, and they began to enter the wooded area. Not too far in, they came to a clearing, Cord stopped at the edge and Mel, standing behind him, could see what appeared to be a series of small huts. Cord silently pointed to Sergeant Masters' group, signalling him to go forward and reconnoitre.

Mel watched as the sergeant and his men kicked open and examined each of the huts around the camp. Finally, the sergeant came up to Cord and saluted. "The area is secure, sir. No hostiles or booby traps detected."

"Very well, Sergeant. Post half the men on the perimeter and have them report in every fifteen minutes. Detail the rest to examine these structures more closely and report anything they find."

With another salute and a crisp, "yes, sir!" Masters turned away and began to issue orders over his radio.

Cord turned to Mel and, lifting his visor, gave her a smile, saying. "Well, fancy a bit of exploring?"

It soon became apparent that her first impressions about the camp had been right. She was not going to find the answers to any of her questions here. Examining the first hut, it was obvious that it had not been used for some time. It was extremely dilapidated and totally empty. When whoever had lived here left, there had been no panic, but an orderly withdrawal; nothing that could have been useful to them elsewhere had been left behind.

The centre of the clearing, which had once been trampled flat by busy feet, was now showing signs of losing its battle with nature. Quite mature bushes were growing in the centre, and vegetation encroached everywhere.

As the day wore on, Mel and Cord made a short excursion

into the thicket and out the other side, but there was little to see. As the sun reached its zenith, they returned to the clearing. As they were eating some of the concentrated rations, Sergeant Masters came up to report. "The encampment is completely empty, sir. We have found no evidence of anyone using this area for at least a year. Do you wish to extend the sweep?"

"Thank you, Sergeant. Yes, extend the sweep another ten yards further south. Use what men you feel is necessary, but we leaving here at 1600 hours. I want to be back in London before sunset. Understood?"

Masters saluted and moved away, barking his orders.

Cord sat down and leaned up against a handy tree. Mel slid down beside him and placed her helmet on the ground beside her. "It's a very nice day," she took a deep breath and, leaning closer to Cord, she sighed and said, "I don't suppose that it's the done thing for a captain to disappear into the bushes with one of his troops."

Cord laughed. "I think you could definitely say the Sergeant Masters would not approve."

Mel leaned back. She luxuriated in the fresh air, and the clear sky still held great fascination for her. She wished she had thought to bring a sketch pad with her. As she began to plan a way to talk Uncle Terry into letting her come outside to do some painting, the early morning start began to catch up on her and she slipped into a light doze.

She was woken by the crackling of her radio at her feet. Cord put his helmet back on to take a report from Sergeant Masters, and Mel lifted hers to her knees to listen in. The sergeant was calling the men in.

Suddenly, over the background chatter, a new, more urgent message began to come in. One of the sweep teams had lost contact with his partner. Mel began to lift the helmet onto her head but, as she did so, the message cut off in mid-sentence.

Mel turned to look at Cord, but he was already on his feet and with a curt, "Stay here," he was gone towards the perimeter. Mel watched Cord disappear into the undergrowth as more urgent messages came over the radio. Just then, without any warning, an explosion took place on the edge of the clearing, at the same point Cord had exited.

As she jumped to her feet, shocked and confused, the area was rocked by another and then another explosion.

Panic began to swell in Mel. She couldn't see Cord; he might be injured. As she moved closer to the edge of the clearing, where Cord had left, she could see some small craters left by the explosions. As she began to call Cord's name, she realised that the way to learn what was going on was to get back to her helmet and listen to the radio.

The helmet was on the ground where it had fallen when she jumped up. As she bent to retrieve it, there were another two explosions. One was very close behind her, and Mel felt the heat of the blast and a sensation of flying.

She crashed into the undergrowth and blackness fell as she cracked her unprotected head against a tree. Her last thoughts before she lost consciousness were about how annoyed Uncle Terry would be with her.

Chapter 3

Mel's return to consciousness was slow. When she thought back, she had hazy memories of voices and being carried, but her first concrete recollection was of a rocking sensation, like being in a boat. She also remembered strange clanking and clanging sounds.

That was what she remembered the first time she woke. It didn't last long, but it signalled the end of her coma, and she slipped into sleep. When she woke again, it was lighter and she discovered the source of the strange noises. Above her was a wooden ceiling festooned with pots and pans and an old fashioned brass lantern. The rocking sensation was still there, and the swaying motion of the objects hanging above made her feel sick.

Mel groaned, loudly.

A figure came into view. It appeared to be an old woman, dressed in a colourful, if well-worn skirt, with a faded red shawl around her shoulders. She looked down at Mel and chuckled hoarsely, "So, back with us at last, eh?"

CHAPTER 3

Mel tried to speak, but all that came out was a croak and, as she tried to lift her head, she began to cough and retch at the same time.

The old woman offered a cup to Mel's lips and, with the old lady's assistance, Mel raised her head and began to drink greedily. "Not so fast," the woman said, cautioning her. "You'll only regret it."

Mel sank back onto the bed, looking up at the woman. "Where am I?"

"Where are you? Well, at least you didn't ask, 'Who am I.' You could tell us that, if memory serves you yet."

Mel considered the question, and her memory began to come back. The trip outside London. The so-called camp site. The explosions. Cord.

"Cord! Where is Cord?"

"Cord? Don't know no Cord. Got some string if you like." The old woman cackled heartily at her own joke. Mel wasn't in the mood to join in.

The old woman pulled some coarse blankets up around Mel, and said, "Now you lay back and rest. We'll be stopping soon and Joel will answer all your questions, and ask a few himself, I'll be bound."

"Stopping soon," Mel said slowly. The fog in her brain was beginning to dissipate. "Are we on a boat?"

"A boat! No, no, we're in a caravan."

The woman moved out of her line of vision, and Mel tried to sit up again, only to be met with another surge of nausea. She had so many questions, but she lost the battle against fatigue, and slipped into sleep again.

The next time she awoke, it was dark, but she did feel better. It helped that the rocking sensation had stopped but, as she lay listening, she realised that she could hear the sound of people sleeping. In fact, someone was snoring loudly.

Realising the futility of trying to wake anyone, she lay back and tried to piece together what had happened to her.

Obviously, she was not in a ground car on her way back to London. She couldn't be in London; nobody used caravans in London. The only caravans Mel had ever seen had been in entertainment videos. And where was Cord? He wouldn't have left her. It just didn't make sense. Unless Cord wasn't in a position to come after her.

Unless Cord was dead.

Unless everybody else was dead as well, and she had been taken by the people who had killed her father.

Cord . . . Dead . . . A tear rolled down her cheek. Fear began to chill her to the marrow of her bones. She felt alone and afraid.

Mel struggled to pull her self together. So far, the only person she had seen was an old woman and, going by her looks, she must be well into her century. These terrorists who could blow up trains inside London and kidnap her were not going to be badly dressed old ladies; they were going to be young and dangerous.

Fear welled up in her again, but she took a deep breath and exercised control. Sergeant Connors had said that when, in a fight, fear was the emotion that had to be controlled, otherwise it

CHAPTER 3

would paralyse and the battle would be lost. Mel began to re-run the events at the camp again, but tiredness overtook her, and she went back into an uneasy sleep.

When she woke again, it was because there was a rough hand on her shoulder shaking her. Mel looked up to see a youngish man, whom she presumed would be Joel, with the old woman hovering behind him. Joel was large, dark haired, and unshaven. Dressed in a vest that at some time, although not recently, had been white, his stomach overflowed the piece of string that served as a belt for his grimy trousers. He had a large gold earring in one ear and there was a strong smell of body odour.

"Where you from, Girl?" he asked.

Mel wasn't too pleased at being referred to as "Girl," but didn't press the point. "London," she answered. "Where am I now?"

"A long ways from London, Girl. A long ways from the Dead City."

"The Dead City?"

The old woman peered around the man, chuckling. "That's what we calls it . . . The Dead City. Ain't been nobody come out or go in for a hundred years. We reckoned they were all dead."

"But now," the man interrupted, glaring at the old woman, "we have you. If it wasn't for that weird costume you were wearing when we found you, I wouldn't have believed it."

"But, I must get back to London." Mel smiled up at the man, "Won't you take me back?"

He wasn't about to be moved by a pretty face. "We haven't

got the time to be flitting about. We're on our way to Exeter for the Spring Fair. This troupe has a living to earn. Ma here will give you some food and find you some proper clothes to wear. We'll talk again later and find out what you can do to earn your keep."

With that, he left, and Mel could hear him outside shouting orders to get under way. The old woman reappeared with a bowl of unappetising looking broth but, as Mel started to eat, it she found she was ravenous and disposed of the bowl's contents quickly. It tasted a lot better than it looked. Mel thought about asking what was in it, but thought better of it.

It left her feeling better, however, well enough to ask some questions of the old woman. Her first questions were simple: who were these people and how did she get here?

The old lady was quite happy to answer her questions. She was in the caravan of Joel Williamson, her son, who was the head of a family of traders, or Tinkers, as they preferred to be called. They spent their lives going from settlement to settlement to sell their wares or skills and to entertain people.

Their last call had been at Norwich and they were now on their way to Exeter for the Spring Fair. They were later setting off than usual, as one of the womenfolk was ready to give birth, so to save time, they cut as close as they dared to London. Normally, they would take a wide detour around the Dead City, as rumours were rife about what happened to people who went to close to the city.

One of the older men remembered an old camp site that they could use to stay overnight, but when they got there they found strange, freshly made holes in the ground. They were about to move on—the Travellers were a very superstitious people and were not about to become a meal for the dead of London—when they found her, lying unconscious in the bushes.

At first, they had thought she was dead but, when she showed signs of life, they decided to bring her with them. She had lain, drifting in out of consciousness, for the best part of a week.

While they were talking, the caravan had got underway again and the rolling sensation had returned. Now she had a full stomach, Mel began to feel sick again, so she closed her eyes to shut out the vision of the hanging pots and pans swaying back and forth. She must have fallen asleep again; when she woke later, she was alone.

The caravan had stopped, and from the light coming through the small, round window, Mel figured it was late afternoon. She eased herself out of bed and gingerly attempted to stand. Apart from feeling a bit light-headed, she managed quite well.

Mel wanted to leave the confines of the caravan and find out more about these people and where exactly she was in relation to London. But, Mel thought wryly, running around naked was not the best way to meet her new travelling companions: she would have to find her uniform.

The inside of the caravan was a mass of cupboards and drawers, but none of them seemed to hold her uniform or any of her other equipment. There was, however, a blouse, skirt, and underwear at the end of the bed, and sitting on top of the pile was a pair of sandals.

It was obvious that her uniform was gone, so she picked up the clothes and began to get dressed.

The blouse was plain and white, and buttoned down the front. It was made of heavy cotton, and the woollen skirt was bright red with a black pattern. The underwear seemed to be made of some sort of sacking material, and was as scratchy as it looked.

Although Mel found them heavy after the synthetic materials she was used to, they were better than nothing. A piece of red ribbon served to tie back her hair and, looking into a cracked mirror on one wall, she decided that she was ready to face this strange world she had been dumped into.

Opening the door, which she had half expected to be locked, she went down a small set of wooden steps and looked around her. There were some eight caravans, all pulled into a circle, in the centre of which a large fire had been lit. Three women, dressed in the same style as Mel, were gathered around, cooking a meal. Several men sat around drinking or playing some sort of game using different coloured pieces of wood.

Mel began to move closer to the fire. A large, open fire like this one was not something Mel could ever remember seeing before. Smoke did not easily escape through the Barrier, so fires of this size were forbidden.

As she drew closer, the men stopped playing long enough to look her up and down as she came towards them. Mel got the feeling that she was being sized up like a piece of livestock. As she passed them, she heard loud grunts of laughter. Well, she thought, at least I'm not being ignored.

"Ah! You be up, then." The old woman came towards her carrying a basin full of potatoes. "You can lend a hand here; all these have to be peeled."

Mel looked in the bowl at its contents. "Peeled? By hand?"

"Of course, they won't peel themselves, you now." The old lady made her way closer to the fire, chuckling to herself.

After a moment's hesitation, Mel followed, deciding that it would be better to join in with whatever there was to do. No use in alienating these people until she knew where she was and whether there was a chance that they might help her get back to London. They sat down on a bench a few feet from the fire, and Mel copied the old woman as she pulled a potato from the bowl and began to scrape it with a knife.

"Mrs. . . . Err, I don't know your name," Mel began.

"You call me Ma. All thems do," she answered, waving the knife in the general direction of the other members of the troupe.

"Ma, I wondered what happened to my clothes, and the white shift I was wearing underneath."

"That black suit you was wearing had to be cut off you. Tough as old boots, it was. Anna, she's the seamstress, has the other bit. Now, that's a fine piece of material, that is. If we could make that, we'd all be rich, so we would. I don't suppose you know how to make it?"

"No, I have no idea. Can I get it back?"

Ma shook her head in wonderment. "I never did feel anything so soft. You won't see that again. I hear Anna's making a shirt for Joel out of it." She gave an indignant sniff, "Not that she'll get anywhere with him like that."

The last reference made no sense to Mel so she ignored it. The shift would be a lot better than this scratchy underwear, but she could live with its loss. But it was important to get the uniform back. There was too much useful equipment with it. The maps, the medikit, even the night-stick would be of no end of use if she couldn't persuade these people to take her back to London.

She asked Ma about getting her stuff returned to her. Ma was silent for a moment. "I'll ask Joel," she finally said, then grabbed a potato out of Mel's hands and clucked her tongue. "Look at the state of this. You've taken more 'tater than skin. That's an evil waste of good food, that is. The way you're handling that knife, anybody would think that you've never peeled a 'tater before."

Mel smiled sweetly. She wasn't about to admit to ignorance about anything; she did, however, watch closely as Ma demonstrated the approved way to peel a 'tater. They had nearly finished the bowl when Joel came and stood over them. He pulled one of Mel's completed potatoes from the bowl.

"Well," he said, looking closely at the potato, "you're no cook, that's for sure. What can you do to earn your living, I'll be asking? Nobody rides with the family for free."

Mel thought quickly. They had forgotten to cover this in basic training but, looking up into Joel's face, she answered. "I can paint and sculpt."

"Paint, eh, and sculpt. Well I don't rightly know what a sculpt is but painting never made a body rich." Then, fast for a man of his size, he reached down and grabbed Mel's arm and hauled her to her feet. He surprised Mel further by spinning her around and looked her up and down with a practised eye. Mel was dumbfounded; no one had ever treated her like this before. Joel's hands came down to her waist, and gripped them lightly. "Good, wide hips, though. You'll bear a man strong children."

Mel flushed red as she heard laughter behind her. Everybody gathered around the fire watched as Joel slapped her hard on the bottom and said, "No doubt some man can get some use out of you."

This caused further laughter from the people present, but Mel held her temper and even managed a smile. The smile wasn't very sweet and it didn't reach her eyes, but it told of trouble for the next person to try and manhandle her like that.

But for now she kept the peace. She had to get her uniform back.

"Joel," she said, managing to sound all sweetness and light. "I was wondering about my own clothes."

He put his hand on her head and ruffled her hair like a child, and Mel felt even further insulted. "Don't you worry your pretty little head about that. I know a man in Exeter who'll pay good barter for that fancy costume."

Someone called him from the other side of the fire and Mel watched him walk away, with her face red and her eyes alight with indignation. That was her uniform and she meant to get it back.

When the meal was ready, Mel sat with the other women to eat. With a bit of clever questioning, she deduced which caravan was Anna's. Still running on the adrenaline caused by her embarrassment, she had already decided to get her uniform and get out of the camp in the early hours of the morning. But a filling meal and the after-effects of the last few days caught up with her and, when she climbed into her small bed in the caravan, she fell fast asleep and didn't wake until late in the morning.

She found the caravan was underway again when she did wake; opening the small door, she found Ma sitting on the steps at the reins of one of the large horses the Travellers used to pull their caravans. The troupe was working their way down a muddy track onto a wide expanse of open ground. Far in the distance, Mel could see more caravans and smoke from a fire.

Ma pointed ahead and told her that they were going to meet other troupes of Tinkers and they would all travel to Exeter together. Mel sat herself down beside Ma and luxuriated in the open air and the sights around her, until they stopped and formed a circle adjacent to the others. Joel hitched his riding horse to the back of the caravan and went with other men to talk to the leaders of the other troupes. It was evident that the women were meant to carry out the chores of securing the horses and setting up camp.

Mel, wanting to appear willing, helped Ma with the horses and other chores. While they worked, Mel got Ma to tell her all about her family and the rest of the troupe. Once Ma started, it wasn't long before Mel had the whole history of the Travellers laid out in front of her.

Joel; he was Ma's only son. She had five daughters; three

CHAPTER 3

of them still survived and were married to men in other troupes or, in one case, to a farmer not far away. Joel had inherited the leadership of the troupe on his father's death some two years ago.

Last year, Joel had lost his wife in childbirth, and the child as well. Apparently, Joel was considered quite a catch and would have to re-marry again, so he could produce an heir and carry on the Williamson's family tradition of leading the troupe. Anna had made her intentions quite clear in that, having lost her husband about the same time, but Ma did not approve of her.

The history lesson went on until the midday break and, after a small meal, Ma decided that, as she had such a willing helper, they could service all the horses' harnesses. After rubbing pig fat into the leather straps, and then cleaning what seemed to be an unending supply of horse brasses, Mel was sweaty and tired by late afternoon.

Finally, as she finished the last horse brass, Ma told that a group of the women were going down to the river to bathe. Ma gave her some soap and a rough towel, and pointed her in the right direction; Mel followed the other women down a path that led to the river.

Still unsure of her position with the other women, Mel hung back slightly. A couple of them glanced back at her, then one of them dropped back to walk alongside her. Mel had already identified her as Anna. She was shorter than Mel, but carried almost twice her weight. What she didn't carry was an attitude of wanting to be friends.

Anna obviously felt that there was no need for introductions.

"You keep your foreign hands off Joel," she said without any preamble. "He's not for the likes of you." She sneered the words, looking at Mel like she had just crawled out from under a stone.

Mel couldn't have agreed more about not being the one for Joel, but she was sore, tired, and had little patience left, so she smiled and answered. "Maybe he thinks that I have more to offer than an overweight outsider like you."

Anna hit Mel with a slap that knocked her off her feet and set her ears ringing in protest. She looked up just in time to see Anna lunging at her. She was making a grab for her hair, her fingers crooked like claws.

Mel rolled over and regained her feet and, as Anna went to slap her again, she grabbed her arm and pivoted her over her shoulder and onto her back. Strike one for Sergeant Connors.

Almost growling now, Anna leapt to her feet, lowered her head, and aimed for Mel's stomach. Mel stepped neatly to one side and as she went past, kicked Anna's feet out from under her, sending her sprawling, face down in the dirt. Anna launched herself from a crouching position at Mel's legs, but Mel just stepped back so she fell down again. As she waited for Anna to regain her feet, Mel noticed that the other women had gathered round to watch the spectacle. She decided that it was time to go on the offensive.

Moving closer, she grabbed the now panting Anna by the front of her blouse, shoved one foot into the pit of her stomach and, falling onto her back, flipped her into the air so that, when she landed hard on her back, all the air, and fight, was knocked out of her. Mel got to her feet and began to brush the dirt off her skirt, keeping a close eye on Anna in case she wanted to carry on proving herself the better choice for Joel. But, after she had been helped to her feet, she contented herself with a look, which, if it had not killed, would have done serious damage. Mel smiled sweetly at her in reply.

They carried on towards the river, with Mel keeping her distance, and when the group stopped and began to get ready to wash, Mel moved back upstream slightly, out of their view. The only person she had really had any meaningful contact with had been Ma, so she thought it would be better if she kept out of the others' way for now. Anna seemed to be some sort of leader, and Mel having defeated her had thrown the others into confusion.

Stripping off her clothes, Mel waded into the river and eased herself down into a sitting position, gasping as she did so. The water was extremely cold, but it was better than nothing. Mel was just starting to wash her hair for the second time — it was so dirty she was convinced that it was full of lice — when she heard the bushes rustle behind her.

She looked up to see one of the younger women coming down the bank towards her. She took off her clothes and entered the water a few feet away. Mel carried on washing her hair and, after a short while, the girl moved closer to her. "You should cut your hair shorter," she advised. "It would be a lot easier to clean that way." Mel smiled encouragingly, but stayed silent and let her do the talking.

"How did you do that to Anna? No one done that to her before."

Feeling a lot better now that she was clean and out of that scratchy underwear, Mel decided that she should cultivate at least one more friend here, so, heaving herself out of the water and onto the bank, she said, "It's all a question of pivots and levers. You use your opponent's weight against them."

The young girl got herself up on the bank next to Mel and began drying herself. Breaking into a fit of giggles, she said, "Well, Anna's got a lot of weight to be used against her."

Peering from under her towel as she dried her hair, Mel looked at the girl sitting next to her. She guessed that she was aged about fifteen, tall and slim, still in the gawky stage. Her short, light brown hair framed a pretty face that seemed to smile easily.

"What's your name?" Mel asked.

"Wilma. What's yours?"

"Melina," Mel stuck out her hand. "Call me Mel."

There was silence as both busied themselves with the job of drying, before Wilma spoke again. "Will you teach me to fight like that?"

"I don't think I will be here long enough for that. I must get back to London." Mel began to put her clothes back on. She picked up the discarded underthings and decided, with a wry smile on her face, that she could do without them for now.

"I heard the men talking last night," Wilma said conversationally. "Joel said that there's a man in Devon who wants anything to do with London brought to him. He pays very well."

Mel's head popped through the neck opening of her blouse,

her hair sticking out in frizzy bunches. She wore a look of amazement on her face. "They are going to SELL me?"

Wrapping the skirt around her hips, Mel felt outraged. Nobody was going to sell her. That was barbaric. She slipped on her sandals and began to comb angrily at her hair with her fingers.

Wilma pulled a simple, smock-like dress over her head and went to stand behind her, saying, "Here, let me do that for you. I've got a brush." As Wilma brushed, Mel could feel the anger draining out of her with each knot and tangle that came undone.

"You really should cut this shorter, you know. It would be a lot easier to manage."

Mel snorted. "I don't plan on being here that long."

The hair brushing went on in silence. Mel's thoughts turned to escape. Perhaps escape was too strong a word; her movements had not been restricted in any way. The people of the troupe obviously did not expect her to leave. Well, that was their mistake.

Her biggest problem was finding her way back. She had no idea where she was, although she was sure that she could work it out if she had access to her maps and compass. Also, the boots would be helpful; these sandals would not stand up to a strenuous hike. She had to get her equipment back from Joel. Wilma interrupted her train of thought with a question. "Tell me about London, Mel. What's it like there?"

Mel looked up at the young girl and smiled. "What would you like to know?"

"What are the people like there?"

"Just like you and me. Two arms, two legs, the right amount of fingers and toes."

"Oh!"

"Oh? What did you expect?"

Wilma sat down beside Mel and smiled shyly, idly pulling hair from the brush. "It's said that the people of London are mutants." She dropped her eyes and stared at her feet. "It's said that they would leave the city at night and kidnap children, to experiment on."

Mel took Wilma's and smiled. "Do I look that different? Those are just stories that adults tell to frighten children. I was told that, if I misbehaved, the outsiders would come and get me. That gave me nightmares for years. I've often wondered why adults feel they have to tell children stories like that."

Mel automatically looked at her wrist for the time; when her gaze was met by only bare skin she sighed and said, "I wonder what time it is."

Wilma glanced into the sky. "Around five o'clock. Why?"

Mel smiled at the easy way she did that. She looked around for the other women; they were still up river in a group. "Well, I wondered how much longer we have before going back to the caravans."

"Oh, we won't go back until almost full dark. We don't get away from the men that often so we like to take full advantage."

"Good," Mel said, getting up and smoothing down her skirt. "Then I've got time to shown you that shoulder throw I used against Anna."

They moved onto a flat piece of ground, and Mel spent the next half-hour demonstrating some of the self-defence moves she had learnt in London. While they were taking a rest, Mel decided the time had come to find out how helpful Wilma could be to her.

"Wilma," she began. "I need your help."

The young girl looked at her enquiringly.

"I don't belong here. I need to get home."

"You're not a prisoner, Mel. You can leave at any time."

"I'm not so sure about that. You said that I was worth something in Devon. I'm not being guarded because Joel believes that if I left I would have nowhere to go. What I need is the equipment in my uniform."

Wilma sat up. "What sort of equipment?"

"Oh, there were maps and a compass. A medical kit, flares, a knife, and my boots. They would be really useful."

Wilma thought for a moment; obviously her loyalties were conflicted. Finally, she took a breath and looked at Mel. "I know where the maps are; my father has them. I overheard him talking about them. I haven't seen a compass, or any boots."

Mel gripped Wilma's arm. "That's wonderful. Can you get them for me?"

Wilma pulled away and began pacing the riverbank. "I don't know. My father said that the maps would be really useful."

Mel smiled. "I don't think a couple of maps are going to make a great difference. Your troupe has spent years going from place to place without them. I don't suppose if I take the maps back, they are going to start getting lost."

Wilma stopped pacing and looked at her. "Why leave, Mel? Stay here with us. We're not a bad people, and it's a good life on the whole, even in the winter."

Mel shook her head. "No, Wilma. This is not my home. My place is in London, with my family and Cord."

"Cord? Is he your husband?"

"My husband?" Mel hesitated for a moment. She hadn't considered that possibility. "No. He's just a friend."

A sudden pain hit her as she thought of Cord. Where was he now? Was he lying badly injured, or even dead, in the medical centre? With an effort, she pulled her thoughts back to the present and her problems now.

"Oh," Wilma remarked. "I thought you would be married. I'm getting married this summer, in Exeter," she finished proudly.

"Married? But you can't be more than sixteen. Isn't that a bit young?"

"Young? No, most girls are married by their sixteenth birthday. I am told that my father has picked a very nice boy for me, with a fine family name."

"You've been told! You mean you're told who you're going to marry!" Mel was aghast. Wilma showed surprise at her reaction.

"Of course. Otherwise how would I meet someone to marry?"

Mel spluttered for a moment. "Are there no boys or young men with this troupe?"

Wilma blushed red. "Of course, but I couldn't marry one of them. They're my cousins or uncles!"

Realisation hit Mel. The troupe members were all related in one way or another, so Wilma would have trouble meeting eligible boys. Now that had been explained, the idea of arranged marriages did not seem so outrageous.

"But," Mel continued, not yet quite ready to give up an argument against a seemingly barbaric concept, "how many times have you met this intended husband of yours?"

Wilma's brow creased. "The last time we met was at the betrothal. I was seven, Randal was nine," she giggled. "I remember he pulled my hair and I kicked his shins."

Mel, whilst accepting that Wilma would have to get married outside of her troupe, still thought that there were too many unanswered questions. "Where will you live?"

"With my husband's family. Eventually, we will get our own caravan, or maybe we'll settle in one of the seaside communities. Randal's a very good carpenter." The pride in Wilma's voice was quite evident. "I would like to live by the sea."

Watching Wilma's calm acceptance of her future, Mel presumed that all girls from this lifestyle had been brought up to believe that this was their destiny, to marry and be a wife and mother. A cold feeling went down her back; if she stayed here long enough, once her curiosity value had worn off, it would be her destiny as well.

"What happens," Mel asked, fascinated by this insight into life outside, "if this Randal turns out to be a wife beater?"

"Oh, Randal won't be like that," Wilma answered

confidently. "Da has known his family for years and, anyway, a man has the right to discipline his wife as he sees fit."

At that comment, Mel almost choked. While she could see that Wilma would never understand her objections and was quite happy to take the route planned for her, she persisted with her line of questioning. "But what if he is violent and beats you for no reason?"

Wilma was now looking a bit put out by this line of questioning. "Well, I can petition the troupe elders and, if he carries on, I can divorce him with no slur on myself. Any children would have to stay with his family."

Mel could see that Wilma was looking a bit confused as to why anybody would question something that had been working for generations, so she did not point out that there were not many women who would leave their children. Or that the woman's only recourse was by appealing to the heads of HIS family.

Wilma asked a question of her own. "Why do you act so surprised, Mel. Isn't this what happens in London?"

Mel hesitated before answering. How much should she tell? She decided that Wilma should know that it was different in London, but not about her full relationship with Cord. She had a strong suspicion that sex before marriage was not encouraged here.

"In London, "Mel explained, "women choose their own partners. Some women never get married at all."

With that piece of information, Wilma's mouth dropped open and her eyes widened in surprise. Mel decided then that she would not broach the subject of women living with other women, or men living with other men, for that matter!

Mel continued to feed Wilma censored pieces of life in London and took hers in return, until one of the women called to Wilma, saying they were going back, They followed behind the others and, except for a glare from Anna, they were mostly ignored.

When they got back, the women headed for the fire to help with the evening meal. Mel felt no compulsion to follow them and, as Ma wasn't around, she decided to take a closer look at Wilma's family caravan, hoping that it would be empty and she would be able to retrieve the maps.

She soon found that was not going to be possible, for as she drew nearer to the caravan, Mel heard the sound of voices coming from it. There appeared to be several men inside and the subject under discussion seemed to be her. Standing underneath the side window, Mel listened in. She immediately recognised the voice of Joel doing most of the talking; another voice asked what he planned to do with her.

"We take her with us to Exeter. The man there will pay good barter for her, if he wants her."

"What do you mean, 'if he wants her'?"

"We were asked to look out for things from London," Joel explained. "The man may not want people."

"And if the man don't want her," asked a different voice, "what then?"

"I could think of a few things to do with her," said a leering voice. The others laughed, evidently finding this remark funny.

When the laughter died down, Joel continued. "We'll have

a marriage bidding. The best dowry from an unmarried man can have her. Can't say fairer than that."

Mel felt her anger begin to rise. That was tantamount to selling her off to the highest bidder, like a prized piece of livestock.

"Eavesdroppers never hear any good of themselves," a voice cackled behind her.

Mel jumped and turned around to find Ma toothlessly grinning at her.

"If Joel catches you," she continued, "he'll take a stick to your backside."

"If Joel tries that," Mel sniffed. "I'll take a stick to his head." Mel shivered. The evenings were still chilly and her blouse was no protection against the cold.

The old woman took her by the arm, saying, "We'd better find you a wrap before you catch your death of cold."

With a thick, woollen shawl around her shoulders, Mel followed Ma to the fire in the centre of the camp, where the other women were preparing the evening meal. Anna was conspicuous by her absence and Ma told her that she had already gone to her caravan because she had a headache. Ma chuckled and Mel guessed that she had heard about this afternoon's meeting. She sat herself down and began to peel more potatoes, listening to the women talk.

Their conversation seemed to be mostly either about their men or about the upcoming trip to Exeter. One of the younger women, about the same age as Mel but with a small child balanced on her hip, decided to include Mel in the conversation.

"What are the men in London like?" she asked.

Mel paused and acted as if she was giving the question a lot of thought. "Oh, I think I can they have all the right equipment, at least."

This broke the ice with the rest of them and they all giggled together. More questions came her way and she answered them as well as she could without letting any more slip than she had already told Wilma.

By the time supper was ready and the men came to the fire, Mel was beginning to change her opinions of the women she had met so far. She began to realise that what she had thought was a lack of spirit, or even forced submission in the women outside, was in fact nothing more than a necessary way of life. It figured that, once the outside world settled down after the Breakdown, one of the main problems would be repopulating the country. The only people who could do this were the women. Almost overnight, they went back to baby-producing machines; over a hundred years of women's liberation just disappeared.

By taking the ages of the women around the fire and how many children they already had, Mel worked out that they had a child about every eighteen months. Many of these children did not grow out of infancy. All of the older women had lost children this way. Life expectancy was pretty low for adults as well. Ma, whom Mel had thought was well past her century, was in fact the oldest member of the troupe at sixty-seven. Men did not usually last past their sixtieth birthday, or women past sixty-five.

Deformities amongst children had also been rife in the early days, as it had been in London, but as London retained its medical knowledge and aborted deformed babies in the womb, outside, it was left to nature.

The leaders of the travelling families now knew all the danger areas, so deformities were now quite rare.

The practice of arranged marriages had also returned by need rather than wish. With such small population left after the Breakdown, and spread out in small communities, inbreeding was bound to become a problem. After a couple of generations, whilst the old knowledge was still remembered, a tradition of pairing up children from different areas quickly became the norm.

This occurred when the children reached an age of seven. It was believed that if a child reached this age then he or she had a good chance of reaching maturity.

If a husband or wife died (women's deaths in childbirth were fairly common) then re-marriage was up to the people involved. Joel's wife had died giving birth to her fourth stillborn child only a few months ago, and he had told one woman's husband that, if it wasn't for the possibility of payment in Devon, then he would have taken Mel for his wife.

This is what had turned Anna against her. Her husband had died suddenly a year ago. Some said she had nagged him to death, and she fancied herself as the leader's wife.

Well, she can have him! Mel thought.

Before the meal started, Joel announced that, as the other caravans had arrived (Mel had not failed to notice them or the extra people eating around the fire), they would be moving on in the morning. Mel realised that she would have to leave tonight, or she would be twenty miles further from London by the next evening.

She sat herself at the edge of the firelight and, as the others ate their supper, she eased herself back into the shadows until she felt safe enough to leave unnoticed.

She made her way to Anna's caravan and tried the door. She was not surprised to find it unlocked, as crime inside the troupe was almost unknown. The same cramped chaos that existed in Joel's caravan was in evidence here, as well. The uniform was easy to find. It hung from the ceiling. The sealing strip had been cut and Mel realised that it was of little use to her. The boots, which were close by, were another thing.

Mel needed them so she had to hope that their disappearance wasn't noticed too quickly. She went through the pockets in the uniform, but found nothing and was about to leave when she saw the uniform's belt lying on the bed and, still attached to it, the survival kit. Opening it up, she found it untouched. Compass, torch, flares, all still there. Mel's spirits rose; the kit would be very useful.

Holding the boots and wearing the belt under her clothes, Mel left Anna's caravan and started to make her way to Wilma's, only to be surprised by Wilma coming out of the shadows.

"I guess you're on your way to get these," she said holding up the maps. "After we talked, I went home and searched for them. They are made of a very strange material. Is it valuable?"

Mel almost snatched the maps from Wilma's hand and then had to smile an apology. "No. It's not valuable in London. It's called plastic and everybody uses it."

"So," Wilma said, with a defensive note in her voice. "You're leaving, then." It was a statement rather than a question.

"Yes, I have to get home. Thanks for all your help, Wilma." She took the younger girl and held her for a moment in a tight hug, surprised to feel some regret at leaving. "I hope we'll meet again."

"When will you go?"

"Just before dawn, while everybody is sleeping."

"Well," Wilma smiled at her. "Look behind this caravan as you leave. I'll try to leave a food pack for you."

Mel hid her plunder and they made their way back to the fire. Nobody seemed to have missed them, although Ma gave her a long, hard look. The men were sitting around talking or playing games. The women were clearing the dishes or putting children to bed. Everybody turned in early in preparation for tomorrow's journey.

Tonight, they were sleeping under the caravan, as the weather had improved. This suited Mel, as there was less chance of her making an inadvertent noise and waking someone up. She waited until she thought it was about an hour from dawn before she began to move quietly out from underneath the caravan. As she stepped by Ma's bed, the old woman put out a hand and grabbed Mel's ankle.

Mel almost screamed, but managed to keep it down to a strangled squawk.

"Going somewhere, Girl?"

"Just the call of nature," Mel answered, trying to keep her voice calm.

"Nature calling, eh!" Ma said. "I reckon it might be, at that." Slowly heaving herself out of her bed, she took Mel's wrist and led her away from the caravan.

"You're leaving," she stated.

Seeing lies would get her nowhere, Mel said, "Yes. I don't belong here. I belong in London."

Ma nodded her head. "Aye, that's true enough. I talked to young Wilma; you've confused her something rare. It's probably best you should leave. You're what they calls 'an unsettling influence'. I saw the look on your face when Joel said we were moving on in the morning. So I packed this for you." She went round the back of the caravan and returned with a sack. "I put in a few things you might need. That stick thing you had is also in there."

Mel opened the sack and rummaged around. There was the telescopic night-stick, a wrap of bread and cheese, a blanket, and a change of clothes.

"You never found a small green box, did you?"

"Aye, I did. I reckon those potions will do more good here than with you."

Mel smiled, Ma was right. It was unlikely that she would need the medikit; it would be a lot more use here. "My gun? It was attached to my belt."

"None of the men could get it to work, so they threw it away." Ma spat into the ground at her feet to demonstrate what she thought of such wastefulness. "Now you get going. People will be awake soon; it's to be an early start."

"What will happen when Joel finds that I'm gone?"

"Oh, he'll rant and rave for a while, but he won't have time for a search. I can handle him. Now, go."

Mel slung the sack of her shoulder and made her way across the circle. When she looked back, Ma was nowhere to be seen. Behind Wilma's caravan was another bundle, containing the food the young girl had promised.

Removing the light sandals and putting on her boots, Mel stepped into the undergrowth, setting off in what she hoped was a southerly direction. As dawn broke, she stopped on a small rise to check the compass; as she looked back, she could see the caravans in the distance and people moving about, getting ready to leave.

As she looked down at the scene, Mel felt some regret at leaving. They were basically a good people, even if they had some old fashioned ideas. Maybe she would meet them again, sometime. But now, working out south from her compass, she turned her back on the camp and began her trek home.

She made about ten miles the first day, moving in a general southerly direction, but with no real idea where she was. The maps she had of Britain were printed before the Breakdown and it was obvious that a lot had changed in two hundred years. What she needed was some sort of indicator that she was on the right road.

The weather remained warm and fine for most of the day, but by nightfall, clouds had begun to build and a stronger wind lowered the temperature enough for Mel to get the blanket out of her pack to put round her shoulders.

As darkness fell, Mel began to look for somewhere to

spend the night. She knew she needed somewhere secure. The men in the troupe had told stories of wild dogs and pigs. She had no wish to run into a pack in the dark.

Finding what appeared to be a rough track, although unused for some time, Mel followed it to a fallen down old fence, beyond which stood the dark outline of a building. No lights shone from the broken windows, so Mel decided to investigate.

The old cottage was deserted, but displayed signs that it had once been regularly used. She wondered briefly what had happened to the people who had once lived here. There were still several pieces of furniture left, and hanging in the corner of the kitchen was an old oil lamp. Mel shook it and found that there was still some oil in it and, with a tinderbox Ma had packed, she managed to light it.

Exploring the rest of the house, she found another two rooms. One had a large tin bath in it, which Mel looked at wistfully. But even if she had the water and a way to heat, it Mel realised that a bath was out of the question. The other room held a large, broken-down bed and a chest of drawers. As Mel brought the light into the room, she could hear the patter of tiny feet as the present occupiers of the room made themselves scarce.

Although Mel had never seen a live rat or mouse before leaving London, she found she had no great fear of them. This was fortunate, as quite a few scattered away from her. This was good enough for tonight, Mel decided, as she threw her pack onto the bed. After a dry supper of bread and cheese, she lay down and tried to sleep.

Although she was tired—walking ten miles in one day was

not easy — she had trouble getting to sleep. When she put out the light, mice or rats running over her continually woke her. She re-lit the lamp and its light kept them at bay until the oil ran out. Then, she was fair game for the nocturnal creatures that lived in the house, unless she used her torch and risked running the batteries down.

So, at first light, she was happy to get up and start moving. After a cold breakfast, Mel sat in the small kitchen and spread out her maps on the rickety old table and tried to work out a route home. What she really needed to know was where she was now.

She knew she had lain unconscious in Joel's caravan for three days and spent another three days with the Travellers, recovering. Ma had said the caravans were doing twenty miles a day, as they had been delayed in Norwich. So six days at twenty miles a day would put her some hundred and twenty miles from London.

Looking at the map in front of her, and measuring the distance according to the scale, as Sergeant Masters had taught her, she traced a route that finally stopped at Salisbury. This, in turn, was surrounded by a large area of open ground called Salisbury Plain. These names struck a chord but the memory refused to surface.

But at least this gave her a reference point from which to start her journey. South across Salisbury Plain to the next large town on the map, Andover. Although Mel was using the larger towns as reference points, she had no intention of entering any of them. According to the Travellers, nobody lived in these areas and they were overrun by packs of dogs and rats.

Her next problem was food. She only had enough for a few days. Ma had told her that there were a few small communities in the area where the troupe traded on their way to Exeter every year. She would have to find one and hope they were friendly. Mel considered trying to catch a rabbit. Deer, she decided were far too big for her to deal with on her own. She had watched the women of the troupe skin and gut rabbits; whether she could also do it, she would have to wait and see.

Now it was daylight, Mel searched the house again for anything of use. She found a knife in a drawer in the kitchen table; its blade was rusty but its edge was reasonably keen. She slipped it into the top of her boot. It was better than nothing.

Mel set off again, her spirits raised by the belief that she thought she knew where she was. It was overcast and drizzling with rain, but she set a fast pace to begin with. This soon slowed, as she had to fight her way through some dense undergrowth. As Mel pushed her way through a particularly thick section, she suddenly fell forwards and rolled down a bank, to come face to face with the thing she most wanted to see.

An ancient stone signpost.

Clearing the weeds obscuring it, Mel felt a surge of pride as she read the inscription. Underneath, an arrow pointing in the direction she was going were the words, London 110 miles and Salisbury 5 miles. Almost spot on, the arrow pointing in the other direction read, Exeter 115 miles.

Mel shouldered her pack and set off in the direction of London.

She had fallen onto an old road, very overgrown, but occasionally she could still see bits of the original tarmac covering. As she worked her way around Salisbury, Mel spied the remains of its cathedral in the distance.

Then, quite abruptly, the trees cleared and Mel found herself on open ground. This was the first indication that she was entering an inhabited area. It wasn't long before Mel entered a small village of ten houses clustered together. The houses had a lived-in look. Windows had been repaired, gardens cared for, the fields surrounding the village had been cultivated and, in the distance, Mel could see someone at work, ploughing.

Sitting on the porch of the first house in the small settlement was an old man, apparently asleep. The building seemed to be bigger than the rest in the village, owing to a large barn-like structure attached to it. A hand painted sign over the door proclaimed it to be a blacksmith.

As Mel approached the house, the old man raised his head and looked at her with watery eyes. "You be not from around here," he said abruptly.

Mel had already considered what to say if anybody asked her where she was from. Saying she was from London would cause too many more questions to be asked, so she had decided on a cover story.

"No," she smiled. "I'm travelling to Norwich. Back to my home and family."

"To Norwich, you say." The old man grinned at her, showing a set of blackened stumps for teeth in the process. "That be a long ways from here."

CHAPTER 3

`"Yes." Mel smiled again, hoping to appear harmless. "And I'm short of food. Is there anywhere around here I can get some?"

The old man scratched himself absently. "Food? Don't know about that. We trades with the caravans that comes through here. You got anything to trade?"

Just as Mel was wondering if she should move on and try to find someone else, another voice came from inside the house; this one was feminine. "Who are you talking to, Da? Is Davy back already?"

The old man indicated over his shoulder with a dirty thumb. "That be my daughter-in-law, Louise." He raised his voice and answered her. "No. Davy's not back yet. We have a Traveller."

From the slightly cynical tone the old man used, Mel surmised that her story was quite believed. The old boy was not as senile as he made out.

Mel smiled to herself. Whether she was believed or not wasn't a problem. She looked towards the door of the house, where a woman was subjecting her to an overall inspection. Mel studied her in return and saw a woman of around her own age, with her light brown hair tied back, and a pleasant, open face, if a bit pinched with some unknown worry.

"A Traveller, hmm," Louise put her hands on her hips and continued. "Well, you had better come in. You look as if you could do with a meal and a hot bath."

Mel nodded to the old man, who grunted and put his head back on his chest and returned to his sleep. Then she followed Louise into the house. She came into a large kitchen with a wood burning range at one end and a large open fire at the other. Between the two was a large circular table with rough wooden chairs around it, and a pair of overstuffed easy chairs by the fire. Over the fire hung a large, black kettle, steam curling from its spout.

As Mel looked at the fireplace, she caught sight of herself in the mirror suspended above. Louise was right; she did look like she could use a bath.

Louise pointed to the kettle, saying, "Hot water there. Everything else you'll need is through that door. You had better pass out those clothes for washing."

Mel carried the kettle through the door to find an old tin bath waiting for her. Now the possibility of a hot bath was very real, she wasted no time in filling the bath and stripping off her clothes. As she handed her clothes out, Louise also gave her some plant leaves, saying, "Crush these into the water. They're very good for aches and pains and they smell lovely."

The aches and pains of her journey disappeared in no time, leaving her so relaxed that, when Louise knocked on the door to ask if she had finished, it was a struggle to heave herself out of the bath. Mel made a mental note to find out exactly what plant the leaves came from.

Dressing in the clean clothes that Louise provided and tying back her hair, she went back into the kitchen to find Louise, her father-in-law, and two other men.

One was about the same age as Louise; he was well built, with thick, well-muscled forearms and a mass of black hair that came down to his shoulders. The other was a teenager with curly blond hair and an angelic looking face.

Louise looked up from the pot she was stirring and waved a hand towards the two men. "The big lump is my husband, Davy, and the innocent looking one is my brother, Josh."

Davy held out a calloused hand and took hers in a crushing grip. "Welcome to our home," he said formally. Josh just glanced up at her and smiled shyly.

He gestured for her to sit down, and Louise began to ladle stew onto the plates in front of them. As he offered Mel a basket containing bread, Davy said, "Da says you're a Traveller. Where are you heading?"

"I'm on my way to Norwich. Going back to my family."

Davy made a non-committal grunt and started to eat his meal. The others followed suit, and Mel copied them. Let them start conversations, she thought.

After the meal, while Mel helped Louise clear the table, the men sat themselves in the chairs by the fire. The old man got out a black, evil looking pipe, and lit it from the fire. Davy fetched his baby son from the bedroom and spent some time playing with him. Louise and Mel joined them, and Mel felt somewhat sad. When she was going through her adolescence, this was the sort of family scene she had always thought she would be involved in if her mother had not died so young.

That turned her thoughts back to London. She had not thought of home lately. Staying alive and making her way back had occupied most of her time. But she realised now that she had another reason to get home; she had to persuade Uncle Terry that the people beyond the Barrier were not dangerous.

The Travellers had some strange ideas about a woman's place, but they appeared to be a good people at heart. Louise and Davy had been so welcoming and trusting, she felt sorry that she was lying to them.

Louise took the baby from Davy and began to make him ready for bed. Josh said that he was going to check on the horses, and the old man went with him. Davy got up from his chair and said that he would make some tea.

Mel had tasted the tea that Ma had made and, although it tasted different from what she was used to, she found it strangely refreshing, if somewhat bitter. When Mel commented on this to Ma, she had just laughed and said that when she made tea, she left the nettle's sting in.

Davy passed a cup to Mel and sat down at the table. Lifting his cup to his lips, he looked at Mel over the rim and said, "So what's a young girl like you doing travelling to Norwich on her own?"

Mel had taken her time in the bath to think of what she hoped was a plausible story.

"As I said, I'm going back to my family." When Davy said nothing, Mel gave a rueful smile and continued. "I hate to admit it, but I've been a fool. I met a man who was with a troupe of Travellers and I thought I had fallen in love with him. So when the troupe headed south for the summer, I went with them. I soon found out that I wasn't welcomed by the by the other members of the troupe, and my big, brave lover was totally under the thumb of his family. So I decided to leave. The troupe leader refused to take me back." That much was true at least. "So I left on my

CHAPTER 3

own."

Davy stared at her over the rim of his cup, and Mel looked back with what she hoped was an innocent expression on her face. Finally, as Louise and Davy's father re-entered the room, he said, "Well, you're welcome to stay here as long as you like. We don't live fancy, but we don't starve."

He smiled and drained his cup, motioning her to do the same. Mel gagged as she upended hers. Davy's brew was even stronger than Ma's.

He took the cup from her hand and placed it in a pail of water. "We'll be turning in now. Up with the sun and abed with the moon, how's we lives. There's a bed over there for you." He pointed to a far corner where a low bed stood, blankets already on it, prepared, Mel supposed, while she was in the bath.

She suddenly got caught up in an enormous yawn. Must be more tired than I thought, she said to herself. She barely made it to the bed before flopping on top and falling into a restless slumber.

The next few hours were a confusion of sounds and images. As far as Mel could remember later, besides realising that the tea had been drugged, Louise, Davy and his father had come back into the room. Louise and Davy were arguing.

Davy had said, "We shouldn't do this."

Louise had said that they had no choice. He had heard what the cultists had told the council. They needed an unknown woman or a baby for the Equinox ritual. The only baby in the village was theirs. Did he want to give their son up to those monsters?

Then Josh came back in, saying that the cart was ready. By this time, Mel was coming round a bit more and, although she could hear everything, the drug they had given her had left her so paralysed that she could not even open her eyes.

The old man then tied her hands and feet and stuffed a cloth in her mouth. She was carried outside and put into the cart. For the next hour, Mel slipped in and out of consciousness; all she really remembered was bouncing up and down. She awoke again when the cart stopped. Mel discovered that she now had some control over her body; she could open her eyes, but she was still tied hand and foot.

The moon was glowing full in a cloudless sky that night and, as a shadow fell across her, she looked up to see a hooded figure above her. "You have done well," the figure said in a hard, grating voice. "We will pray for you and bless your crops at the Equinox."

He snapped his fingers, and Mel felt her arms and legs being gripped as she was lifted from the cart. Her struggles came to nothing and no noises passed the gag in her mouth. Out of the corner of her eye, she saw Davy and his father re-mount the cart. Josh was already sitting in the back, and Mel saw him look back at her and the unknown others as they carried her into a dark building.

He looked sad.

Chapter 4

In all her travels so far, Mel had never felt the fear she felt now. The shock of waking up in a caravan and being so many miles from home was nothing compared to this. She handled that by keeping calm, holding her fear in check, and working the situation until she was in control.

But this was different.

Bound hand and foot, the only part of her body she could move were her eyes. She couldn't even scream because of the gag in her mouth. She found herself shaking uncontrollably. Tears ran down her cheeks unchecked.

Inside the dark building, she was taken into a room that was lit only by flickering torches. Smoke from the only source of light hung heavily in the air. She was placed on a table and another dark, sinister figure loomed over her.

The face that now looked down on her was as old a face as Mel had ever seen. As she stared into the milky white eyes, her breathing laboured through the gag, he brought his face so close that Mel could smell his rancid breath. She tried desperately to escape, to roll off the table, but strong hands held her firmly as she was examined.

The creature said in a voice surprisingly clear and resonant, "She will suffice. The Spring Equinox is in five days. Give her Rembis to calm her down and make her sleep. Have one of the Sisterhood attend her. She is not to be molested."

Mel was hauled up and carried into a stone, cell-like room, where she was laid on a hard bed. The gag was removed but, before she could react, a burning liquid was poured down her throat, making her gag and retch. A warm sensation flooded through her body, and she felt herself relaxing as a feeling of detached calm came over her.

Mel was beyond any words or action as rough hands tore her clothes from her unresponsive body. The room emptied and she was left lying naked on top of the bed. Although the small cell was cold and damp, she felt warm and drowsy. She fell into an uneasy sleep full of nightmares.

Hooded figures, with chalky white skulls as faces, chased her down long, never-ending stone corridors. Skeletal hands reached out and groped at her naked body. There were doors all along the corridor; each one was locked, except the last one. When Mel opened it, she saw her father there waiting for her, his arms open wide. But as she ran into the safety of his embrace, he changed into the old man with the milky white eyes. The figure laughed, saying, "You're ours now." She saw Cord emerge from the shadows, but he changed into Ma, who shook her head sadly and said, "You should have stayed where you were safe." Mel tried to turn and run, but skeletal hands gripped her arms and legs and she began to scream.

Mel woke with a start, covered in sweat and gasping for breath. Not yet fully awake, she felt a pair of hands holding her and she began to struggle, trying to escape. Mel opened her eyes and pushed the hands away from her. They belonged to a young, thin-faced girl, dressed in a dirty, ragged smock. She looked as terrified as Mel did.

She was saying in a quiet, shaky voice, "Please be quiet. You're safe now. It's the Rembis; it gives you bad dreams. Please be quiet."

As Mel's racing heart began to slow, she began to take in more of her surroundings. She was in the small room they had taken her to last night. She presumed it was morning by the light coming into the cell through a small window at the top of one wall. Mel began to shiver, realising that she was still naked, although someone had put a thin blanket over her. She pulled it closer around her, and moved up the bed until her back was against the cold stone of the wall.

As she regained her composure, Mel looked at the girl. "Where am I? Who are you? Who were those men in cloaks?" As her memory of last night's events came back, the questions tumbled out one after the other.

The girl smiled nervously at her. "Please, I will try to answer your questions." She picked up a dirty piece of cloth and began to wring it in her hands as she continued in a voice that was almost a whisper. "You are in the Temple of the Brother Druids. My name is Olanda, and I have been instructed to care for you. The men you saw last night were the Brothers."

Things began to drop into place inside Mel's head.

Druids. The place on the map marked Stonehenge. Long forgotten history lessons telling of Druids and their worship of the sun. When the old monk with the rancid breath was leaning over her last night, he said something about the Spring Equinox. But what did that have to do with her?

Mel looked closer at Olanda's face. Although it looked young, no more than late teens, the girl's eyes were lifeless and dull.

"I was drugged and brought here. Why?"

Olanda's expression went bland and she shrugged her thin shoulders before answering. "Oh, I expect you're here to join the Sisterhood. The Brothers always need women to serve their bodily needs."

"Is that why you're here? To serve their bodily needs?" Mel shivered. She could guess what that meant.

"Yes. I was sold to the Brothers by my family two years ago." Olanda stopped for a moment as she remembered. "I was one of the blessed ones," she continued proudly. "At the initiation, I was impregnated. My son is destined to become a Brother."

"The initiation?"

Olanda's eyes glazed slightly as she recounted her story. "When a new sister is initiated into the Sisterhood, she is taken by each brother in turn on the altar of Persephone. If she conceives, it is taken as a sign." Her voice had taken on a chanting quality, as if she was reciting something that she had been taught by rote. "If the child is male, then it is known that he will rise far in the

Brotherhood and his mother will be granted entry to the Garden of Eden and everlasting life."

Mel lay back, watching Olanda, who had a slight, satisfied smile on her face as she thought of her initiation.

Now she was no longer tied or gagged, her terror had receded. But the more she learned about the Druids and their practices, the more worried she became. Finding herself as the centre of attraction at a mass rape was not on her list of things to do before she died.

Mel turned her thoughts back to her unwilling arrival here. "Olanda," she said, "last night, an old Brother in a white robe said that I was to be made ready for the Spring Equinox."

Olanda started out of her memories and, to Mel's surprise, dropped to one knee, saying, "Chosen One."

Mel lifted herself onto one elbow, watching Olanda with bemusement, and then said, "Olanda, what is the Spring Equinox?" Mel had a sinking sensation in the pit of her stomach that whatever the answer, the reply would mean trouble for her.

A look of wonder was on Olanda's face as she raised it to look at Mel. "The Spring Equinox is one of the most important times for the Brothers. To be the Chosen One is the greatest of honours," she bowed her head again. "To serve the Chosen One is also a great honour."

Olanda's mood was so reverent that Mel was beginning to get caught up in her mood. "What happens at the Spring Equinox?"

Olanda looked up with an expression of mild surprise on her face. "Why, that is when a virgin is sacrificed to the gods who will then look favourably on this year's harvest."

Mel gave a short laugh. "Well, I don't qualify then."

"You don't understand. You are not a member of the Sisterhood, or known to the Brothers, and as long as you are left untouched here, you could be."

Mel fell back onto the hard lump that served as a pillow, not knowing whether to laugh or cry. "That's a fine piece of twisted logic. What happens if you can't get a virgin?"

"Oh, then a child will do, but it is not as good." Olanda took Mel's hand in hers, sensing that she wasn't as pleased with her position as Olanda thought she should be. "It is a great honour to be given in this way to the gods. You will live in their splendour for all eternity."

"Oh! That will be nice." The sarcasm went straight over Olanda's head.

Mel fell silent as she watched Olanda busy herself. When she picked up the wooden bowl she had brought with her and made to leave, Mel asked one final question. "When is the Spring Equinox?"

Olanda rapped on the door. "In four days. The ceremony is at noon." The door was opened by one of the Brothers and, as she left, Olanda said, "I will return shortly with food and drink. Please try and rest."

The door closed behind her and Mel heard the sound of bolts being driven home. It sounded very final.

Laying back and thinking about her position did little good. She did not know enough about her surroundings to contemplate escape. Besides, her brain was still fogged with the drug they had given her. Olanda was right in one respect. She needed to sleep. Pulling the blanket round her, she willed herself into a light sleep.

Mel awoke to the sound of her cell door being opened and, although she felt uneasy, she couldn't remember any nightmares, not clearly at least.

Olanda entered carrying a tray with bread and fruit; there was also a large jug. Putting the tray down on the floor, Olanda bowed her head and asked if she was hungry.

The first rule of being a prisoner, Mel decided, was to make a friend in the enemy's camp. So she summoned up a broad, friendly smile, and said, "Yes, yes I am."

In fact, she was ravenous. The light outside the small window had dimmed, so Mel figured that she had not eaten for over twelve hours. The bread was a bit stale, but the fruit was fresh and she ate it with relish. It was not long before she noticed Olanda watching her intently.

Mel picked up an apple and offered it to the young girl, saying, "Please, won't you have some as well?"

Olanda looked scandalised. "Oh, no. I couldn't. This food is for you. The Brothers would beat me if I ate the food meant for the Chosen One."

Mel grimaced at the term "Chosen One." All this food would appear to be some sort of fattening the calf for slaughter.

"Well, I tell you what," Mel said in a low, conspiring tone, "I won't tell if you don't. Besides," she carried on—she could see that Olanda was not yet fully convinced—"I hate to eat alone. You wouldn't want the Chosen One to be unhappy, would you?"

With a nervous smile, Olanda took the apple and bit into it. They ate in silence and Mel took the opportunity to think of the questions she needed to ask. The problem was whether to ease the answers out of Olanda, or be more direct.

The young girl was still very nervous; apparently the well-being of the Chosen One was her responsibility. So Mel decided to get to know her better first, to put her at her ease.

"So," she began. "Tell me about yourself and the Sisterhood."

The story Olanda began to recount was, to a girl born and bred in modern London, a horrifying one.

Olanda's family lived some twenty miles away on a hill top farm and, when she was fourteen, her father had sold her to the Brothers. There were just too many mouths to feed, and a bad harvest meant that if they didn't get enough grain to feed the livestock through the winter, the whole family would starve. She was the youngest girl, therefore, the most expendable.

A travelling Brother had told them about the Druids and the Sisterhood, and offered to take Olanda in exchange for a supply of grain. Her father had brought her here and left with the grain. She had heard nothing of them since. She laid no blame on her family for leaving her; in fact, when her son was old enough to be left, she hoped to join an expedition of Brothers who took the word of the Druids around the countryside, and visit her family.

At first, Mel was disgusted with what Olanda's father had done to her but, as the girl's story continued, telling of her large family, hard winters, and springs not much easier, Mel supposed and hoped that Olanda's father thought he was doing his best for her.

Olanda's community was very small. There were always mouths to feed. Everything was balanced on a knife edge. If spring was too wet, the harvest failed. If it was too dry, the harvest failed. They were also open to attacks from animals and humans alike. Olanda's abiding memory of her childhood seemed to be hunger; at least here the meals were regular, if meagre, even if it meant being a slave to these men.

Olanda's initiation at such a young age meant that she could not see anything wrong with what had happened to her. Mel guessed that a woman's liberation speech would not be understood, so she wisely kept quiet and just listened to her attendant's story.

Once she had started, Olanda began to speak quite freely. She told Mel of the people in the surrounding area, how they traded with the Brothers, and how, in return, the Brothers protected the area from bandits and other rogue groups.

Normally strangers such as Mel were left alone but, with the Equinox coming up, the word had been sent out to the village councils that a sacrifice was needed.

The blacksmith's family had been in an awkward position. If they had let Mel go, then their own baby could have been taken. If they had resisted, the chances were that they would have all been killed. The Druids could be ruthless when crossed.

With this new information, Mel felt slightly better disposed towards Louise and Davy. She had really been a victim of bad timing; if she had arrived a week later, she would have had no problems.

Mel's eyes were opening to the world outside London. She had thought that the Travellers had a reasonable lifestyle, and the blacksmith's family had also seemed to cope well. There were bound to be hard times, but not normally life threatening.

The fact that the smaller communities had to align themselves with people like the Druids to be safe from greater dangers spoke volumes as to the fragility of life outside. Olanda had told her of raids on her settlement from bandits, and the villages around here needed the Brothers to defend them or they would just be controlled by another group. Better the devil you know than the devil you don't.

Mel thought of all the technology available in London, food replicators, solar heating, medical knowledge, and the good it could do in the outside world if the Barrier came down. When she got back, she would have to convince Uncle Terry and Parliament of the need to re-integrate themselves with the rest of England.

Mel smiled wryly to herself. First, she had to get out of here. Olanda had fallen quiet while Mel had been thinking. Mel looked at her and decided it was time to be more direct.

"Olanda, help me escape from here."

All the colour drained away from the young girl's face, her eyes widened in disbelief. "No! No! You can't leave here, Chosen One. You are for the Equinox."

"My name is Mel. Not Chosen One."

"No! You are the Chosen One. The Elder Ones have said it is so. You are the one who will appease the gods. You must be prepared and made ready. You cannot leave."

Mel took Olanda by the shoulders and shook her. "Olanda! Look at me!"

Olanda began to squirm and, in a voice laced with hysteria, shouted. "NO! No! You are the Chosen One. If your blood does not drain into the earth, then it will not be replenished for the growing season. The crops will fail and all will starve."

With a strength fuelled by her fear, Olanda squirmed free and backed towards the door, which had been opened by one of the Brothers investigating all the noise and, with a look of terror on her face, she turned and fled the cell.

Mel sank back onto her bed, stunned.

The direct approach had failed spectacularly; now Olanda was terrified of her. Mel's spirits sank. Talking to people and making friends had worked so well up until now. Mel was at a loss what to do next. She lay on her bed, thinking of options and discarding them until she fell asleep.

She awoke refreshed, with none of the uneasiness she had felt before. Mel hoped that this meant that the drug they had given her had worked its way out of her system.

Light coming through the window told her that she had slept through the night, so she eased herself off of the bed and tested her condition. Besides a bit of stiffness, she seemed fine. A few of the relaxing exercises she had been taught in London soon loosened her up.

Now her eyes were accustomed to the gloom, she explored her cell more fully. Apart from the bed and a small, low table, there was only one other object in the room. A leather bucket stood in one corner. Its use was obvious, and nature was catching up with her so, feeling slightly repulsed, she put it to good use.

By moving the bed under the window and standing on tiptoe, Mel's chin came level with the windowsill. Window was too grand a term for the aperture she looked out of. There was no glass, only steel bars, and the hole was too small to climb through, even if she could dig out the bars.

There was not a lot to see, either. The bottom of the window came level with the ground, and all Mel saw was the occasional pair of legs going past. There was no hope of escape through here. Mel pushed the bed back into its original position and wrapped the blanket tighter around her. The air in the cell was damp and Mel wondered if she would ever be warm again.

However, her fighting spirit had recovered from last night's low. Eventually, they must let her out of this prison and, when they did, she would find some way to escape.

The pulling of the bolts on the door caused her to look up. The door opened and the old, blind Brother from her arrival entered.

He stood just inside the door and stared at her with his milky white eyes. He was stooped and leaned heavily on a cane. The robe he wore still retained some of its former whiteness, but patches of it were stained dark red. Mel tried not to think what those stains were; hopefully, he was just a messy eater.

He spoke in that surprisingly clear voice that seemed to belie his obvious age. "Sister Olanda has told me of your words to her."

Mel said nothing. To deny it would have been a waste of

CHAPTER 4

time. She waited for him to continue.

"Talk of leaving is foolish. Accept your fate for the good of all Brother Druids and even greater glory will be yours."

"You'll excuse me if I don't cheer." The sarcasm was ignored and he continued as if she had never spoken.

"If you continue this way, I will have you drugged until the ceremony."

That was a real threat. Mel would need all her wits about her if she were to escape.

The old man gave a thin smile. He knew his threat had hit home even without seeing the expression on Mel's face. He turned slightly and beckoned behind him; another sister entered. "This is Sister Eva. She has been instructed not to speak to you. She will obey."

A sudden worry hit Mel. "Where is Olanda?" she asked.

"Sister Olanda," he stressed the title that Mel had left out, "is undergoing penance for her crime of eating food meant for the Chosen One and for listening to your words of heresy."

Mel's mouth went dry. "Penance?"

"She will spend some time in the penance cell. Where the pain of punishment will put her back on the road to salvation."

Mel's heart sank. She never meant for anyone to get hurt. One day, she vowed, she would return here with a squad of Protectors and clear out this nest of perversion.

The old man gave an evil, gap toothed grin. "Prepare yourself, Chosen One. In two days, you will join the gods in their home. You can tell them that their subjects obey without question." With those words, he turned and left, the door locking behind him.

Sister Eva, who was a lot older than Olanda, laid her burdens on the floor and knocked timidly on the door to be let out. She had said nothing, not even raising her head to look at Mel.

Examining the bundle on the floor, Mel found another blanket and a white, full-length smock. Although she felt it might have too much to do with the forthcoming ceremony, she slipped it on. It was made of thick wool, and at least it was warm. There was also more food and drink.

Having eaten and drunk her fill, she sat back on the bed and waited. There was nothing else she could do. The silent Sister Eva delivered more food at dusk and, when night fell, again she tried to sleep. She worked on her hate and loathing of the Druids to keep her determination and spirits up, but it was difficult; eventually she slipped into a light sleep, her thoughts on how she was going to escape still unresolved.

Mel had been dozing for a couple of hours when she was woken by noises from outside the window. Looking up, she saw a dark shadow looming across the opening. Her hopes rose. Could it be that she had gotten through to Olanda, after all? Moving to stand beneath the window, Mel whispered, "Who's there?"

"My name is Iain." The voice had a strange accent that Mel couldn't place. "I'm here to help you."

Mel smiled to herself. A window too small to get through, a guard always on the door, and a building full of fanatical Brothers. Help was needed, but would not be easy to supply.

"But how did you know I was here?"

CHAPTER 4

"Answers later," came the curt reply. "I don't have much time. Just be ready to move when they bring you out to start the ceremony."

Silence descended. Mel could still hear the figure's soft breathing but, as she opened her mouth to speak again, he continued their whispered conversation. "Don't drink anything. They will drug the wine to make you more cooperative at the sacrifice."

A sudden realisation hit Mel. She was being naïve. Just because she had promised not to be obstructive, she had assumed that she would not be drugged. But nobody goes to his or her death quietly, so they would be bound to use drugs to make everything run smoother. Mel's attitude hardened; she must trust nobody.

Iain spoke again, his voice so soft now that Mel had to strain to hear it. "I must go. Somebody's coming. Remember to act drugged when they come to collect you. They must not suspect anything, and don't do anything until you get an obvious sign."

There was a rustling sound and the shadow across the window lifted. Mel went back to the bed and wrapped the blanket around her to ward off the chill air.

Her head was full of questions. Who was this Iain? How did he know about her? Could she trust him, and did she have any choice? She let out a deep sigh. The answer to the last question was easy: no, she didn't have any choice. She was in deep trouble and a point in her unknown rescuer's favour was that she would have drunk the wine without his warning.

However, Mel was not entirely convinced. It could still be some underhand trick by the Druids. She would have to bide her time until the ceremony and play the cards as they fell at the time.

By her reckoning, there was another day and a half to go before the Equinox, so hopefully any drugged drink should appear before tomorrow morning.

With so many questions and probabilities floating about in her head, sleep became even more elusive. She dozed on and off until dawn. Soon after that, Sister Eva appeared again with fresh fruit and wine. She left them on the table and retreated without a word.

Mel sniffed at the wine suspiciously and tasted a small amount; it seemed fine, but she drank sparingly. If there were no ill effects, she would finish it later. The fruit provided enough moisture for now.

Her biggest enemy at the moment was boredom. She spent the morning doing the body-strengthening exercises she had been taught in London. Just before midday, Mel had another visit from the old Druid and, with him, he brought Olanda.

The old man stood for a moment, hunched over his stick, staring at Mel with his opaque eyes. Mel shivered. Although it was logical that he should be blind, with eyes like that, it seemed to Mel as if he could look right inside her. Mel's heart began to beat faster, wondering if he had come to tell her that they had caught her unknown helper. But he remained silent, and gestured to the young girl behind him to come forward. "I brought Sister Olanda to resume her duties as handmaiden. She has been suitably scourged of her sins. Show the Chosen One, Sister."

Olanda, who had kept her eyes downcast since entering the room, looked up at Mel as she slipped her smock off her shoulders and onto the floor. Her body was painfully thin, her ribs easily visible beneath her skin. She turned slowly until her back was towards Mel.

Mel gave a gasp of shock and disgust. Criss-crossed on Olanda's thin back were dozens of angry red wheals. They stretched from her shoulders to her thighs; some showing dried spots of blood where the skin had broken. Mel hissed, and couldn't stop herself turning away.

The old man smiled at Mel's evident disgust. "This is what happens to those who transgress." He signalled to Olanda, and she picked up her smock and left the room, her eyes downcast again.

The old Druid spoke again. "In one day, Chosen One, the ceremony will begin," his voice betrayed his excitement. "It will be glorious!"

Mel took a deep breath and swallowed the bile that had built up in her throat. She controlled the urge to attack the monster in front of her. "You make me feel sick." Her voice was laced with loathing, but it was wasted. The old man just smiled and continued to stare at her.

"You don't understand, Chosen One," His voice changed to one that was addressing an ignorant child. "Sister Olanda is much happier now she has been instructed in the way things are." He turned towards the door and lifted his stick to knock for to be opened. "You will make a good sacrifice. You are strong of mind and body. The longer you take to die, the more the gods will smile on us."

Mel felt her terror building again, her knees going weak, but she would not let it show in front of this monster.

The old man turned again in the doorway for some final words. "One day, Chosen One," he said as he left, "one day, and the glory of an eternity in the presence of the gods will be yours."

When he had gone, Mel sank onto the bed, shaking with a combination of fear and anger. She returned to her exercises with a savagery unfelt before. She would be ready for the mysterious Iain tomorrow, and if he didn't show, she would find some other way of escaping.

The wine offered that evening had a strange smell to it, but not so strange that Mel would have noticed if she hadn't been forewarned. The fruit satisfied her thirst, and she poured the tainted wine into the bucket.

When Olanda returned to collect the remains of her supper and empty her toilet, she feigned a restless sleep.

That night, Mel lay awake waiting for her would-be rescuer to come back. When he didn't appear, worry set in, but she forced herself to examine her fears logically. He would only come if he had something to tell her. He wasn't about to drop by for a cosy chat when discovery would almost certainly mean death.

So, laying aside her fears as best she could, Mel dozed fitfully throughout the night. The next morning, when Olanda delivered her breakfast, she noticed that she was now limping.

Olanda was so thin and childlike that Mel ached to take her in her arms and protect her. But the girl immediately shied away when she tried to approach her. However, Mel decided one way or the other, she would be out of Olanda's life in the next six hours, so she tried to apologise. "Olanda," she began. "I'm sorry that you were punished because of me."

"Please, Chosen One," the girl spoke so softly that Mel could hardly hear her. "You have no need to apologise. You have helped me see the way more clearly. The pain of my punishment will serve to remind me of the true path to glory."

Mel sighed. Olanda was so beaten down that the worse the things that happened to her, the more perverse pleasure she obtained from it.

Olanda left silently and Mel was left alone with her own thoughts. As she ate the bread and fruit provided, she wondered what she would have been like if she had lived Olanda's life. A few days ago, Mel had been outraged at the idea of being given to someone as a wife. Olanda had been sold into sex slavery for a supply of corn.

Mel was an intelligent, educated Londoner, and she realised that these people did not need lecturing, but educating. She could see that if she had been brought up in the same way as Olanda she would have accepted her fate as well. Now that the possibility of death was just a few hours away, she was beginning to realise the hold that life had on a person. It was not that easy to throw away.

Mel picked up the flagon of wine; it was larger than usual and full to the brim. She poured some of it into the bucket and soaked the rest of it up with the straw from her bed. Then she lay down and pretended to sleep.

A couple of hours later, the door opened and one of the Brothers came in and examined the flagon. Mel lay on the bed and moaned and shuffled about, as if in a drugged sleep. Satisfied, the man went away and Mel got up and risked some loosening-up exercises.

Time was the enemy now; she had too much of it to think about what could happen in the next few hours. She began to run scenarios in her head of what could happen when she was collected for the ceremony. But she stopped that when she remembered what Sergeant Connors had told her about the dangers of over-planning. It was dangerous if you convinced yourself that you knew what was going to happen. If something went wrong and you weren't ready to improvise, then, with that moment's hesitation, the battle could be lost.

The hours passed slowly until finally Mel heard noises on the other side of the door. Breathing deeply, forcing herself to relax as the door opened, she went into her act of a drugged sleep. Someone took her shoulder and began to shake it.

"Chosen One," it was the old man's voice. "Chosen One, wake up now. You must leave here."

"Don't want to," Mel slurred her voice as if she was sleepy. "Want to sleep."

Arms gripped her and pulled her to her feet.

"Want to sleep," she mumbled, struggling weakly. Mel hoped she wasn't overplaying it, but the only reference she had to go on was her own reaction to her earlier drugging.

CHAPTER 4

An arm went round her waist to support her, and another voice said. "Come into the daylight, for a walk."

"A walk," Mel mumbled. She kept her head down in case her eyes were to give her away. "Yes, a walk would be nice."

She allowed herself to be ushered through corridors and up a flight of steps, collapsing her knees occasionally to keep up her act. When they emerged into a small courtyard, Mel took the risk of raising her head to see where they were.

Some thirty feet or so from the door stood an impressive circle of stones. Mel recognised them from pictures back in London.

Stonehenge.

Gathered in the centre of the circle was a large group of Brothers and, behind them stood the Sisterhood. Spread at intervals around them was a series of containers raised up on pedestals. Beside each one stood a Brother with a flaming torch in his hand.

No faces were visible. The Brothers and Sisters had hoods pulled down over their faces. As Mel looked around, the sun emerged from behind a cloud, its brightness dazzling her.

In the centre of the circle stood a low altar stained red with blood. The old monk hobbled his way to stand behind the altar, and the two brothers holding Mel urged her the same way. As they did so, Mel decided that she was fed up with being so cooperative and began to put up a struggle. Nothing too violent, just enough to slow their progress. She looked around, hoping for a sign that would tell her that Iain was in the area.

The Brothers began a low chanting and the Sisters joined

in. As they got closer to the altar, Mel could see that there was an arrangement of straps fixed to it. Their purpose was clear. They were to hold the victim down securely. Her heart began to beat faster, pumping adrenaline into her system. If nothing happened soon, Mel knew that she would have to make a move before they strapped her down.

As they brought her to stand in front of the altar, the chanting rose to a higher pitch; some of the Sisters were now swaying back and forth, moaning. The old monk, pushing back his hood to display his dead eyes, turned towards the assembled company. Flinging his arms up and wide, he began to speak, his voice almost quivering with excitement. "We come to give thanks to the gods for allowing us to live through another winter. We offer a sacrifice, a virgin to grace their tables."

The wailing became higher pitched, and some of the Sisters screamed and fell to the ground. The old man's voice boomed around the circle. It was as if the stones themselves were amplifying his words. "We ask only that you smile on our harvests and protect them from the demons of bad weather." He reached behind and picked up a large knife with an ornate, white bone handle and held it above his head. "Bless us," he boomed. "Bless all your children for another season."

The chanting stopped as if someone had thrown a switch. All that could be heard were a few low moans from the women. The old monk turned and brought his hands together in front of him, taking a double hold on the handle of the dagger. "Light the fires!" he called. The Brothers standing by the bins plunged their torches into the containers. "Prepare the Chosen One!"

CHAPTER 4

With a sinking feeling, Mel realised that she, too, had been mesmerised by the unfolding ceremony. Chances to escape may have come and gone and she had not noticed. Now she began to struggle in earnest, but to no avail. The two monks holding her were strong and, as she tried to get a kick in, another Brother grabbed both her legs, and she was hoisted bodily onto the altar. Mel squirmed and struggled even more, but the Brothers hold on her was too firm. As one of the monks leaned across her to retrieve a strap, an explosion took place in one of the fire bins, then another and another.

Shrapnel from the metal bins shot into the crowd and the onlookers began to scream as they were hit by red-hot pieces of metal.

The old man, sensing that something was going wrong, raised the dagger higher as if to continue the sacrifice. Suddenly, as if by magic, a metal shaft appeared in his chest. He gave a strangled gasp and began to fall forwards, the dagger still held for the killing blow.

One of the Brothers holding Mel had fallen, pierced by a large sliver of metal; a second had released her in the panic and confusion. Only the monk across her legs remained.

Mel gave one large heave and threw herself sideways off the altar as the old man fell where seconds before she had been lying. His head hung inches from her face, and blood bubbled from his mouth onto her robe. A death rattle sounded in his throat as Mel stared into those milky eyes.

Getting to her feet, Mel looked around. The rest of the Brothers were milling around in shock and panic; nobody was taking any notice of her.

Suddenly, a Brother strode through the disarray and took her arm. As Mel tensed herself to launch an attack, he said, "It's me, Iain. This way, quick."

Iain pulled her towards the building. As he did so, another Brother, his hood thrown back and showing blood on his thin face, stopped them.

"Where are you going?" he asked.

Iain looked into the man's eyes. "Our Father has been slain. The Second has told me to return the Chosen One to her cell. Until a new time can be set for the ceremony."

"Who are you?" This Brother did not seem as stunned as the others. "I am the Second. I gave no such orders."

"Excuse me, Second," Iain smiled politely. "You must join your Father." With that, he pulled out a knife from under his robes and plunged it into the monk's chest.

Mel was shocked. All this death and destruction had numbed her senses. She stood staring at the body of the Second until Iain took her hand and pulled her after him.

"This way," he said. "We have to go out the front entrance."

The building was deserted. Once out through the door, Iain pulled off his robe and threw it to the floor. Mel didn't have the luxury of being able to do the same, so she picked up the hem of hers and followed as best she could.

Once they were under the cover of trees, Iain slowed the pace of their escape. After half a mile or so, he stopped to listen for sounds of pursuit. Satisfied that they were not being followed, he looked at Mel and smiled. "There's an old cottage over there," he said, pointing. "If all has gone to plan, there should be someone there to meet us."

He pushed his way through some dense undergrowth and Mel followed, to find herself on the edge of a hidden clearing. At its centre was a small cottage, which looked as if had leapt straight out of an old painting.

Mel made as if to go towards the cottage, but Iain held her back, saying, "Wait." He lifted his hands to his mouth and made a hooting sound with them. A figure came to the door and waved at them. "Right," Iain waved back. "It's safe. Let's go in."

As they came to the door, the question of how Iain had known about her predicament was answered. The figure waiting for them at the door was Josh, the blacksmith Davy's young brother-in-law. His face was flushed with excitement as he asked Iain. "It went alright then? No problems?"

"No problems at the moment, laddie," Iain answered. "But those freaks are not going to be very pleased." He dropped into a chair and looked up at the young man. "Are your family safe?"

"Yes. Davy has taken Louise, Da, and the baby to Sevington with him. They'll be gone for at least a month."

"Good," Iain smiled at the boy's enthusiasm. "Then you had better be on your way and catch them up."

"Right." Josh picked up a sack and made as if to leave.

"Wait!" Mel said, her voice shaking slightly as reaction to the last hour's events caught up with her. "What IS going on?"

Her mind was in turmoil. She had almost been sacrificed to some obscure gods, showered in shrapnel, taken on a cross country run, and brought to a cottage straight out of Hansel and Gretel, only to be met by one of the people who had gotten her into this mess in the first place.

"Oh, that's easy." Josh dropped his sack and began to explain, his eyes sparkling with excitement. "When Da, Davy, and me got back from taking you to the Druids, we found Iain has arrived for a visit. Louise had already told him what had happened and he came up with a plan to rescue you." Josh looked at Iain with eyes full of hero worship, as if he always had the answer to everything. When the older man said nothing, he carried on. "It was important that the baby wasn't put at risk, so Davy left for Sevington with the others. I came here to the cottage with Iain."

He took a deep breath. "Well, Iain found out where you were being kept. That took ages; he had to get one of the Brothers drunk enough to make him tell us." Josh's voice was more and more excited by the moment. Iain sat in his chair, smiling indulgently.

"Once Iain made contact with you, we made up some explosive packages and sneaked them into the fire bins the night before. I hid in a tree with a crossbow, and Iain dressed up as one of the Brothers. The fire bins went boom, I shot the old one when it looked like he was going to continue, and the rest you know."

Josh crossed his arms with the air of someone who has just performed an easy task. Iain looked at his young friend and said. "And now it's time you were gone."

Josh bent down to pick up his sack and, as he did, Mel took his free hand. "Thank you, even if you did get me into this mess in the first place. But I understand why," Mel hesitated for a moment and then continued. "Maybe I'll visit here again. But not at the time of the Equinox." She leaned forward and kissed Josh on his cheek. He flooded red and left the cottage, almost at a run.

Mel looked after him in amusement. She wasn't used to having that affect on young men.

A soft chuckle came from Iain's chair. "You've had quite an affect on that young man."

Mel turned to face him. "And what about you?"

He looked her up and down before answering. Mel felt very self-conscious. She must look a right mess, the once-white robe she was wearing was ripped and stained with blood, and her hair had suffered from the run through the trees.

"Oh, you've had quite an affect on me, as well."

This time it was Mel's turn to blush, though he may not have noticed through the dirt and grime on her face. "That's not what I meant," she said, trying to cover her confusion. "You're not from around here, are you?"

"No. I'm from Scotland."

"Scotland. That's a long way from here. What are you doing down here?"

He waved a hand airily above his head. "I wander the English countryside, reporting on the state of England for my government, and in my spare time, I rescue damsels in distress." He stopped as Mel gave a small laugh. "I often stop by here, if I'm out this way. I was married to Davy's sister, but she died in childbirth. I like to keep in touch."

There was a moment's silence before Mel said, "I'm sorry. I didn't know Davy had a sister."

"No reason you should." He sat up straighter in his chair and looked at her more intently. "Well, that's where I'm from. How about you?"

Mel hesitated for a moment. Should she tell the truth, or her "going to Norwich" story? She took a deep breath and decided that it would be best to be consistent in her stories.

"I'm from Norwich and I'm on my way back to . . . "

"Meet your family," Iain finished. "Yes, Louise said that was the story you told her." He raised one eyebrow and said no more.

Mel shifted in her own seat as she considered her options. Obviously, her story had not gone down as well as she had hoped with the blacksmith's family. While she thought, she studied the man opposite her. She tried to guess his age; considering the faster rate of ageing outside, she gauged him to be in his late thirties.

He had dark red hair, shoulder length with some grey in it, and his face had a fine sprinkling of lines about it. Not an unpleasant face at all, she decided. Not as outwardly handsome as Cord's, but nice, regular features. His body carried little fat, and she guessed his height to be a little taller than hers. But most of all, as she studied him, she got a sense that she could trust him, that he was a good person. After all, if you couldn't trust a man who had saved your life, who could you, trust?

Well, thought Mel, *Confession is supposed to be good for the soul.* "I'm from London," she said, taking the plunge. She waited to see if there would be any reaction. None came, so she carried on being good to her soul. Once started, she couldn't help but tell the whole story—her father's death, the investigation, the trip outside, and waking up in the Travellers' caravan. Iain said nothing, just nodded his head occasionally.

Finally, when she had finished, she thought maybe the church did know something after all; there was a certain amount of relief to be had in sharing your troubles with someone else.

Iain stretched in his chair. "I know the Williamson family. Joel's a good troupe leader, if a bit single minded. Ma's the brains and driving force behind him."

He lapsed into a thoughtful silence, and Mel began to scratch her leg where the mud and dirt she had collected over the last few days was irritating her. She asked where she could wash.

"There's a bath in the bedroom, but you'll have to wash in cold water. No fires until after dark. Louise left you a change of clothes, as well. You can get water from the stream out back."

He helped her carry the water in and left her to her own devices. The water was very cold, but it helped invigorate her. She stripped off the robe the Druids had made her wear and, with a feeling of vengeance, ripped it into strips to use as towels. Wrapping another piece around her head to help her hair dry, she put on the clothes that Louise had provided.

There was none of the itchy underwear she had worn before, for which she was grateful, and at the bottom of the pile, she found a thick, woollen cardigan, which she hugged around herself. She dragged the bath into the garden and emptied it, thinking wistfully of the self-cleaning, built-in jet massage tub back in London.

She went back into the living room, only to find it deserted. She felt a moment's panic before Iain come in, carrying a dead rabbit by the ears.

"Dinner," he said. "Once it gets dark." He laid his catch on the table and looked Mel up and down. "Well. Don't you clean up nicely."

Mel sniffed and wrinkled her nose. "At least I smell clean, which is more than I can say about some other people."

"Point taken," he answered, smiling. He disappeared into the bedroom to wash. Mel searched the kitchen for a pot and fetched some water from the stream, mildly surprised to find that it was already getting dark. She looked at the rabbit lying on the table, and hoped Iain knew how to skin and cook it. She hadn't a clue where to start. She sat herself down in one of the overstuffed chairs and before she knew it had dozed off.

The sounds of Iain cooking and the mouth-watering smell of rabbit stew woke her an hour or so later. She felt relaxed and refreshed and, she realised, for the first time in two weeks, safe.

Iain brought her the same feeling of security that her father had done. A pang of guilt shot through her as she realised that she had not thought of her father lately, or of Cord, for that matter. Mel wondered if London had written her off as dead. She had to get back.

Iain brought two bowls of stew to the table and smiled at her. It was very nice smile, Mel decided. "I hope you're not a vegetarian," he said.

Mel showed her surprise. "No, I'm not. You know of vegetarians, then."

"Of course." He sat down opposite her. "We have vegetarians in Scotland, you know. We also have all the other fads that come with a modern society. Scotland is just as sophisticated as you Sasanachs."

The term *sasanach* fazed Mel for a moment, so she filed it away to be explained later.

"We also keep up with the technology, " Iain continued. "But we try to keep to our old traditions as well."

Mel dipped her spoon into the stew and tasted it. After a day without food, it tasted wonderful. "How much do you know about London? Most people I've met so far think it is inhabited by ghosts."

"I could hardly take back full reports to Scotland if I didn't visit places like London and Birmingham, could I?"

Mel's spoon hovered over the bowl. "But, how do you get past the Barrier?" She felt mildly shocked. Iain talked so casually about visiting London. She remembered how she used to feel so safe behind the Barrier, but it was beginning to appear that anybody could get in when they wanted to.

Iain laughed, as if he had guessed what she was thinking. "Nothing's totally impregnable, Mel. There are far too many old tunnels, sewers, and gaps to keep out anyone determined to get in."

She remembered Cord saying the same thing. "So how many times have you been there?"

"Three times, the last time about a year ago." He looked

at her across the table. "Something wrong with the stew?" he asked.

"No, no. It's lovely." Mel dipped her spoon into the broth and began to eat. Iain smiled and followed suit.

"What did you do there?"

"Oh, I'd wander around, talk to people. Try to find out what makes a Londoner tick. They, well you, have a problem, you know."

"A problem?" Mel felt herself go on the defensive. Iain had already admitted that he spied for his government; how far could she trust him?

"Yes, a big problem. Overcrowding. London is ready to burst at the seams and people seem to be ignoring it."

"Not everybody is ignoring it," Mel bristled, stung to defend her home. "My father and the president were leading a campaign to turn the Barrier off. But, when my father was killed, the tide of opinion turned against it."

"Well, that would be the answer. Remove the Barrier and begin to reclaim the land around London. But it has to be done carefully. When Newcastle's Barrier went wrong and turned itself off suddenly, over seventy percent of the population committed suicide. They couldn't take the sudden exposure to the outside world."

Mel finished her meal and pushed her bowl away. Iain picked them both up and dropped them into water. Mel leaned back and began to review the events of the last week. She had to admit that she had not been as successful as she would have wished. She had thought that she would have to simply follow her maps back to London and arrive home safely. She now realised that there were a lot of dangers between her and London.

What she needed was a guide.

"Iain," she paused, wondering how to ask for help. She shrugged her shoulders and plunged straight in. "Would you help me get home? Back to London."

"Want to leave us so soon? There's so much you haven't seen, yet." He put a hurt expression on his face, which made Mel smile.

"The first people I came into contact with wanted to sell me. The second drugged me and gave me to a set of mad monks who wanted to sacrifice me. I think I would be safer at home!"

He laughed. "Yes, I'll help you get home, Mel. We can start first thing tomorrow." He gestured to the bedroom. "You take the bed and I'll sleep here in the chair."

Mel began to argue that it was his house and he should have the bed, but he insisted and, in the end, she was too tired to argue. So, she placed her borrowed clothes on a chair and slipped under the heavy covers of the bed and dropped into sleep. But it was not the restful night she had hoped for.

As Mel slipped deeper into sleep, lulled by her feeling of safety, nightmarish images began to haunt her dreams. Hooded monks chased her, their bodies just skeletons. Bony hands reached out for her, grabbing at her. The old monk appeared, an arrow in his chest, blood running down his mouth, calling to her, "Come to us, Chosen One. You are our salvation, come to us." Olanda appeared and called to Mel. "Help me. Help me, Chosen One." But when Mel got close to her, Olanda grabbed and held her fast. The old monk, a bloody knife in his hand, came closer. Her father, Cord, Ma, and others she had known became indistinct blurs on the edge of her vision. She called to them, but they just moved further away. The old man lifted the knife for the killing blow, and Mel screamed.

She awoke with a start, covered in sweat, to find Iain shaking her shoulder. She began to struggle again, until she realised who it was, and then threw her arms around his neck and held onto him as if she was drowning.

"Okay, its okay," he soothed. "It was just a bad dream. Reaction to all you've gone through." His hand was behind her head as she pressed her face to his chest.

Her racing pulse slowed and Mel regained enough composure to disentangle herself from him. "I'm sorry," she apologised, glad that it was dark and he couldn't see her blushing. "Did I wake you?"

He looked at her, smiling. "If you had screamed much louder, the Brotherhood would have been round here to complain about the noise." He stood up. "If you're alright now, get some sleep. Tomorrow will be a long day."

Mel lay back, but as he went to leave, she suddenly felt afraid and lonely. She came to a decision. "Iain, don't go. Don't leave me alone tonight."

He looked down at her and she saw the question in his eyes. "Are you sure, lassie? You don't owe me anything."

Mel gave a small, nervous laugh. "I owe you my life," she said simply.

He picked up her hand and kissed it, then leant over and

pressed his lips to hers. As he did so, Mel was mildly surprised by her reaction; she pulled him towards her and passed her hands up inside his shirt, pulling it from the shorts he was sleeping in.

She had missed a man's touch more than she realised. As he pulled the blankets down and worked his mouth down her body, Mel began to pull more urgently at his clothes; her release came with his. Full, but too quickly. They made love again, slower and less urgently. Mel fell asleep in Iain's arms and the nightmares stayed away.

CHAPTER 5

When Mel awoke the next morning, Iain's side of the bed was empty. As she stretched lazily, the memories of the previous night came back to her and she groaned aloud as she felt embarrassment and some guilt. The embarrassment was there because, once she had decided she wanted to make love with Iain, she had basically ravaged the poor man. The guilt was there because of Cord. Mel knew why she had done what she had done. She had been frightened and lonely, and Iain had been there when she needed comforting. *And,* she thought impishly, *he hadn't done a bad job of it, either.*

But she could have wished for better self-control.

Mel sighed and lifted herself up on her elbows to look out the window. The sun was just beginning to rise. Waking up at dawn had become a habit. She splashed some cold water on her face and got dressed. Taking a deep breath, she went into the kitchen. She would have to face Iain eventually; better sooner than later.

He was at the stove. "Rabbit stew alright for breakfast?

Not that there's any other choice." Mel sat down at the table and he placed a bowl in front of her. Sitting down to eat his own, he said, "Eat it all up. I want to make twenty miles today."

Mel looked up. Twenty miles in one day, on foot, was pushing it a bit, she thought. "Why so far?" she asked.

"Well, that will bring us to a small community I know. I have friends there who will take us in for the night. Plus, the more distance between us and the Brotherhood the better."

Mel heartily agreed with that ambition, but still thought twenty miles was a tall order. But she had put herself in Iain's hands, so shrugged her shoulders in agreement.

"Don't be too relaxed, Mel," Iain said. "There's some tough country to cover and bandits to avoid."

"Bandits?" Mel's curiosity was piqued. "There are bandits around here?"

"This area is quite well populated," Iain explained. "And where you get prey, there are always predators. Most of these bandits are outcasts from settlements, having committed one crime or another. They band together in small groups and spend their time fighting each other, raiding the weaker settlements, or attacking Travellers on the road."

"They sound like old time highwaymen," Mel commented.

"Maybe," Iain sniffed. "Except that these highwaymen don't give you the choice of 'your money or your life.' They kill or worse first, and then rob. It's safer that way, at least for them."

Iain stood up and opened a cupboard, pulling out a

shoulder bag. Mel gave a whoop of delight. "My bag! I thought it was lost." She took out of his hands and emptied its contents onto the table. Mel was pleased to see her bag again; the things in it were hers, links to London.

She opened one of the maps and spread it out on the table. Iain peered over her shoulder. "These maps are a bit out of date," he remarked. His closeness and his male scent turned Mel's thoughts back to the previous night. The memories were pleasant and she had to fight the urge to pick up where they had left off.

With an effort, Mel slid round the table until she faced Iain. His only reaction was to move closer to the maps, umming and ahhing over them like a collector.

"Iain," Mel began. "About last night . . . "

He looked up at her. "Yes, I should apologise. I took advantage of you."

"No, no. I was quite willing to be taken advantage of. It was very nice, but I should have had more self-control. I'm sorry, but I don't want to lead you on."

He looked at for a moment, then, smiling her, said. "There's someone waiting for you in London."

Thinking of Cord, Mel replied, "I hope so."

Iain smiled again and scooped the maps and other things back into Mel's bag. Handing it to her, he said, "It's almost full light out there now. We'd better get going."

Pulling the cardigan around her, Mel followed Iain out of the cottage and into the surrounding woodland. Looking back at the cottage, she felt sorry to be leaving such a lovely place, but glad to be leaving the area.

She turned her back and resolutely followed Iain.

That day's travel was a hard slog for someone not used to walking great distances. Iain pushed hard until noon before he stopped for a break, for which Mel's aching legs were grateful. A drink of water and some bread accounted for lunch, and they were soon on their way again. Shortly after they had restarted their trek, they came across the first indication that the area was not completely uninhabited. They were making their way up a small hill when they heard voices coming from in front of them.

Iain held up his hand, and they both crouched down and worked their way to the top of the hill on their bellies. Below them, in a small valley, they could see a collection of old farm buildings, and several people milling around.

Iain reached into the pack on his back and pulled free a crossbow. Fitting it with a bolt, he slung it across his chest in a handy position.

"Who are they?" Mel whispered.

"A small bandit group, and a bit of a surprise. They weren't here the last time I came through."

Mel looked down on the scene. "There are women there, as well!"

Iain glanced across at her. "Yes, there are. Some of the outcasts would have taken their families with them. Others may have joined on their own, thinking it's a romantic way of life. They soon learn different. Some may have been snatched from settlements. Girls aren't as useful as boys, so their families would probably not bother to ransom them."

"That's terrible." Mel was shocked.

"Life can be very tough for women out here. Basically, their function is to serve the men." Iain began to move down the hill, saying, "We'll have to go round."

They doubled back and Iain took a circular route around the encampment. He stopped twice to avoid sentries before he decided that they were clear enough to take a less cautious pace.

Finally, as the afternoon turned into dusk and the sun began to set in the west, a red ball of fire casting long, deep shadows, they stopped for a break. Mel leaned tiredly against a tree. Iain looked at her and smiled. "I don't think that we are going to make John's place tonight. That detour delayed us somewhat. "

Mel yawned and sank to the ground. "Well, I'm finished. I could sleep right here."

Iain stood up and held out his hand to her. "Well, you COULD sleep here," he pulled her to her feet and she groaned as every muscle in her body protested. "But you'd probably end up as a meal for a pack of dogs, or an overnight guest of that group of bandits we passed."

Dog packs had not so far been a problem. Iain had told her that they were mostly nocturnal and not that common where there were large settlements. The local population would band together and clear the area if the packs became too large. The bandit groups would also keep the dog population down, more for their own safety rather than a sense of civic duty.

"As I remember," Iain remarked, "there's an old farm over

CHAPTER 5

the crest of that hill. We'll spend the night there."

Sure enough, they could see the small collection of farm buildings spread out below them when they got to the top of the small hill. They paused just long enough to make sure the buildings were deserted before descending.

The two barn-type buildings were no more than fallen-down lean-tos, but the main house was in much better shape. Someone had replaced all the windows and repaired the roof. Whilst the inside was sparsely furnished, there was a supply of dry wood and a large jug holding water.

Iain explained that they were on the outskirts of the settlement that his friend, John, ran, and that the house was maintained for anybody caught away from the community at night.

By the time the sun had set, Iain had lit a fire in the stove and found an oil lamp, and set Mel to plucking a pheasant he had trapped earlier. Mel, not wishing to look incapable, did her best, but let Iain gut and cook it.

Once the meal was over, they settled down on an old mattress, fully dressed, and Mel found, annoyingly, that tiredness had deserted her. So she asked Iain about life in Scotland and the other Barriered cities. She felt that if Iain could spy for his government, the least she could do was the same for hers.

"Birmingham is fast heading for the same over-crowding problem as London. But they've had population controls a lot longer. I suppose the main difference between the two cities is that London has a kind of democracy, while Birmingham has a kind of dictator."

Mel bristled at his suggestion. "What do you mean, a 'kind of democracy'? Londoner's vote every five years; even the president has to stand for re-election. One man, one vote. That's always been the basis of democracy."

Iain smiled at her spirited response. "Over the past five years, the president has pushed through more and more emergency powers for himself. All he has to do, if it looks like he might be defeated or impeached, is declare a state of emergency, and democracy will go out the nearest window."

"I didn't know that." Mel had no reason not to believe Iain; he had no reason to lie, as far as she could see. But that did not mean she wasn't going to check out his statement as soon as she got home. "Is that how Birmingham got a dictator?"

"Birmingham never really had a chance to have a democracy. After their Barrier went up, fighting broke out between factions, all wanting to take control. Like London, they needed one man to take a lead. The difference was the man that came to the fore was a minor royal, called David Soames. He was an Earl, and something like fortieth in line for the throne. He raised an army and expelled all the leaders of the different factions, and declared himself King.

"With a clear leader in control, the people saw that life was a lot calmer, and backed him when other people objected to what he had done. He remained King until he died, and the leadership passed to his eldest son. Life remained the same under him, and his son, so nobody overly objected. Before they knew it, the people of Birmingham had a dynasty.

"There have had six so far and, on the whole, they have

been benevolent despots. The third King of Birmingham, Samuel, was a bit debauched, but nothing too serious. The present King is Mark. He knows they have a population problem and is trying to prepare his people for the day the Barrier is turned off. But the agoraphobia problem of London is just as relevant to Birmingham. It's a slow process."

"What about the other Barriered cities? You said you were there when Newcastle's Barrier was turned off."

"The Newcastle Barrier came down about fifteen years ago. But it wasn't turned off. They were hit by a virulent plague, and it decimated the population. The technology of the Barrier failed and there was no one to repair it. It fell overnight, and the effect on the people was devastating. Seventy percent of the remaining population suicided out of panic brought on by acute agoraphobia. This is why London and Birmingham must prepare their people for the outside. Even if they didn't have population problems, their time is limited."

"Why?"

"Because, Mel, the rest of the country is beginning to pull together and, once they realise that London and Birmingham are so rich in technology, they will want it. If the cities won't share then the rest of the country will try to take it. That means a civil war, just as the country is recovering."

"But, what about Scotland? They must be at risk, as well."

"Scotland is in a different situation. While we have access to most of the technology, we haven't become dependent on it. Also, we have tenfold more space than the cities.

"We have farms, factories, and mining operations. We trade with Sweden, Norway, and Ireland. Our Barrier is not beset with holes or tunnels running under it. The only other way into Scotland is by boat. We watch those places that can be landed at; the rest of the coastline is craggy and inhospitable. The Barrier stops the casual visitor. Scotland will rejoin the British Isles when the time is right."

Mel lay back, silent, thinking about all she had been told. She was fascinated; she had been brought up to believe that London was probably the only place in Britain that still held life. She had seen for herself that was patently untrue. Compared to London, life outside was primitive, but it was still life.

"The Travellers talked of Exeter becoming an important place. They had been told to look out for things from London. Is there some sort of government there?"

"That's what I had heard. I was on my way there when you distracted me. The last time I was there, about five years ago, it was just a large market town. People would go there in the summer for a big fair and market. But rumour has it that more and more people are settling there, so some sort of government may have formed.

"If that's true, then a nation-wide government may come sooner than we thought. So it follows that the cities may have less time than they hoped for."

Mel mulled this over. In the last hour, she had learnt more about the world she lived in than in ten years of school. From an original five Barriered cities, only two remained. It stood to reason that those two must also fall in the end. It must be better

CHAPTER 5

to re-join on their own terms than be forced into it. She had a lot to tell the president when she got back.

Iain had closed his eyes, and Mel could hear his soft, regular breathing as he slept. She took longer to fall asleep. Too many questions floated around in her head, and not enough answers.

When she did fall asleep, she was awakened about three hours later by the sound of howling dogs. She got up and looked out of the grimy window, where she could see a pack of about twenty dogs milling around. She jumped slightly as Iain came up behind her as she watched them. Without conscious thought, she leaned back into him, as if for protection.

"They know we're here," he said softly.

They watched the dogs snuffling around, squabbling amongst themselves, for a short while. Then Mel gave a large yawn; Iain put his hand on her shoulder and said, "They can't get in here and they'll be gone by morning. Let's get some sleep."

Mel nodded tiredly and returned to their bed and, despite the dogs outside, slipped easily into sleep.

Sure enough, the next morning, the dogs were gone. Iain said he would check the area, just to be sure, and disappeared outside. He returned within half and hour, his arms full of wood to replace the kindling they had used. After a cold breakfast, they set off again.

The going was a lot easier now, as they were crossing open fields instead of fighting their way through trees and thick undergrowth. Within a couple of hours, they came to fields that had been ploughed up and cultivated and, shortly after that, they saw their first local inhabitant.

As soon as the man, who was walking behind a horse pulling a plough, saw them, he lifted a crossbow out of a holster on the front of the plough and aimed it casually in their direction.

As they drew closer, Iain raised his hand in greeting and called out, "George Stout. Just because I beat you at poker the last time I was here is no good reason to shoot me. That way, you'll never get your stuff back."

A grin broke on the man's weathered face; he spat into the ground before answering. "Iain McEvoy," he held his hand out, "turning up like a bad penny, again."

Iain took the dirty, callused hand, saying. "Well met, George." He indicated the crossbow, now back in its holder on the plough, "Since when do you go armed in the fields?"

"Been about a year now. We lost some people to dogs and bandits, so now we go armed. We also carry these," he held up a tube in his hand. It had piece of cloth attached to the end. "It's a flare. If I light this, the watch at the big house sends help."

"You've been having bandit problems, then," Iain said frowning.

"Aye, the Gov'ner will tell you more, if you and your friend have a mind to visit," George said pointedly, looking for an introduction.

"George, this is Mel, ex-damsel in distress. Mel, this is George, master ploughman, crack crossbow shot, and lousy poker player."

George made a noise of disgust in his throat and held out

a hand to Mel. "Ex-damsel in distress, eh! There's a story to be told there, I'll wager. Don't believe him about the poker, either. He cheats!" He turned his attention back to Iain. "Go up to the big house; the Gov'ner's there. Even if he's not pleased to see you, the twins will be. They're too young to know better."

"Thanks George, I'll see you later, if the dogs don't get you."

Iain looked thoughtful as he led the way to the large house in the distance. "That's another indication," he said to himself.

"What's an indication?" Mel asked, mostly to remind him that she was still there.

"Oh, what? Oh, an increase in bandit activity around here. If there is some sort of government in Exeter, then there will be some sort of law enforcement as well. So they push the bandit groups out of their area, which means more down here where the pickings are easier. Doesn't solve the problem, though; just gives it to someone else."

He lapsed into silence as they walked up the gravelled drive towards the house. Mel saw a figure disappear from the roof and, shortly after that, a large, red-haired man emerged from the house, preceded by two young boys about ten years old. Whilst the man strode towards them, the two boys were less inhibited, and ran as fast as they could towards Iain.

He scooped both of them up and, to the sound of loud squealing, hung them both upside down for a moment. By the time the man had reached them, they were both on the ground, laughing and trying to avoid Iain's fingers as he tickled them.

The man stood in front of Iain and, putting hands the

size of small shovels on his hips, looked him up and down. His craggy face frowned, his large, bushy eyebrows almost meeting in the centre of his forehead. Then his face broke into a wide grin and he held out one, large, hairy hand, with the words, "Well met, Iain McEvoy."

Iain grinned back at him in response and took the proffered hand, only to be pulled into a rib-breaking hug. Released and trying to get his breath back, Iain replied, "Good to see you as well, John."

"It's been too long a time." The giant slapped Iain' shoulder with his hand, which threatened to topple him over. "Almost two years, I reckons."

"Well, I had to go home for a while. But how are things here? The boys have sprung up; won't be long before they're fighting you for control."

Iain laid a hand on each boy's head, each of whom was busy staring, unblinkingly, at Mel. Their gaze was even more disconcerting when Mel realised that they were identical twins. She smiled back at them, but their stares never wavered. That left her at a loss as to what to do; she had little experience with children.

She tried to ignore them, but their unwavering stares drew her eyes back to them; she was mesmerised. In a booming voice that matched his build, John broke the spell. "Don't stare, lads. Go back to the house and tell your mother that there will be two more for the midday meal."

The boys turned and ran towards the house, and John turned his attention to Mel. "And what do we have here? Good breeding stock, I'd say."

"What!" Mel had a flash of déjà-vu. The expression on her face told both men that she was none too pleased at being referred to as good breeding stock.

Iain laughed. "Don't be insulted, Mel. That's a compliment as far as John's concerned. He has a bit of a blind spot where people are concerned; tends to treat them all as livestock."

"Aye, no insult intended. Come up to the house. Mary will be wanting to see you, Iain." John put his arm round Iain's shoulder and began to lead him towards the house, talking and waving his free hand as if Mel no longer existed.

As Mel looked after them, she couldn't help a small grin cross her face. *I'll just follow on behind, shall I?* she thought wryly.

She followed them into the house and downstairs to a large kitchen, where several women were at work preparing food. John announced, at the top of his voice, easily cutting through the noise of a busy kitchen, "Mary, look who's come to visit."

A small woman, slim, her long, jet black hair just beginning to show some grey, turned and, giving a big smile, crossed the kitchen to plant a kiss on Iain's cheek. Mel noticed that she had the same dark beauty she had seen in the troupe of Travellers.

Small she may have been, but she soon proved who was in control. As John went to sit down, she stepped up and stopped him.

"Hold it, you," she ordered. "If you are going to stop for your meal, you can get those dirty boots off." To Mel's amusement, John did just that without a murmur. Mel's respect for Mary rose accordingly.

Mel gently bumped hips with Iain, to remind him that she had not yet been introduced. "Oh," he said. "Mary, this is a friend of mine, Mel. Mel, this is the woman who puts up with John, Mary."

Mary looked at them quizzically. "Puts up with John? That sounds like my husband has been tactless, again."

"Mel didn't like being referred to as breeding stock."

Mary gave a snort. "The big oaf. I'll give him what for when I get him alone tonight." She waved them over to a table on the far side of the kitchen. "Sit, sit. Now, how long can you stay?"

"Only the night, I'm afraid," Iain answered. "I've promised to get Mel home as soon as possible."

"Oh," Mel cut in. She had been very impressed with this house and its occupants. She had also taken an instant liking to Mary. "Let's not rush things. I could certainly do with a rest, even if you couldn't." She looked at Mary. "As long as it's not going to put you out."

"No, no," she answered. "We love having guests. It's the only way we get to know what's going on in the rest of the country. In fact, we'll have a Gathering, in the courtyard."

"Please, don't go to too much trouble." Mel felt a bit overtaken by events.

"No trouble. We haven't had a Gathering for weeks. I'll send messengers to the outlying farms. They'll all come; everybody loves a good Gather."

Iain excused himself, saying that he would tell John about

the Gathering. Mary looked up as he left, saying, "Men! As soon as the hard work starts, they disappear. Now," Mary leaned closer, "tell me how you met Iain."

Mel had intended to be cautious about how much she revealed to Mary, but the other woman was such a good listener that she found herself tell her all about the Druids and how Iain had rescued her. After that, without even realising how it happened, she found herself involved in the planning for the Gathering.

During a lull in the preparations Mel asked Mary about Iain.

"He turned up here about five years ago. John was out hunting and got himself trapped by a pack of dogs. Iain saved his worthless hide but got himself injured in the process." Mary nodded to a woman who brought them a cup of tea. "He stayed here until he recovered, the two of them became as thick as thieves, and now he calls in whenever he's passing. He's always welcome here. One of John's strong points is that he never forgets a favour, and the boys think the world of him."

Mary said that she needed to see the stockman for a sheep to put on the spit tonight, so they both went outside, where Mel found Iain and the boys building a bonfire in the roasting pit. Then, it was back into the kitchen with the other women, to help organise the Gathering.

The house, Mel learnt, served as a focal point for the community. Mel had thought at first that maybe John and Mary acted like Lord and Lady of the Manor, living in the Big House while those who worked the fields live in smaller accommodation around it. But it wasn't so.

All the rooms were occupied, or in use. When their men folk were working in the fields, the women would bring their children to the big house. The community would look after the younger ones while the older ones got a rudimentary education in one of the larger rooms. If the men went away for any length of time, then their families would move in until they returned.

One wing of the house was given over to a hospital and care home for the elderly. There was even a maternity wing, so the women didn't have to give birth without help.

It seemed everybody mucked in together. There was a strong feeling of family that spread throughout the community. Mel felt some sadness at having to leave so soon. This set up, she thought, was almost ideal. The community was large enough to defend itself and everybody seemed to be happy with their lot.

Mel got so involved that, before she knew it, the day was ending and people were arriving from all directions. The festivities soon got underway.

As the evening progressed, Mel found herself being led around by Mary and introduced to numerous other people. At every stop, drinks were offered and, not wanting to appear standoffish, Mel drank them all. She soon found herself getting rather drunk.

There was no room in London for vineyards or hop fields, so the only alcohol came from the replicators. This, Mel soon found out, was not very strong, unlike the local brew, which was. By the end of the evening, she had told Mary and her friends all about London and all that had happened to her since.

Mel dimly remembered being helped to bed in the small hours of the morning, but nothing more until she woke the next morning. Although she didn't so much as wake up as come round, feeling worse than when the Druids had drugged her. She was also a bit surprised to find herself in a double bed, with the other side showing signs of having been used.

As she lay on her back staring at the ceiling, her eyes refused to focus on anything close; she tried to review the night's events. But her throbbing head would not let her concentrate.

The door opened, and Iain came in carrying a tray with food and drink on it. "Oh, come round at last, have we?"

"No!" Mel snapped back. "I've died and gone to hell. My head hurts." What started as a sharp retort, ended in a plaintive whine.

Iain sat on the bed and offered a cup from the tray. "Here, drink this. It'll help your poor head. Down it in one."

Mel decided that she was too ill to argue and did as she was told. The offended face she made told the whole story. "That's disgusting!" she spluttered.

"That's why it's good for you," Iain said, smugly. "The local brew around here is rather potent; it needs something strong to counter it."

For all its abominable taste, the concoction did help. Mel could fell her head clearing enough to ask some questions. "Who put me to bed last night?" was the first one.

"Mary did," came the reply. "I joined you later."

Mel raised a questioning eyebrow at him. Iain laughed.

"Don't worry, I stuck to our agreement. It's just that, if you turn up with a woman who's not a relative, then you are presumed to be together. You said that you didn't want to be any trouble, so I accepted the room for you. Anyway, the only thing you could do by the end of the Gathering was snore!"

The Gathering? What did she do at the Gathering?

As her head cleared, the memories of last night's celebrations began to come back. Mel suddenly put her hand over her mouth as one particular memory returned. "Iain, I think I told everyone, well, Mary at least, that I was from London," she confessed in a small voice.

Iain patted her hand. "Don't worry. John and Mary know all about London. They don't think you're a ghost."

"Ha, ha." Mel was not in the mood for humour.

Iain placed the tray on her lap. "Here. This is lunch. Eat well; I have a plan to get you home quicker."

Although the sight of food made her stomach turn over, she began to eat. She was also put out to find it was after noon.

"So," she asked around a mouthful of food. Once she had started, her appetite came back. "How am I going to get home quicker?"

"Well, it depends. Have you ever ridden a horse?"

Mel almost choked; Iain slapped her on the back until she stopped. "A horse!" she finally spat out. "No, never. You don't get many horses in London."

"That's what I thought. So, if you ever decide to get out of that bed, we'll throw you onto the back of one and see if you fall off correctly or not."

Mel, still eating, contented herself with a baleful stare for his offhandedness.

Iain ignored her and continued. "John will lend us a couple of horses and that will double the distance we can travel in a day. And if we run into trouble, they can run faster than us, as well."

Mel fell into a thoughtful silence. Until she had left London, she had never seen a live horse, let alone rode one. She had helped Ma take care of the ones the Travellers used. They were great, hairy beasts that they called Shires. She knew that there were other horses in the camp that were ridden, but she had never considered riding one herself. But now she found the idea quite intriguing.

Iain said that Mary had left some suitable clothes out for her, and would she hurry up, otherwise it would be time for supper.

Mel found a pair of trousers and a thick jumper at the bottom of the bed; she wore her own boots. After all they had been through, they were still unmarked. But getting up had made her head throb again, so she carefully made her way down the stairs to meet a smiling Mary at the bottom.

"Ah! Good morning," Mary spoke in a disgustingly cheerful voice. Mel restricted her answer to a grunt; Mary gave a light laugh and said, "Iain and John are waiting outside with the horses."

Mel went out into the courtyard where she found Iain, John, and two saddled horses, their reins being held by another man.

"Oh!" John said in what Mel thought was an unnaturally

loud voice. "Up at last. Can't say I hold with this sleeping all day."

"Don't mind him," Iain laughed. "He's so healthy the only excuse he'll take for not being able to work is death."

"That's unfair," John protested. "I have been known to allow women in the last stages of pregnancy time off to give birth . . . occasionally."

"Ha, ha. Yes, very amusing," Mel shaded her eyes from a sun that seemed much brighter than yesterday. "Well, I actually died during the night. Can I go back to bed now?"

Iain came over and took her elbow. "No. The best thing for a hangover is a lot of fresh air. You'll feel right as rain in no time."

Mel didn't think that she would ever feel as right as rain, but she turned her attention to the horses. They looked. . . . large.

Iain nodded to the man holding the reins. "This is Martin. He looks after the horses around here. There's not much he doesn't know about them."

Mel came alongside the nearest horse and hesitated, unsure of how to proceed.

"This one's name is Candour. She has a lovely temperament; just slap her on the neck to let her know you're there." Martin's voice was soft and gentle as he lifted Mel's right leg and placed it in the stirrup. "Put all your weight on that leg and lift. and swing the other up and over her rump."

She did as instructed, and suddenly found herself sitting astride the horse. Martin lifted the reins back over Candour's head and pressed them into Mel's hands. "Hold these lightly in between your index finger and thumb, wrap the rest of them around your other three fingers."

Iain came alongside as Martin was adjusting her stirrups. "How do you feel?"

Mel cleared her throat nervously before she answered. "Tall," she finally said.

John gave out a deep rumble from his chest, which Mel presumed was laughter. "Aye," he commented. "I can see that. If you haven't been brought up with horses, they might seem a bit big."

The next hour was spent with Martin leading Candour round by the reins, so Mel could get used to the walking motion of the horse. Then, a long rein was fitted and Martin coaxed the horse into a trot.

The sudden increase in the bouncing motion of the horse took Mel by surprise and she found herself and the horse parting company; she managed to fall on her backside. Mild shock at where she found herself etched itself on her face.

John walked over and put his hands under Mel's arms, lifting her back onto her feet. "Don't worry about falls," he said as he helped her remount. "Horses were made for two things. Riding and falling off of."

Mel soon realised that the way to stay on a horse was to go with the motions, not against them. However, when Martin got Candour to break into a gallop, Mel lost her seat again. This time she felt herself going, and managed to half dismount and half fall off.

"Well done, well done," Martin praised. "You've kept hold of the reins and managed to land on your feet. Now," he continued, smiling, "back up you go." Mel groaned softly, but did as she was asked.

Mel was discovering something that people had known for years about horses. There was a thrill to being on the back of a powerful creature like a horse, and being in control. Mel, like many before her, was hooked.

Martin was already back into his lessons. "Now, when the motion of the horse gets too much, lift yourself out of the saddle and use your knees as shock absorbers." He tugged on the reins and Candour set of again.

This went on until Iain came alongside on the other horse. It was mostly black, with a white face, and looked like it would live up to its name, Spirit. It shuffled and fidgeted as Iain got a strong hand on the reins.

"So," Iain said, looking down at Martin, "do you think she's ready for the Gather day races?"

"Not quite. But she's ready for a short ride," Martin removed the training reins and continued, "Remember, take it easy, use your knees to guide the horse, and don't get over-confidant!"

Mel nudged Candour with her heels and followed Iain's lead towards the open fields. The ride was short, just a big circle around the field, but they went through all she had learned and, by the end, Mel felt much more at home on a horse.

Mel was also impressed with Iain's abilities. He rode easily in the saddle, giving the impression that the horse and rider were one; he had a fine, upright stance in the saddle that Mel tried to copy.

Finally, when they were on the far side of the field, Iain turned back and broke into a gallop. Mel nudged Candour with her heels and followed suit. The gallop was both frightening and exciting. She was half-afraid that Candour wouldn't stop but, when she pulled on the reins as she had been taught, the horse responded beautifully.

They took the horses back to the stables where Martin showed Mel how to care for her mount. When the horses were unsaddled, groomed, and fed, Iain, Mel, and Martin stood outside Candour's stable where Iain's questioning look asked Martin for his opinion.

"Well," he said, "you're not the most natural rider I've seen, but you do have good sense of balance. If you take it easy over the next day or so, you should be fine."

Iain took Martin's hand and shook it. "Thanks for all your help. We'll take good care of the horses."

Martin gave a thin smile. "Be sure you do. A cared-for horse could save your life."

"Well!" Iain looked at Mel as they walked back to the house. "That was strong praise from Martin. He doesn't lend horses to just anybody, you know. If John overworks any of the horses, Martin will let him know in no uncertain terms. John may be in charge around here, but the horses are as good as Martin's property."

Mel was pleased with Martin's reaction. She had to admit that when she had first mounted the horse she had felt pretty apprehensive but, by day's end, she had felt quite at home. Now that everything was in place for them to depart the next morning, Mel felt sorry to leave, as there was such a feeling of family here.

Dusk was falling as they entered the house. Mary was in the kitchen cooking the evening meal with just a couple of helpers; the other women had returned to their own homes. She refused Mel's offer of help, telling them that John was waiting for them in his office.

They found John sitting behind a very old desk in a cluttered room just off the main hall. He waved them in and pointed in the direction of a table on which maps were spread out. Iain studied them for a moment and then asked Mel to fetch her own maps from the bedroom.

When she returned, she found both men leaning over the map table. John waved his hand over them, saying, "These are the most up-to-date we have of the countryside you'll be crossing. They go almost to the edge of the dead land, just outside of London."

Iain spread out Mel's maps and John began to compare them. "All these places," he said, pointing to towns marked on the older maps, "are deserted. The nearest settlement we found to us, going south anyway, was a place called Hogs." He looked closer at Mel's maps. "That would be here, close to this old town called Farnham. The main settlement was high on a hill and the people weren't that friendly, as I remember."

Iain pursed his lips in a silent whistle. "You've mapped all this since I was last here?"

John shrugged. "When all the planting was done last spring, I took three others and set out to find out how populated the southern countryside was. It's beginning to get a bit crowded around here. Children are growing up and, whilst the eldest boy automatically inherits the father's land, the younger siblings have nothing. They want the opportunity to hold land of their own and, if they don't get at least the chance, then I'm afraid that there could be trouble between those that have and those that don't. This mapping expedition was to find out what was available."

"And?" Iain prompted.

"And, like I said, the nearest settlement is over thirty miles south. Some of the land is usable now; other land, such as where towns once stood, can be reclaimed but it will need a lot of hard work."

"Do you mean clearing away the old buildings?" Mel asked.

John spread his hands wide. "That's only part of the problem. All the old towns have new inhabitants, rats, dogs, even wild pig packs. Your new home will also be hours away from help, should you run into trouble. It will be dangerous, especially for the first few years."

"Well," Iain looked thoughtful as he spoke, "the answer would seem to be that you say to those who want their own land that the land is there for the taking. If you can take it and keep it, it's yours. Some will die trying; others will come back with their tails between their legs. But those that succeed will have proven themselves the best to control the land."

John nodded his large, shaggy head slowly. "That's what I thought. We'll give them what supplies and help we can, but it will be up to them to keep the land. I also thought that if we had several outlying homesteads close enough to each other, it might help in controlling the bandit population. It's got a lot worse in the last few months."

"Yes, I think I might have a reason why." Iain sat on the edge of the desk and crossed his arms. "There are rumours of a man in Exeter beginning to take control in the area. If this is true then one of the first things he would have to do is get the bandit problem under control. It's my guess that he's pushed them out of the area and they've ended up here. Are they proving much trouble?"

John's brow creased. "The first time we realised any change was after an attack on an outlying homestead, Steve Hardman's place. Joe Moore is his nearest neighbour and when he didn't turn up for a regular visit, Joe went to look in on them. He found the house burned to the ground, Steve and Julie, his wife, dead, and their three daughters gone.

"Joe came and told me, and we got together a few others and went looking for the girls. We found their camp and took them by surprise and rescued the girls. Only we weren't quite quick enough. The eldest girl, Jolie, she's fourteen, had been raped several times, and the younger ones had been abused. They're all still alive, but Jolie is unlikely to ever recover fully. Maria and Lindy are living with Joe and his family, and seem to be recovering all right.

"Jolie stays here with us. Mary is slowly getting her

through it, but she still shows the effects of the attack. It breaks me up when another man enters a room where Jolie is. She backs away like a frightened rabbit. We hung those bandits we didn't kill, and we cleared out a few other camps, as well. I hoped any other would take note and move on, but we are still getting attacks, increasing over the last few months."

There was a heavy silence in the room. John's story had affected them all. Mel could see the pain in John's eyes. The hangings had affected him, as well. He hadn't wanted to become an executioner, but he had been left with little choice. There were no jails, or time, or resources to confine criminals. He had tried to set an example of what would happen to people like this. Mel hoped it would work.

John sighed and looked at Iain. "If you get to Exeter, be sure and tell whoever's in charge down there what sort of problems he's causing for us."

"Don't worry on that score, John," Iain had a glint in his eye. "You can count on it."

"Thanks." John spoke with great sincerity. He folded Mel's map so the route back to London on hers was above the route on his. "Between here and here," he indicated their present location and Farnham on both maps, "we found only one other human inhabitant. A half-crazy, old man called Seth; he lived here at what's called Sandhurst on your map. It's an old army camp, and he was the only one left. Grew enough to live on and spent most of his time fighting off rats and dogs. He had some interesting tales to tell, and it's about fifteen miles from here, so you might want to stop there overnight. Old Seth's a bit crazy, but harmless enough."

Iain nodded. "We'll do that, then. What were his stories, then?"

John shook his head. "I'll leave him to tell them. I thought they were just ramblings, but Mel's map brings a grain of truth to a lot he said." John went back to the maps. "Not far from there is what was once known as a motorway." He traced a finger down the light blue line on Mel's map. "A lot of it still exists. We kept coming across it while we were travelling. It leads almost to the dead zone; after that you're on your own."

He folded the maps and handed them to Iain. "When will you leave?"

"Dawn," Iain answered. "A good meal and an early night, and we'll be away at first light."

"Well," John went over to a cabinet, poured three drinks, and handed one each to Iain and Mel. "Here's to good luck and a safe journey."

Iain and John downed theirs in one gulp. Mel sipped hers cautiously. She had no wish to repeat last night's experience. Once bitten twice shy.

They ate with the rest of the household; Iain told them all he could of the news from outside their community before making their way to bed. Mel was a bit worried about them sleeping together again, but as soon as her head hit the pillow, she was asleep.

The next thing she knew, Iain was shaking her awake. It was an hour before dawn and she had to pack her things and get ready to leave. As dawn broke, they were in the courtyard;

horses saddled, and ready to go.

John and Mary were there to say goodbye. Mel took Mary in a hug, and kissed John on the cheek. Iain kissed Mary and slapped John on the arm, Mel and Mary rolled their eyes at this macho parting. They mounted and turned the horses towards their hosts. Iain looked down at them, saying, "I'll see you in a couple of weeks, John, when I return the horses."

John held up one hand as a salute. "Good journey."

They turned the horses and trotted out of the courtyard and across the fields. Mel looked back once, but John and Mary had gone in.

Time to move on again.

They passed around cultivated fields, passing small farmhouses; some obviously had been standing since the Breakdown, others were more crudely built. Most were up at this early hour, and anybody they passed seemed to know Iain. Mel recognised a few from the Gather.

Iain remarked how much the settlement had grown since he had first seen it. Mel wondered how the land had been settled in the first place.

John's family, Iain explained, had been living in the big house for generations. When the Breakdown had happened, John's great-great-great grandfather had closed off the area around his land and, with his family, had held against all who had tried to take it over. There were many fights, even against government forces. But, they had succeeded.

Then when things calmed down and the survivors were left to fend for themselves, without interference from one tin-pot government or another, refugees from the radioactive areas in the north had begun to make their way south. John's ancestor realised that his family couldn't run the whole settlement on their own, so he handed out parcels of land and those who proved they could work it were allowed to stay.

The refugees worked the land and paid a tithe to the Lord of the Manor. As time went by, the title of Lord was lost, and John's predecessors became working heads of the community. He retained the right to try and punish those who broke the community's law, and to take land away from people not pulling their weight. When John died, his sons would take over and carry on the family line.

Iain glanced at Mel as they trotted the horses alongside each other. "John now heads a large, self-contained settlement. They have all that they need: blacksmiths, carpenters, weavers, thatchers, etc. They even have a doctor, although you probably wouldn't recognise her medicine. They have all they need to survive and grow. However, John has realised that if they shut themselves off from the rest of the country, they'll become afraid of strangers and new ideas. So, he trades with other communities, mostly with coastal places for food like fish, and he welcomes people like the Travellers. In fact, that's how he met Mary. She was with a troupe that passed through; she stayed behind and they started a family. John's settlement is a prime example of how the country can pull together. One day, maybe one of John's grandsons will help form a government for the whole of England. They have gone from individuals, growing just enough for themselves and their families to live on, to growing enough to trade as well. This will allow the manufacturers, such as the blacksmith and the carpenters, to work at their craft without the worry of growing food to feed their families.

Iain continued his story. "Once this begins to happen, the people will start to rediscover the old sciences. There's a man I know who lives on the West Coast, who has made a crude battery. Once electricity has been discovered, then some will develop the telegraph, then the radio. Sociologists in Scotland believe that, left to their own devices, in another hundred years, the outside population of England will be back to pre-Breakdown technology, especially if places like London and Birmingham lower their Barriers and take their place in a New England."

Mel looked across at Iain, a puzzled look on her face. "Why don't you tell the people how it's done? It would save a lot of time."

Iain shook his head. "No, to give all the technology at once would be dangerous. You have to be careful who you give knowledge to. If information on gunpowder and ballistics were to fall into the hands of someone like the Druids, it would be very dangerous. After the Newcastle Barrier fell and the locals got their hands on modern weapons, there were many small wars. Fortunately, as the ammunition ran out, they didn't know how to make more. It's better to leave people to their own devices and give them a little nudge in the right direction occasionally."

Mel saw his point. The thought of Druids with guns and bombs sent a shiver down her spine. "But you said that John and Mary know about the cities. Surely they must know about the technology, as well?"

"Oh, I've told them about the cities, but not what's available in them. John's only real interest is how to plough his fields quicker and grow his crops bigger. Guns and bombs don't hold much interest for him."

They rode on in silence. Fording a small stream, they came to the edge of a wooded area. Iain suggested a short rest. Releasing the horses to graze, Iain pulled the maps from his bags and spread them on the ground. According to John's map," his finger traced across the map, "this stream goes all the way to Sandhurst. According to yours, it disappears about a mile from here."

Mel looked closer at the maps. "Disappears? How can that be?"

"Before the Breakdown, if a stream or river was in the way of building, then they would divert it underground. When John's ancestors reclaimed the land, the stream would have been brought back to irrigate the fields." Iain shaded his eyes and looked up at the sun. "Come on, let's get moving. I want to be at Sandhurst before dark. I'm curious as to what this Seth has to tell."

Mel pulled herself back onto her horse. "What do you think his story will be?"

Finding a break in the trees, Iain nudged Spirit forward. "John knows my interest in the time before the Breakdown. I expect he has some stories from his grandsire's time."

Conversation came to a halt as they fought their way through some thick undergrowth. They tried to follow the stream as much as they could, but they often had to take detours. As the sun was setting, they finally came across a path that had been used recently. But as they did, trouble found them.

They both heard the sound of dogs barking. Iain stopped for a moment, to try and determine where the sound was coming from. It soon became obvious that there was a pack of dogs behind them, and coming in their direction.

They began to push the horses as fast as they could on the narrow path, but low hanging branches were always a danger. Mel glanced behind, almost unseating herself as a thick branch scraped the top of her head. What she saw made her spur Candour to go faster. A large black dog led the pack, and only two hundred yards behind them.

"Mel!" Iain called sharply. "Concentrate on your riding. If you fall off, you're finished."

The trees thinned out in front of them and a low fence appeared, Spirit instinctively jumped it and Mel had just enough time to ready herself before Candour followed suit; even so, she struggled to keep her seat as her horse landed with a bone-jarring thump.

On the other side of the fence stood a series of long huts,. Most of them were falling down, but by a hut that looked liveable, there was a figure chopping wood. As the two horses landed, he looked up with a start and reached for a bow by his side.

"DOGS!" Iain yelled.

The figure quickly fitted an arrow and fired over the lead dog's head and into the pack. There was a yelping sound and a dog fell, bringing down several more in its wake.

Iain skidded Spirit to a halt and dismounted. Gripping

hard on the reins, he took a fast shot with his crossbow. The bolt landed in between the lead dog's feet, stopping him in his tracks.

Mel almost fell off Candour, and took Spirit's reins from Iain as he was trying to reload his weapon one-handed. The other man let go another arrow into the pack and the dogs began to mill around, confused and excited by the smell of blood coming from their comrade. The man pulled open a large side door in the hut, and Mel pulled the horses inside. She tried to calm them down as the door was slammed shut behind them.

Iain came over and began to talk to the horses in a low, calming voice while Mel went over to a grime-encrusted window and looked out on the pack of dogs. They were attacking their fallen member.

Survival of the fittest in action.

Chapter 6

The man, Mel presumed he was Seth, began to divest himself of various pieces of clothing, muttering to himself all the time. Looking him over, Mel thought that he looked even older than Ma.

Straggly clumps of white hair stuck out in all directions from his balding head. His face was deeply lined and the colour of leather, most of his teeth seemed to be missing, and those that were left were a dark yellow. He may have been tall once, but was stooped with age. His eyes were the only things that showed that life still had a hold on him.

He hobbled slowly over to the window and stood next to Mel. The old man's body odour made her move away slightly, leaving her to wonder how long it had been since he had bathed.

"It'll be a couple of hours before they'll go away," he said, his accent thick with age. "Damn near got that black hellion this time. Never met a dog with so much luck." He cackled with laughter and moved to stand by the door. He then looked Iain up and down, as if he had just noticed him.

Iain gave a large, disarming smile and held out a hand, saying, "You'll be Seth, I'm guessing?"

The old man's eyes clouded with cautious suspicion. "I may be. I mayn't be. Who wants to know?"

Iain dropped the proffered hand, but kept smiling. "I'm Iain and this is Mel. A friend of ours told us about you, John Ferguson. He lives in a settlement just north of here."

Seth snorted. "I remembers him. Said he was 'looking about the countryside.' Looking about! I told him he should be home looking after his family." Seth gave the impression that this looking about was the height of folly. He went silent for a moment, and then continued. "I suppose you expect me to feed you, now you're here. Well, when the pack has gone, we can see what meat they've left us."

Mel was nonplussed for a moment, and then she realised that he meant eating the remains of the dogs that were killed. That thought made her stomach flip; she didn't fancy eating dog meat.

Iain went to the saddlebag on his horse, and pulled out the mutton joint that Mary had given them for their journey and held it out towards Seth. He came closer and sniffed at it like a dog.

"Mutton," he said his voice full of wonder. "A long time it's been since I had mutton. Gets fed up with dog and rat."

Mel stomach lurched again and she tried not to think about eating rats.

He went off to a far corner of the hut where a pile of pots and pans were stacked, and began to sort through them. He began to throw them into the middle of the hut; Mel had to smile as Iain deftly side-stepped a flying pan. Finally, finding a large roasting pot, he waved it at them and said, "This way, this way."

He led them into a room in the back where there was a low cot in one corner and old overstuffed chairs were scattered about. Against one wall stood a black, pot bellied stove, its fires already lit.

Filling the pan with water, and finding some scrawny looking vegetables, he began to cook the mutton, humming happily to himself and ignoring both of them.

Iain took Mel's arm and led her back to the horses. "While he's cooking, we had better see to the horses. They need rubbing down after that run."

They busied themselves with the horses' welfare, feeding them grain from the supply they had brought along with them. When Iain was happy with their state, he asked, "Well, what do you think of Seth, then?"

Mel shrugged. "I think he's been on his own too long. He's got some strange eating habits. Did you see those dead rats hanging above the stove? Yuck!"

Iain face creased into a grin. "Get hungry enough and you'll eat anything. I know."

Mel debated asking him what he meant by that, but decided that she didn't want to know.

They went back into the living area and sat down on an old sofa, waiting for Seth to finish cooking. When it did arrive, the meal was quite tasty. Seth had added something to the meat which gave it a strange, but not unpleasant, flavour. Mel didn't enquire what had been added, but did make sure that the same number of rats hung above the stove.

At the end of the meal, Seth leaned back and gave a self-satisfied belch, and Iain began to ask about John's visit.

"Aye, I remembers him. Big strapping lad, he was." Seth demonstrated his size with his hands. "Said he wanted to 'repopulate' round here. Too late, I told him. Round here's already populated, with dogs and rats." He broke off into chortling laughter, which turned into a coughing fit. Mel pounded him on the back, raising quite a cloud of dust, until he came to a wheezing halt.

"Thank'ee, Miss," he finally gasped. "Been a long time since I was nursed by a pretty girl, a very long time."

"How long, Seth?" Iain asked.

"Ah," Seth looked sad for a moment. "Must be five summers since the missus died. Damn sight longer since there were youngsters here." He shook his head slowly; Mel could see his eyes getting damp.

"Where did they all go?" she said softly.

"When I was just a lad, there was a split. The younger folk, there would have been about a hundred of them, said that the community was dying and they needed to go to the coast to be near other settlements. The older people disagreed, and when the youngsters moved on, they stayed behind. My Ma and Da decided to stay. I was born late to my Ma; I was about ten when the others left.

"Mind you, when I came of age, I left too. I had an urge to see what was on the other side of the hill. When I met my

Missus, I decided to come back and raise some children, but we were never blessed that way. Slowly all the old 'uns died off and there were only the two of us left."

"Why didn't you leave then?" Iain asked.

"Before he died, my Da told me why he never went with the others. He said he had to keep the records up, so people would know what had happened here. He showed me where it was and what to do, but now the machine don't work any more."

There was silence as Seth retreated into his memories. Mel glanced at Iain and saw a puzzled frown on his face. She was puzzled herself. What did Seth mean by 'keeping up the records'?

"Where are the records kept, Seth? Maybe we can help fix them."

Seth looked up from his reminiscing. "Do you think you can?"

"I can't promise anything, but both Mel and I have some knowledge of the old technologies." Iain smiled reassuringly at the old man.

Seth went to the window and looked out. "The dogs have gone, but it's getting dark. If you want, we can take a look now."

Mel and Iain both nodded and reached for their coats. Seth picked up an old oil lamp and lit it. They left the hut and followed him across the camp to the far edge, where Seth walked straight into a large bush. Mel and Iain stopped for a moment until Seth reappeared, saying, "Come on, come on, this way."

Iain looked at Mel and shrugging his shoulders, followed

Seth. Working their way inside the bush, they found, hiding in the centre, a concrete building. The door was open and they could see the light from Seth's lamp inside.

"This definitely looks pre-Breakdown," Iain whispered to Mel. "Let's go inside."

He heaved on the door to open it fully, and went inside, Mel at his heels. The room was of moderate size and there was a waist-height shelf around three of the walls. Sitting on the shelf were several computer monitors; the light from the lamp reflecting eerily in their black screens. On a lower shelf were keyboards.

"It's a computer room." Mel was slightly awed by this unexpected discovery. This was not something she had thought she would see outside London. "I've seen stuff like this in the museum. The keyboards are for inputting data. Before voice recognition became standard."

"Aye, my Da called in the com-put-er room. He said it was left to him to look after by his father, and his father before him. I carried on as he asked, but everything stopped working about a year after he died." Seth turned to the computer behind him. "This was the only one we used. Da said that his great-great-grandfather had begun the records. I remember as a child that he would come here at the end of every day and make his report, as he called it."

While Seth was talking, Mel began to look at the other consoles. All were covered in a thick layer of dust and none showed any sign of life. Then she noticed a red light in a panel on the wall winking steadily. It was hardly noticeable because of

CHAPTER 6

the dust covering it. When Mel wiped the panel clean, the reason for the light became clear.

"Iain, look at this." She pointed to the legend below the flashing light. It read Battery Power Low.

"Battery power," Iain mused. "Batteries are unlikely to last two hundred and fifty years. They must be recharged somehow."

"Well, there's no main power. Maybe there's a wind generator around," Mel offered.

"No. That would take a tall tower. We would have noticed even the remains of one of those," Iain stroked the stubble on his chin. "I know. Solar power! There must be solar panels on the roof."

"And," Mel continued, "the roof is covered in branches and leaves, so the panels are not getting any sunlight to recharge the batteries."

Iain turned to Seth. "Seth, how long has this room been covered by trees."

Seth scratched his head. "I planted them just after Da died. He seemed to think this room was important, so I thought it would be best hidden."

"And in doing that you cut off the supply of sunlight to the panels. The system probably has a failsafe, so the batteries are never full discharged, and you don't lose all the information stored."

Iain smiled at Seth, who had a look of bafflement on his face. "We think that there are panels on the roof that convert sunlight into electricity. So, when the trees grew up over the roof, the batteries went flat and the computers stopped working."

Iain went back to the door and looked out. "It's almost fully dark now. First thing in the morning, we'll clear the roof, and, providing dust hasn't affected the systems, we should be able to get the computer going again after a few hours."

They went back to the main hut and settled down to sleep. At first light, they were up and cutting back branches to reveal the silver glint of the hidden solar panels. A couple of hours saw them finished, and they retired for a late breakfast.

"How long do you think the batteries will take to recharge?" Mel asked as they finished their breakfast.

"They'll take days to fully recharge, but it's a bright day, so we should be able to try this afternoon."

After the meal, Seth went off to work on his garden and Iain went to check on the horses, leaving Mel to her own thoughts. She felt full of nervous energy. On the one hand, she was eager to get back to London; on the other, her curiosity had been piqued about what was in the files of the computer. Her thoughts went to Cord. She wondered briefly if this could be a subconscious effort to delay possible bad news. The news that Cord had died at the campsite.

No! She wouldn't believe that until it was proven. She had to believe that he was still alive.

Mel watched Iain talking to Seth and wondered how they would get on if he and Cord were ever to meet. Probably one of two ways, she supposed. Instant respect or instant dislike. There would be no middle ground with either of them.

Iain said that he was going to help Seth cut some wood for

the stove, and left Mel on her own, again. Bored, she gathered together the breakfast things and washed them clean. After that, she surprised herself by beginning to clean the hut, as well. I must be getting domesticated, she mused to herself.

The other two came back with armfuls of wood, and Iain got Seth to tell them more about life in the camp.

"Well, this was a reasonably happy place before the younger ones moved on. After they left, there was population of about seventy left. By the time I left, that was down to forty. I came back after a year and they were down to less than twenty. There had been a sickness and the older ones had no resistance to it. But my Ma and Da were still alive and pleased to see me. I had brought Annabelle with me, and we settled down and tried for children, but none came. My Da explained some of what the computers were about, but died sudden-like in his sleep.

"Ma died not long after, but we carried on, trying to survive. We thought about packing up and following the others, but we didn't know where they had gone exactly, so we stayed. One by one the others died, by illness, dogs, or rats.

"The dog packs were getting bigger, and smarter. When there was more of us, we would hunt out the breeding places to keep the numbers down. But with fewer people to hunt them, the dogs multiplied quickly. Eventually there was only me and Belle left. We were too old to start again, so we made the best of it."

A look of immense sadness came over his face as he continued. "Then, Belle died of a fever. That would have been five year back now. I just live day to day, waiting for my call to come." He gave a long, drawn out sigh and went silent, lost in his memories.

Mel moved closer to Iain. She could feel Seth's loneliness. Iain spoke kindly from her side. "I will be coming back this way in about a week or so. Why don't you come to the Ferguson settlement with me? I'm sure that John could use your knowledge of the past to teach his people some things."

"I don't know," Seth said slowly. "I ain't been around people in a long time. Although, I don't fancy dying alone."

"Well, you think about it. I'll call in, anyway. You can decide then."

They returned to the computer room and, as they entered the windowless room, the lights automatically came on. A light on the monitor was flashing and when Iain pressed a key, the stack began to make a whirring sound and the monitor flickered into life. A box appeared on the screen asking for a login name and password.

Taking a deep breath, Seth laboriously typed in COLMORRIS. "Morris was my great-great-great grandfather's name. He was a colonel here at the time of the Breakdown, "Seth explained. Then he typed in ROSE. "His wife's name." The screen went black for a moment and then displayed a list of options.

Seth hesitated, not sure how to continue. "Place the cursor on the line that says DAILY LOG and press the enter key," Iain prompted. Seth did as he was told, and the words REVIEW OR ENTER? appeared. Iain leaned across and pressed the R key. They were then asked for a start date.

Seth looked up at Iain and Mel inquiringly. "Well," Iain

CHAPTER 6

said. "The best place to start is at the beginning. Put in June 6, 2067. That was the year the first bomb went off, if I remember rightly."

As they watched, letters began to flow across the screen.

This is the personal log of Colonel William Stuart Morris. Second in command, Sandhurst Officer's training camp.

Brigadier Harcourt has informed me that we are to speed up training as the union riots are expected to increase in ferocity when the new anti-union laws are implemented from tomorrow.

I have to ask myself if this government knows what it is doing. They appear to be asking for a direct confrontation with the people of this country.

I fear for the future.

Iain and Mel watched fascinated as the history of the Breakdown unfolded before them. What followed were detailed observations on the most unsettled time Great Britain had ever faced. At first, the entries were daily. They told of new orders, or problems arising throughout the country. Colonel Morris also had access to communications from other countries, and reported on their problems

The reports were sometimes very personal, and he talked about the Manchester bomb, telling of his search for information on his parents and his sister's family, who still lived there.

After a month of daily reports, they became more irregular. Sometimes weeks, or in one case a month, passed without any entries. Iain guessed that he had been sent off on missions, maybe to try and restore order in different parts of the country.

Then there was a gap of over a year. When the entries

restarted, the first one was long and rambling about how he had tried to get into London to find his wife and younger children. How he had searched the refugee camps, but to no avail.

He spoke of how he hoped that they were safe behind the force wall that had been put around the city. Now he was left with only his eldest son, who had joined his father in the armed forces when the bombs had been detonated.

His last entry said that he was being sent north to assess the situation in the areas closest to where the bombs had been detonated. His son, reporting his death at the hands of half-maddened radiation-affected survivors, authored the next entry.

His son, Bruce, then took over the job of keeping the records, and they returned to being more regular. His reports spoke mostly of the camp, and how they were coping with the troubles outside, and of the refugees arriving almost daily. He wrote of attacks on the camp, which were easily repelled as the defenders were much better armed. After a few months, he reported that they had stopped accepting any more refugees because of overcrowding. The flow of people finally abated, and the reports said that they would go months without seeing other people.

Bruce Morris then began to talk about diseases long-since conquered, like bubonic plague and cholera. He wondered if they were all natural, or if they were man made.

Five years after the Breakdown, Bruce Morris sent out parties of men north and south. Based on the information they brought back, he estimated that, outside of the Barriered cities, there were only some hundred thousand people left alive.

CHAPTER 6

Those who had survived the mini-civil wars, disease, and famine had settled into small communities and were wary of strangers. The scouts told of being shot at and being generally unwelcome. Bruce considered this to be a sensible way to run a community and adopted the same ethos.

As the community settled down, the reports became monthly, and took on the form of a progress report. The camp had a population of over five hundred at the beginning, and they were using the land around them to grow crops. Morris reported their frustration at their ignorance of how to grow the things they needed. Finally, they risked going into the nearby towns to raid libraries for books on agriculture and, slowly, they learned the art of self-sufficiency. But many of the very old and the very young died in the first few years.

After that, the reports settled into the regular goings-on at the camp. Deaths, births, the progress of the harvests. Iain and Mel skimmed through these entries, although Iain did remark that there were historians in Scotland who would kill to see these writings.

The passing of Bruce Morris was noted, and then his son, Glen. The population of the camp reached a high of over seven hundred in Glen Morris' time. Infant mortality was high, but they were happy that they could maintain a constant number. Then, there was another three-month gap in the reports.

When they returned, James Morris was reporting the death of his father, Glen, along with seventy percent of the camp dwellers, from a virulent plague that had swept through the camp in an especially cold and bleak winter. James first report made depressing reading.

Spring has arrived and brought none of the joy we associate with it. The winter's plague has hit us very hard; we number now some two hundred and ten. There is a consensus growing among the surviving younger ones that we should move to the south coast. They believe that if there are any large communities in the country, then that is where they will be.

I find that I cannot disagree with them. The birth rate has fallen to almost nothing, and the rat and dog population has increased and threatens to overwhelm us. I don't believe that this community can recover from the blow it has been dealt, and I see no reason why they should die with it.

'I, along with some thirty others, will be staying. I feel I have a responsibility to my father and my grandfather to keep up this record. They hoped that one day someone would read this journal and it would help them to understand better what happened in those dark days, now some hundred and fifty years ago. I, too, still have that hope. I also believe that man is a resilient beast and I am convinced that one day he will overcome the odds and repopulate this country again.

The others are staying because they feel they are too old for change, or they have lost hope and wish to die in familiar surroundings. That is their choice, and it will be honoured. But the younger generation wishes to move to a community that has a better chance of survival. I wish them a speedy and safe journey.

The reports after that went back to the mundane. James Morris recorded Seth's departure and his return, and wrote that

CHAPTER 6

he was cheered by the news of other communities, and that they were trading with each other. Seth reported his father's death, and carried on filing reports until the computer stopped operating.

Mel felt emotionally drained by the end of the reports. She had just read the whole history of a community. Life, death, and survival. It was all a bit much to take in at one sitting. Iain was quiet, as well; he stood, watching Seth closely.

"Well?" he asked him. "Will you start making entries again? Now it's repaired?"

Seth smiled sadly. "What is there to report? Every new ache and pain I feel, what I had for dinner last night? No, I think I'll leave it alone. There's no more I can add."

Iain put a hand on his shoulder. "I think you're right. It's an amazing piece of history. I'll help you seal the room. Maybe someone else will find it in a hundred years and it will help them understand what went on."

They went back to the hut and ate their meal in a very subdued mood. It was now into the small hours of the morning and, as he cleared away the remains of their meals, Iain said to Mel, "It's very late and it's been a long day. We'll leave tomorrow, but at our own pace. A late start is in order, I think."

Mel had trouble sleeping. She had read so much about the people here that she felt a connection with every one of them. Their struggle for survival had touched her deeply. Thoughts turned over inside her head for some time.

It was nearly noon the next day before Iain and Mel were mounted and ready to leave. They had said their goodbyes to Seth and he had disappeared somewhere. Iain told Mel not to worry; Seth had been on his own for a long time and could take care of himself. He would call back here on his return and try to persuade him to come to John's settlement.

So, with no further sight of Seth, Mel felt they left Sandhurst on a low instead of a high. She tried to build up her spirits by telling herself that she would be back in London in a couple of days. But it only partly worked.

They made their way across country to where they hoped to pick up the old road. After an hour's riding, skirting the heavier clumps of trees, they found the remains of the hidden road in a large, narrow valley. It was hemmed in on each side by trees and steep banks. The tarmac was still visible in some places, although vegetation was pushing its way through in a lot of places.

They rode slowly on the road for several hours before they came across a section that had completely disappeared. No trace of the old road could be seen, just a thick copse of trees from one side of the valley to the other.

"Is this as far as the road goes?" Mel looked and sounded puzzled. "We can't be that close to London, yet."

"No, I read about this happening up north. Before the Breakdown, all the old roads had tarmac on them. After fifty years or so, when the surface began to break-up, the locals would go to a road that wasn't being used, strip the material off the top, and melt it down to use on their local roads. This must be one of the sections that was re-used."

"However," Iain continued. "It does give us a problem. We don't know how far this section stretches." He glanced up at the sun sinking in the west. "I think we should leave the road and try and find somewhere to spend the night."

They went through a gap in the surrounding banks and found themselves in what appeared to be an old surface mine. There were several buildings still standing, so they settled in for the night in the least dilapidated structure. They laid out their blankets, ate a cold supper, and settled down for the night.

The next morning, they returned to the road. The missing section of road was about half a mile long and the brush became dense in places. Mel was glad that they had not tried to tackle it in the dark.

They came across two more missing sections during that day's ride. This slowed their progress, but Iain did manage to trap a rabbit in one area for their evening meal. The banks around them were too steep for the horses to climb when night fell on the second day of their journey, so they built a big fire and camped in the middle of the old highway. Cautious of rats and dogs, they kept watch in turns during the night. On watch in the small hours, Mel had the feeling that she was being watched. When she threw more wood onto the fire, the flames leapt up to reveal hundreds of tiny points of lights in the surrounding bushes.

A shiver went down her spine when she realised what the lights were. Rats and other small animals, watching her. She hoped that Iain was right and the fire would keep them away.

With the dawn, the lights disappeared, and Mel was happy to get back on their way. As they set off again, Mel asked how much further Iain thought they had to go.

"We should be at the outer limits by late afternoon. " Iain

shifted his position in his saddle. "After that, all we have to do is get you back inside."

"And how are you going to do that?"

"We'll cross that bridge when we come to it. The only thing I know for certain is that you won't be going back in the way you left."

Mel had already figured that out. There wasn't exactly a bell you could ring at the gate.

They rode on in silence. Mel's thoughts were confused. Before long, she would be home. Before long, she would know whether Cord was dead or alive. Before long, she would have to leave Iain. That thought saddened her; they had been through a lot together.

Iain was quiet. Mel wondered if he would miss her as well.

As Iain predicted, as the sun was beginning to dip westwards, they had reached the end of the road and were passing through what had once been a built-up area. The skeletons of factories, houses, and tall buildings were all about, their only occupants now birds and animals.

Mel realised that she must have passed through this area when she had lain unconscious in Joel's caravan. She was glad she hadn't been awake; the whole area had a depressing feel to it.

Iain stopped his horse and looked about. He waved his arm and said, "All this was once London. People stayed here until the food supplies ran out. But they were widely spread and easy pickings for the soldiers of the factions that fought for control after the Breakdown. They moved into the countryside after a generation or so. They couldn't grow the food they needed around here and they needed to band together for protection."

"I wonder how many survived," Mel said, trying to imagine thousands of people living, breathing, and dying here.

Iain shrugged. "Not many. It was about that time that disease took hold. People did not have the resistance they should have had. Research in Scotland has found that all the once-conquered diseases, at least in Europe, like cholera, typhoid, and scarlet fever, killed millions. But those who were left alive at the end of the epidemics were tougher for it. It also stopped all the minor wars; the survivors were too busy trying to stay alive to worry about who controlled which piece of ground. My father is a researcher; he says that it was nature taking its revenge after the Breakdown. Who knows, maybe he's right."

Mel sat on Candour, staring at the bleak landscape until Iain took her elbow and pulled her from her reverie.

"We'll make our way to Richmond. There's a large, old house there, which I've made habitable. I think we should spend the night there and see about getting back into London in the morning."

Mel opened her mouth to object to the delay, but said nothing. Another day wasn't going to make much difference. She nudged her horse in the ribs, to follow Spirit.

A couple of hours later, they were riding in open countryside again and just cresting a small hill when Iain pulled his horse to a stop, and said, "Here's something that might interest you." He pointed ahead.

Shading her eyes from the sun and following the line of Iain's finger, Mel looked into the distance, and her heart missed a beat. There on the horizon, the sun reflecting in a hundred different ways off its Barrier, was London.

Mel let out her breath slowly in a large sigh. Iain chuckled next to her. "I know how you feel. I always feel like that when I get back to Scotland. Home is where the heart is, as a great poet once said."

He fell silent and let Mel gaze at her home for a short while before leaning across and pulling on the reins of her horse, saying, "Come on. By tomorrow, you'll be home."

As they went down the hill, London disappeared behind broken buildings. Iain led her to a large house that once must have been quite imposing, but now looked like all the others they had passed that day: Run down and sad.

Once they were inside the grounds of the house, Mel could see that one wing was in much better shape than the others. Pushing open a door, Iain bowed from the waist and waved Mel inside. What awaited her was impressive after the decay that was all around them.

This one room, in a once proud and grand house, was in very good condition.

"Not bad, hey lassie?" Iain smiled and said, "Welcome to my town house. When I first visited London, I came across this place on the way. I needed somewhere to stay so, as this room was in the best condition, I did some repairs. Replaced the ceiling and windows, blocked up all the holes that rats could get in, raided the rest of the house and others around here for the best furniture. The books came with the house; I think this must have been the library."

Mel looked around her. The room was some forty by thirty-five feet square and, in one corner, was the biggest bed she had ever seen. There were ornately carved chairs placed around a large oaken table. A large, well-stuffed, leather sofa and matching easy chairs were placed in front of the fireplace, and two of the walls were taken up with floor to ceiling bookcases, crammed full of books.

Mel ran her hands over some of the lower ones; printed books were rare in London. You downloaded what you wanted off a central net onto a reader. Even so, there were many titles she had never heard of.

"What do you think of the bed? I had the devil's own job of getting it here. I dragged it half a mile and had to dismantle it to get it in."

Examining the bed, she saw that it was enormous. Four finely carved posts held up a canopy, and there were curtains on each side. "This whole room is quite something. If somewhat dusty," she finished, looking at her hands.

"Ah, well," Iain shrugged and grinned. "A good cleaning lady is hard to come by these days."

Iain had also repaired the kitchen area to serve as a stable. They groomed the horses and set up their feeder bags. Martin, the groom, had given them an ingenious device that would allow a measured amount of feed to come through in intervals. This would allow Iain to leave the horses for up to a week. The last part of the journey would have to be done on foot.

Mel slapped Candour on the neck, and she nuzzled her hand in response. Mel was sad to leave her; she had become quite attached to her.

"They will be safe here, won't they?" she asked for the third time.

"Quite safe." Iain smiled to reassure her. "There's enough water and feed for five days at least. I should be back in one."

They returned to the room and Iain lit some sweet-smelling candles that Mary had given them to ward off the dark. After toasting some of the bread on the fire, they retired for the night in the sumptuous bed.

As she lay in bed, Iain snoring gently at her side, Mel found that she was too keyed up to sleep. Random and sometimes silly thoughts kept popping into her head. Like, when she got home, she would have the longest ever bath and get a change of clothes. The set she was wearing now had not been off since they had left John and Mary. She had a fancy that if she were to try and fold them, they would snap in two.

She also tried to plan what she was going to say to Uncle Terry. She had to make him realise that nothing she had seen on the outside could threaten the people of London, and that there was so much London could do for the outsiders.

Mel wondered if she could get the president to appoint her a sort of ambassador to the rest of England. The thought of spending the rest of her life quietly in London was not as comforting now as it had been a month ago.

Inevitably, her thoughts became apprehensive as they turned towards Cord. Somehow, she knew he wasn't dead; why she was certain of this she did not know, but it was a very strong feeling.

Her thoughts drifted to Iain. She would have to leave him soon. Memories of the cottage at Stonehenge surfaced. Part of her, she found, was sorry that they had not made love again. That was her heart speaking, she supposed. Her head told her that she had made the right decision.

She smiled again as she thought of that pretty cottage; it seemed like a lifetime ago, not just a couple of weeks. Mel fell asleep and dreamed of Cord and home. Pleasant images; the nightmares stayed away.

The next morning, as they packed what they could into packs they could carry on their backs, Mel asked again how she was going to get back into London.

Iain smiled at her. "The same way I got in when I first entered London. About a mile into the cleared area there is an inspection shaft that leads to the old underground train tracks. I hope you're not claustrophobic, because we have a long, dark walk ahead of us."

"Claustrophobic!" Mel made a snorting sound. "Not after living in London all my life!" She gave a small laugh, but, even to her, it sounded nervous.

"Well, then," Iain opened the door, "are you ready to go home?"

After checking the horses one more time, they set off. An hour's walk brought them to the campsite where Mel's life had so irrevocably changed. There were six, small, fresh craters in the area, but no sign that anybody from the city had ever been there.

Mel stood trying to remember more clearly what had happened, while Iain examined the area. He returned to say that, apart from some wheel marks left by the ground car, there was no sign that this campsite had been used in years.

"But the explosions, who set them off?" Mel queried.

"Well, you saw yourself that the Travellers carry nothing more destructive than crossbows. You'll have to look elsewhere for your terrorists."

"Then some other outsiders set them off."

"Possibly." Iain came and stood next to her. "Possibly not."

"Maybe they came from north of London." Mel was becoming more confused. From what she had learned of the outside, there wasn't anybody who would attack London. All the people she had met had ignored the cities as irrelevant to their lives.

"But," Mel shook her head, "if outsiders didn't set the booby traps, then someone in London must have."

Iain picked up his pack and slung it across his back and started walking, saying. "That seems logical."

Hurrying after him, Mel thought about Iain's words. If the bombers did come from London, then it must be the Isolationists who were behind them. There was no one else in London who would do this sort of thing. But then, if the Isolationists had set the traps, then they would have had to leave the city to do it. This was the one thing they wouldn't do.

After tripping in a pothole and almost falling flat on her face, Mel realised that she had better keep her mind on the walk.

She put this new theory to the back of her mind; more to tell Uncle Terry when she got home.

Not long after they left the campsite, Iain stopped by a bush and began to feel around in the dirt at its base. He grunted, pulled hard, and lifted up a steel cover to reveal a dark hole in the ground. A metal ladder was attached to the side and led down into its dark depths.

Laying his pack on the ground, Iain pulled free a couple of branches he had picked up at the campsite and, wrapping them in sheep fat-soaked rags, lit them.

Handing one to Mel, he asked, "Ready then?"

She nodded, and he held her pack as she led the way down. Iain dropped both packs and pulled the cover back over the hole to hide it. As Iain stepped off the last rung, Mel looked around her. They were in a small tunnel that started / ended at the ladder. Holding up her torch. Mel could see that this tunnel led into a larger one, just ahead.

Iain took the lead and led her into the next tunnel. This one was just as dark but a lot higher. The light from the torches created a multitude of shadows that seemed to have lives of their own. Wooden blocks on the floor showed where the railway tracks once ran. They had been taken to use in London at some time.

"We are now," Iain's voice echoed strangely off the walls, "on what was known to the millions of people who used to live in old London town as the Piccadilly Line. We are just outside an area called Earl's Court."

"So where do we go, now?" Mel hoped it wasn't too far.

The tunnel smelled and felt damp, and as they began to walk, she could hear the sound of dozens of rats making themselves scarce.

"We follow this tunnel until we come to a dead end. Beyond that is where you modern Londoners still use the Underground system." He looked back at Mel, "What's the last station on your Underground?"

"Knightsbridge. It's a few hundred yards from the Barrier."

Iain set off again. "I'll soon be able to tell you how far we have to go then."

It wasn't long before the tunnel widened out to take in a platform. On the wall was a faded red and white sign which read Earl's Court.

Iain heaved himself onto the platform and pulled Mel up after him. Going to the wall, he rubbed at it until he revealed a complicated map of faded, coloured lines. Mel recognised this as a larger version of the Underground maps she was more used to. Iain pointed to the dark blue line and the words, Earl's Court.

"We are here and Knightsbridge is here. So, two more stations and we will have passed under the Barrier."

Iain jumped back down to the lower level and Mel followed. Another hour saw them pass both Gloucester Road and South Kensington. Shortly after that, they came to a dead end.

Iain slapped the wall with his hand. "Beyond here is your London."

"It looks pretty solid," Mel remarked.

Iain went to one corner and pulled at it. A large section

moved away to reveal another brick wall behind it. Pushing against that one, enough bricks fell to allow Mel to climb through.

"There, once you get to the other side, put the bricks back. Don't worry if you have to tell where you came back in. I have plenty of other places to use."

There was a moment's silence between them. They both knew that this time would come, but neither knew what to say. Iain broke the silence.

"Well, I suppose this is goodbye. Don't forget what you have learned about the outside. Tell them we are not all baby-eating mutants."

Mel laughed to hear her own fairy tale coming back at her. "And you must convince outsiders that we're not evil ghosts." She looked at the tall Scotsman standing in the gloom in front of her. "What are you going to do next?"

"I'll pick up the horses, take them back to John. I'll pick up Seth. John will look after him. Then I'm going to Devon, to find out what exactly is going on there."

Mel took his arm and leaned forward to kiss him on the cheek, saying. "Take care, Iain. I hope we'll meet again soon."

At the last moment, Iain moved his head and their lips met. A light kiss turned into a longer and more passionate one. When they broke, they both were breathless. Only the crackling of the torches broke a heavy silence. Neither wanted to break the spell, until finally Iain said, "Pah! Cobwebs!"

Mel laughed, and took that as a cue to leave. She climbed through the hole and began replacing the bricks. With the last brick in place, she slid down the wall and sat at its base.

She sat there a while. She felt drained at the parting with Iain and at finally being home again. Away down the tunnel, she could see the bright lights of Knightsbridge Station beckoning to her. With a deep sigh, she pulled herself to her feet and started down the tracks to the platform. It was deserted when she got there and, as she pulled herself onto the platform, she caught sight of the station clock. It read 15:30. Knightsbridge, being the last stop on the line, was not widely used, so nobody saw her climb the steps towards the surface. In fact, the whole station was deserted. The entire system was free to travellers, and completely automatic. There was no need for guards or ticket inspectors. But at every station there were public restrooms, so that was where she headed next.

Standing in front of a mirror, Mel took in her reflection. She had felt dirty last night. After a trip through the tunnels, she felt the even more so.

Her hair was lank and greasy, and the once-white blouse that Louise had given her was covered in dark smudges and cobwebs. The trousers Mary had lent her were dirty and torn, and her face was smudged with dirt. Only the boots she had brought from London had stood up to her travels.

She cleaned her face as best she could and tried to brush the tangles out of her hair with a comb she got from the small replicator. She considered getting a change of clothes as well, but decided she would wait until she got home.

So, with her hair tied back, she left the station and went out into the filtered light of London. As she looked up into the sky to see the hazy force field, she realised that she was finally home.

The road outside was deserted as well, but there was a public call point. Mel could not put off the moment of truth any longer. She would call the barracks and see if Cord was there and, if he wasn't, she would call Uncle Terry.

The call went trough to a switchboard and a computer-generated picture of a pleasant looking young woman asked how she could help.

In a strong voice, Mel said, "I would like to talk to Captain Cord Taylor, please. Melina Wilson calling."

A second's delay, and a reply came. "Captain Taylor is not available. May I connect you to someone else?"

"Where is Captain Taylor?" Mel's voice cracked with frustration.

"I do not have that information. Please select another . . ."

The picture disappeared, to be replaced by another. This one was definitely more human looking. "Please confirm your identity by placing your wrist under the scanner."

Sighing, Mel did as requested and let the light of the scanner play over the chip embedded in her wrist.

The man on screen looked at her with curiosity on his face as he said, "Please remain where you are, Miss Wilson. Your call has been logged and a security unit is on its way to meet you."

"Wait!" Mel had to know. "Where is Captain Taylor?"

The operator glanced to one side and then smiled at her. "Captain Taylor is in hospital. He is expected to make a full recovery. Please stand by for pick up."

Mel went outside and sat down on a bench, her spirits lifted by the knowledge that Cord was alive. Soon a ground car came silently to a halt in front of her, and a man dressed in the familiar all black of the Protector forces got out and looked at her, asking, "Miss Wilson?"

Mel nodded and climbed into the rear seat. She let out her breath in a big sigh, suddenly feeling very tired.

After a few moments of travel, she realised that they were heading away from the medical block. "I wish to go to the medical centre first," Mel stated.

Without even turning his head around, the trooper in the front seat replied, "Our orders are to take you to the Palace directly, Miss." Mel was torn; she wanted to see Cord, but she had so much to tell the president. She leaned back in the plush seat and closed her eyes. She knew Cord was alive. She would see him soon.

When they arrived at the Palace, there was only her uncle's aide, Laura, to meet her. She looked her up and down. Mel was sure she saw her lip curl in disgust at what she was wearing. Laura informed her that the president had been informed of her re-appearance and would join her as soon as possible.

Laura then took her elbow, almost gingerly as if she thought she would catch something deadly, and led her into the Palace, saying, "We have prepared a room for you. I'm sure you will want to bathe and change your clothes. Do you require food?"

"Yes. Thank you, a steak dinner and chocolate ice cream to follow. Did Uncle Terry say how long he would be?"

"The president was not specific. He has been attending an emergency debate on the Barrier. It was called because of your disappearance; your return will have thrown things into confusion, I expect."

Laura showed her to the room she had stayed in after her father's death. It seemed so long ago now; so much had happened since then. She showered and put on a jumpsuit from the replicator. It seemed very tight and close fitting after the loose clothes she had been wearing for the last month. But, the underwear was as wonderful to wear as she remembered.

Her meal arrived and, as Mel hadn't eaten since that morning, she attacked the food with relish, only to be slightly disappointed by its bland taste. Somehow, the food outside tasted better. However, there was no chocolate ice cream outside. That still tasted as good as she remembered.

The com-unit bleeped for attention and, when Mel answered, she found the president looking back at her an expression of disbelief on his face.

"Lina, it is really you? Where have you been? No, wait. I'll be back in less than half an hour. We'll talk then."

"Wait, Uncle Terry. What about Captain Taylor? What's his condition?"

"I'll have Laura connect you with the medical centre. They'll give you an update. We'll talk soon."

The screen went blank and Mel leaned back in her chair, wondering at the terseness of the call. The unit bleeped again and a picture appeared of a dark haired man dressed in a doctor's white hygiene suit. "Miss Wilson? I am Dr. Jameson. I am in charge of Captain Taylor's recovery."

"Can you tell me what injuries Captain Taylor suffered?"

"The captain suffered a broken arm, a fractured leg, and several broken ribs. There was no internal bleeding and he is presently sleeping whilst undergoing bone regeneration. I have recommended that he be wakened tomorrow, as his bones have knitted well."

Regeneration treatment consisted of feeding minute amounts of electricity through the broken bones so that they knitted in weeks rather than months. As the body had to remain completely still during this process, it was standard procedure to sedate the patient. Mel guessed that Cord had been asleep most of the time she had been away. "When will he be well enough for visitors?"

"We will wake him early tomorrow. He should be fully conscious by midday."

Thanking the doctor, Mel broke the connection and leaned back in her chair with a contented sigh. She felt a lot better now she knew what had happened to Cord, although she was a bit put out by the fact that, while she was worrying about him, he was sleeping!

Mel went to the window where she saw the president's car draw up at the entrance. Maybe now she could get the full story of what happened out at the campsite. She went downstairs to meet Terrence Charterhouse at the door.

Charterhouse stopped when he saw her on the stairs, a strange, unreadable expression on his face. He came forward and took her hands in his. "Lina, it is really you. I still wasn't convinced. Where have you been? Are you well? When you didn't come back, I felt responsible. I should never have let you go."

Mel smiled up at the president. "I'm just fine, Uncle Terry. You can't blame yourself. I did insist, if you remember rightly."

He took a firm grip on her arm and led her into the sitting room, guiding her to one armchair and taking the other for himself.

"Where have you been?" he said after a moment's silence.

Mel leaned back and countered with a question of her own. "Before I tell you what has happened to me over the last month, I need to know what happened after the explosions went off and I was knocked unconscious."

"I'll have a copy of Sergeant Masters and Corporal Connery's reports downloaded into a reader for you. But for now, here are the edited highlights. When Masters lost contact with the perimeter patrol, he went to investigate. As he did, he heard explosions behind him and turned to see you and Captain Taylor being blown into the bushes. As he came to assist, another explosion went off and knocked him unconscious. When he came round, he was in a ground car heading for London. Corporal Connery had taken command, picked up all the casualties, and ordered the patrol back to London. Unfortunately, she didn't know that you were in the group. We kept the knowledge of your presence on the expedition as quiet as possible. As far as Connery knew, a standard complement of twenty personnel were on the trip, so that was how many injured and bodies she returned with."

"Bodies?"

"Yes. Three Protectors were killed outright by the booby

traps, and another two died back in London. When they reached London, all the injured were sedated until their conditions could be assessed. This included Sergeant Masters, as he was drifting in and out of consciousness with a concussion. When I was informed, I asked after your condition. That's when it was realised that you were not with the rest of the unit. By then it was dark, and we had to wait for dawn before we could send out another patrol to look for you. When they arrived at the site, you were nowhere to be found. All that was there were the holes made by the explosions and some strange wheel tracks that nobody could identify."

"They were caravan wheel tracks," Mel said quietly, as she assimilated all this information.

"Caravan wheel tracks!" The president's eyebrows lifted and he looked at Mel with an astonished look on his face. "Well, that's what happened; the reports are much more detailed. Now, what happened to you?"

Mel took a deep breath and began to relate her story. She left nothing out and told the president all about the Travellers, Stonehenge, Iain, the Ferguson community, and Seth.

By the time she had finished, the ornate grandfather clock in the room was showing midnight. Her voice had become slightly hoarse; Mel had not spoken so much in days. The president was silent for quite a while, before smiling and saying, "Well, Lina, you've given me a lot to think about. You had better get to bed now; you look worn out. I want you to have a full check up at the medical centre in the morning. Laura's made the arrangements."

CHAPTER 6

Mel stood up and stretched. "They are waking Cord, Captain Taylor, up from his regeneration treatment tomorrow, as well. I would like to be there when they do."

Charterhouse stood as well, and gave Mel another tight hug. "Well, welcome home again." He ushered her towards the door. "When you've finished with the doctors, I want you to write up all that you told me this evening. I will have to make a full report to Parliament of what happened to you, and the news services will want something as well. You've been hot news for the last month."

As the door closed behind her and she went up the stairs, Mel felt relaxed. She hadn't had the chance to talk to Uncle Terry about her idea of going back outside again, but there would be plenty of time in the next few days.

She undressed and slipped into bed, luxuriating in the pleasure of the smooth, self regulating, heated cover. No more scratchy blankets. As she drifted off to sleep, her thoughts turned to Iain. She tried to work out where he would be now; most likely in the house at Richmond.

Sleep claimed her and she slept soundly, uninterrupted by nightmares.

The next morning, after a late breakfast, there was a car waiting to take her to the medical centre. When she arrived, she insisted on looking in on Cord in the regeneration tank. After that, she was taken to another part of the complex and subjected to a barrage of tests.

Several frustrating hours later, she was taken to the recovery room by Dr. Jameson, himself. He warned her that Cord would not show too much awareness at first, until the all the drugs they had given him worked their way out of his system. The doctor expected him to be more aware tomorrow.

Mel was disappointed to find that he was right. She had hoped to tell Cord all about her time outside, but she had to settle for holding his hand for an hour. But she was rewarded when his eyes flickered open for a moment, and he smiled at her.

Mel returned to the Palace and was shown to a computer terminal where she entered a full report of her travels. She tried to report everything faithfully, but decided to leave out her night spent with Iain. That was personal and she wanted it to stay that way.

To be sure that her report would not be misinterpreted, she summarised her feelings at the end, pointing out that while there were dangers outside, they were not as bad as generally thought.

Mel wrote that the Druids and the bandit groups were the exception rather than the rule, and that London could do a lot to bring stability to the rest of the country. She saved the report onto the public mainframe and downloaded copies into readers for herself and the president.

She presented the reader to Uncle Terry that night at dinner. He scanned it quickly, and said, "Thank you. It looks very comprehensive; I'll read it fully later and have a condensed version issued to the media and Members of the House."

Mel looked up from her coffee. "Can't we discuss it now, Uncle Terry?"

The president smiled at her impatience. "No. Let me digest

this and draw my own conclusions. I will also need to talk to my cabinet. You've only just got back. Slow down, and take a deep breath. As my mother used to say, 'it will all come out in the wash'."

Mel thought that sounded fair, but couldn't help feeling a bit frustrated. She wondered exactly how long it would take to reach a decision. Her father always said that there was nothing slower than the bureaucratic mind.

"So," the president said, brightly, "what do you plan to do now? You know you're more than welcome to stay on here."

"Thank you, Uncle Terry, but no. I need to get home, contact my friends, and think about maybe going back to collage. I'll leave in the morning."

"As you wish, Lina." He smiled sadly at her. "In one respect, at least, you're much like your mother. Once your mind is made up, it very difficult to change it. But do remember that there is always a place here for you."

Mel got up and walked behind her Uncle. Putting her arms around his neck, she kissed him on the cheek.

"Thank you. I will remember that." She opened the door and, saying goodnight, she went up to her room. The clothes she had worn for so long outside were neatly folded and on the dresser waiting for her. Putting them in a holdall, she realised that she was packed and ready to go. A blouse, a pair of stiff leather trousers, and a scratchy undershirt was all she had to show for a month in the wild. But, she thought, thinking of that night in the cottage, she had a lot of memories.

The next morning, a car took her home to the apartment

she once shared with her father. Nothing had changed. It seemed to Mel that somehow it should look different, but it was all the same. She opened the door to her studio and stood in the doorway looking at her sculpture.

She remembered how important it had seemed to her before she left. The big surprise she was going to spring on everyone when she unveiled her statue of herself in the nude. Now it seemed so insignificant.

That was the moment she realised that she could not just pick up her life where she left off. She needed now to do something different; she needed to make a difference, and bringing London out to join the rest of the country was going to be it.

Mel had a memory flash of Joel saying he didn't know what a sculpt was. One day, she would bring him here and show him. Maybe he had a talent for sculpture but was too busy keeping his troupe alive and fed to find out. Who knew how many poets, writers, and other artists there were outside too busy just surviving to ever find out.

But she was home now and must let her friends know. She could see now it wasn't going to that easy to fit back in again.

But she would try.

CHAPTER 7

Mel got something to eat and sat herself down in front of the com-unit. She selected Myan's number and had the pleasure of seeing the most amazed expression on her friend's face when she answered.

She wanted to come over straight away, but Mel put her off until the next day. She needed to see Cord again and have some time to herself. She then contacted her Uncle Granville. He didn't seem so surprised; Mel guessed that he already knew she was back through his contacts in the media. He invited her to visit and she promised she would soon.

After that, she walked to the medical centre to see Cord. As she walked the streets of London, she couldn't help noticing how gloomy and dull it seemed after the bright sky outside.

Cord was more alert than the last time she had seen him, but still kept falling asleep, sometimes in the middle of a sentence. So Mel restrained herself from talking about her experiences until he was better.

However, the next morning, when Myan arrived, she was

anything but restrained. She burst into tears and babbled on about how worried she had been, and how she was sure that she had been raped and murdered by the barbarians outside.

"Barbarians?" Mel questioned. "The people outside are not barbarians. Well, most of them aren't, anyway. They're much like us, except their lives are harder and more primitive."

"But, surely there are tribes of cannibals and mutants living outside?" Myan asked, her eyes wide at the thought.

"No, of course not. Whatever makes you say that? Those tales are just made up to scare children." Mel took Myan's hand in hers. "I can honestly say that I didn't meet one mutant or baby-eating cannibal."

"But all the vid shows since your disappearance have been telling of nothing else!"

Mel sniffed and said, "Well, they will have to change their tune when my report is published. But, what have they been saying."

She turned to the wall and said, "Vid on." An eight-foot section of the wall formed itself into a giant screen, which was split into twenty sections.

"News channel"

One screen expanded to take up the whole area. The sound came on and the smiling face of the perfectly proportioned, computer generated presenter appeared, solid and unmoving.

"News of Melina Wilson. From one month ago," Mel said clearly. "Transmit."

The face of the presenter flickered and a news report started. The date and time in the lower right hand corner told her that it was four days after she disappeared.

Four days? thought Mel. *Well, there was a lot of confusion.*

It has been confirmed today that a regular patrol group was attacked at the edge of the control zone. This is the first such attack for over sixteen years. Government sources also confirmed that Melina Wilson, daughter of Melville Wilson, Vice-President, who was recently killed in a train accident, was a member of the party. Her condition is at this time unknown.

Over the ten days, there were similar reports, detailing the dead and injured. Mel was always listed as missing.

Two weeks after she disappeared, there was a documentary on what Mel would face outside. Some of the wilder ideas put forward—and it seemed to Mel that these were given a lot of consideration—were about mutated humans living in primitive, Stone Age like tribes with strange, ungodly rituals and practising human sacrifice.

Well, there were the Druids who made human sacrifices, but if you believed the presenters of this show, the whole of the outside were sacrificing people left, right, and centre.

At first, Mel was indignant that anybody could believe such sensationalist rubbish, but when she thought deeper about it, she realised that the people of London had nothing to compare these stories with. The media was there to educate and inform, not to be questioned.

Mel herself had never questioned the news reports before she went outside. She only questioned now because she had extra knowledge that other people did not. Mel suddenly realised the power of the media.

Well, she thought. *That would all change when her report was made public.* She would make herself available for interviews; she would change people's ideas of what life outside the Barrier was like.

But having decided that, there was a tickle of worry at the back of her mind. Myan was a typical Londoner; she would never think to question what was told to her. She had a life to live; why worry about what went on outside when she was safe behind the Barrier.

Mel imagined that many others thought just like that.

Finally, over two weeks after she disappeared, it was announced that Mel was thought to be dead, and a program followed on her family and her short life. There were interviews with her friends, including a now-embarrassed Myan.

After that news, reports were sporadic and mostly concerned with the progress of the injured.

The day after her arrival back in London came the announcement of her return. A program followed this on how being lost outside for a month would affect her. The assembled panel of experts—Mel wondered how they could be called experts if they had never set foot outside the Barrier—discussed how she may have problems re-adjusting and may need counselling for the rest of her life. Mel gave a short, derisive laugh, and looked at Myan, who was looking back at her with her hands clasped together in front of her and a worried look on her face.

"Vid off!" Mel said, tersely. The wall took on its sky blue colour again, and silence descended over the pair.

"How do you feel, Mel?" Myan asked in a worried voice.

"I feel fine. According to the medics, I'm just slightly undernourished, that's all. You can't just order nutritiously balanced food from a food replicator out there, you know."

"Was it terrible?"

"NO! No. It was not terrible." Mel took a deep breath. "It was... interesting, fascinating, sad. Sometimes it was scary, but not terrible."

Mel turned to face Myan and recounted the whole story. When she had finished, she looked at her friend and said, "That is what everybody will learn when my report is published, and the sooner that happens, the better."

Myan stayed until late in the evening before leaving. Lying in her bed that night, Mel thought more about what she had seen that day. She worried at the hysteria that followed her disappearance. The information that had been broadcast was, at best ill informed, at worst sensationalist. She was angry that people like John and Mary could be portrayed as primitive and vicious, when she had seen for herself how they had made a good life for themselves and the people who depended on them. She fell asleep having decided that it was her place to put right the wrongs that had been done to her friends.

The next morning, after an early breakfast, she went back to the medical centre to find Cord wide-awake and pleased to see her.

When she found out that he had no memory of events following the explosions, Mel told him everything the president had told her, and then told him what had happened to her in the last month. She left a reader at the side of his bed so he could read it later.

"Well," Cord said, in a low, hoarse voice. "You've had quite a time. I've often said that we don't know enough of what goes on outside. Your information should go a long way to dispelling people's fears about the outside."

He lay back and closed his eyes. Mel realised that he was asleep again, but was content just to sit there holding his hand until the doctor arrived on his rounds. She took that opportunity to discuss Cord's state of health with him.

The doctor assured her that, now he was awake, it was just a case of him regaining his strength and he would be as good as new. The doctor said he expected to be able to release him in a couple of days.

Mel left the medical centre feeling as if a great weight had been lifted from her. When she got back to the apartment, she decided to contact the president and see if she could discuss the programs she had seen yesterday, but his aides told her that he would be unavailable all day and they would inform him that she had called.

She looked at the glowing figures of the timepiece on the wall. *Only back a short time and already clock watching,* she thought wryly to herself. Mel smiled as she remembered how lost she had felt, not having an accurate way of telling the time when she was outside. She had just gotten use to thinking like the locals, splitting the day into three sections, Morning, Afternoon, and Night, when she had returned to London. In the end, she decided that she preferred to know what the time was.

She glanced again at the wall. It was just past noon. Getting a snack from the dispenser, she sat down and began to idly surf through the channels on the video. An hour later, the president returned her call.

"Lina, what can I do for you?"

"I was wondering about my report. When will it be released?"

A tight smile appeared on the president's face. "Not for a few days yet, dear. My advisors are still going over it. If you don't mind, they would like to talk to you about it. Just to clear up some points they're not quite clear on."

"That's no problem, Uncle Terry. I'll be glad to help in any way I can." To tell the truth, she was bored and any distraction was to be welcomed.

"Good, good. My office will contact you to arrange a time and date. Tell you what, if you come to dinner tonight, I'll ask for a preliminary report so you can see what their thoughts are."

"I would love to. I'm feeling a bit lost at the moment."

"That's settled then. A car will pick you up at eight. See you then." The connection broke and Mel sat back wondering what sort of questions the president's advisers would have for her.

Still full of nervous energy, she went into her studio and looked at her sculpture. She stared at it for some time before coming to an almost sudden decision. She would not do any more to it. It felt like it was a part of another life, a life that included her father, and before she went outside.

She would leave it as it was. A testament to the person she

was.

However, she still felt full of artistic energy, so she replicated some paper and charcoal sticks and began sketching impressions of the Traveller's camp. Mel had finished three sketches before the house computer reminded her that she was to dine at the Palace tonight.

When she went to her room to change, she surprised herself with her choice of dress. For the young, the jumpsuit was nearly always the costume of choice. The colours may change, but the shape remained the same. Mel decided that she needed a change.

Looking through her wardrobe, she found the dress she had replicated for Myan's last birthday. A full length, deep red, backless gown with a long split down one side. Piling her hair high on her head, she went down to meet the car.

She guessed she had made the right choice in attire when the driver did a classic double take. The president was just as impressed, remarking that he felt underdressed.

The meal was eaten with just small talk being made, but as they settled into easy chairs for coffee, the president handed Mel a reader. The preliminary report wasn't very long and gave no real indication as to what conclusion the president's advisers were coming to about Mel's time outside.

When Mel said as much to Charterhouse, he just grinned at her impatience. "When you've been in politics as long as I have, you learn that civil servants can not be rushed. The people who are dissecting your report will be thorough. I believe you know one of them. Dr. Marks."

Mel nodded; she had liked the old scientist a lot. He seemed like the classic, absent-minded professor, but she now knew that, even though he was over a hundred years old, he had one of the keenest minds in London.

"So," Mel handed back the reader, "do your years of political experience tell you when they will be ready to publish?"

"I would expect a least a month."

"A month!"

"Yes. I don't want to rush them. If we go too early with this, and people are not prepared, we could cause panic."

"But . . . a month." Mel felt deeply disappointed. She had hoped that she might be on her way to Exeter by next week. She decided not to mention her idea of being a roving ambassador for London just yet. The time didn't seem right somehow.

Charterhouse leaned forward and patted her arm. "Don't look so disappointed, Lina. Patience is a virtue, you know." He sat back and absently twirled the coffee in his cup around. "I would also like you not to discuss your time outside with anyone before the report is published. We have contacted the media and they have agreed to wait until the right time before broadcasting anything."

"But I've already told Cord everything."

"Captain Taylor understands the need for patience. He's a military man, after all."

Some instinct that Mel did not quite understand stopped her telling the president that she had told Myan everything as well. She would contact her herself and tell her to keep quiet, rather than allow some faceless civil servant do it.

Mel finished her coffee and, wishing the president goodnight, went back to her apartment. She sat thinking for some time, an uneasy feeling inside her about what she had seen on the news items and the delay in publishing her report.

The next morning, she contacted Myan and asked her not to tell anyone else what she had told her about her time outside. Myan actually appeared to be relieved to do so; Mel wasn't sure whether Myan believed what she had been told.

The president's office called and asked her to meet the committee studying her report that afternoon at the parliament building. Mel arrived early, to be met by the ever-enthusiastic Dr. Marks. The interview was quite short and, mainly, they asked her to confirm that what she had written in her report was correct. They asked for more details on the rumour that there was a government being formed in Exeter. But Mel told them that all she knew was already in the report.

The committee thanked her for her time and said she would receive a copy of the report as soon as the president had read it.

The committee of four was friendly and seemed to be a reasonable cross section of ages. There was Dr. Marks, the eldest. A judge named Elvia James, who was on her way to being venerable. A civil servant called John Davis, who said he was secretary to the Undersecretary for State, and a General Henry, whom Mel had once met at the barracks.

As she left, she thought over what they had asked her, and felt that it was a good sign that they had wanted to confirm her report, and that they were taking it seriously.

That evening, she went to visit Cord and was pleased to find him wide awake and out of his bed. He had done some gentle physiotherapy and had been told that he could leave the medical centre if he had someone to look after him for the next month.

"So," Cord said, with a twinkle in his eye. "Fancy a job as my nurse? Because if you don't, the Protector force will send a couple of pretty nurses from here, to attend my every need."

"Oh, I couldn't see you suffer like that, could I?" Mel kissed him lightly on the lips. "But don't think you're going to get off easy. I will be taking advice from the doctor about exercise, diet, everything. You'll be under my command this time, Captain."

Mel spent the rest of the evening with Cord and talking to his doctors. The next day, a car delivered the invalid to her home and the medical centre set up a personal link to her house computer.

For all her light-hearted joking about the arrangement, the situation did make her feel nervous. They would be living together, twenty-four hours a day, for up to a month. This, she realised, was to be the first big test of their relationship.

Her worries were unfounded. The next three weeks were the happiest she had been since her father had died. Each morning was spent doing strengthening exercises on Cord's legs and, in the early days after Cord's release from the medical centre, Cord would rest in the afternoons and Mel would work on her paintings of the outside. As Cord got stronger, they took walks in the park and spend time getting to know each other.

Mel's paintings of her memories of the outside fascinated Cord. There were ten complete now, and Cord asked her what she planned to do with them.

"Well, I thought I would exhibit them, once the government releases my report. Then people will be able to see how much life there is outside."

Cord put his arms around her from behind and rested his head on her shoulder. "I think they will cause quite a stir," was his only comment.

After three weeks, Cord returned to light duties and Mel was left on her own again during the day. It was only when she was satisfied that her paintings were not going to get any better that she began to wonder why she had heard nothing from the president or the committee about her report.

She made a couple of attempts to contact them, but got the impression that she was being given the run-around.

Then, one afternoon, Granville Wilson came to visit.

She had not seen much of her uncle since she had been back and, following the president's wishes, she had not discussed her adventures with him. She had been mildly surprised that he had not pushed her on the subject.

Mel met him at the door and showed him to a seat in the living room, where he got straight down to the reason for his visit. "Mel, I need to hear about your trip outside, in your own words."

"I've just been talking to the president's office and they told me that my report has been issued to the media. I know you're in that business. I thought that you would have a copy."

"Indulge an old uncle. Please"

Mel thought this meeting had taken a strange turn, but did as he asked. Her uncle's frown deepened as she related her story.

CHAPTER 7

When she had finished, he leaned back and studied her closely. Finally, just as she was ready to burst with frustration, he smiled a sad smile and said, "Well, I think you had better read this."

He handed her a reader and she began to scroll through its pages. As she did, her sense of disbelief grew. Eventually she exploded. "This is all rubbish, made up rubbish. There's no mention of the Travellers, of the Fergusons. The Druids are made out to be mutants. In fact, the report tries to make out that they kidnapped me and kept me for the whole month, before brainwashing me and sending me back."

Granville took the pad from her and put it in his pocket.

"That's what going out on the morning news. The government's official line will be that, outside the Barrier, there are only savages and mutants."

"But . . . Why?"

"Why? The overriding reason is fear." He spread his hands in a helpless gesture. "Fear of the outside. Fear of the unknown. For the top people in government, fear of losing power. Then, of course, there is the carefully cultivated xenophobia. Have you checked out the kind of programmes that were run while you were away?" Mel nodded. "That sort of programme has been running for the last hundred years."

Mel watched her uncle with a growing sense of alarm. What he was telling her was making sense. Iain's comments to her at the campsite, *"If it wasn't someone from the outside, then it must have been someone from inside London who set the bobby traps,"* also struck home now.

"But," she tried to think of an argument against what

Granville was telling her. "There is no great danger outside. The Druids, for all their religious mania, would not stand a chance against our superior technology. The same for the bandit population. The rest of the country, at least in the south, is just trying to survive."

Mel looked at Granville. He just shrugged his shoulders. "I know all that, Mel. The problem is that the people of London don't."

"Well, isn't it up to the government to educate the people?" Her frown deepened as she thought about this shocking, new information. She knew from what Iain had told her about the Barrier failure at Newcastle that you couldn't just turn off the Barrier and hope for the best. But, surely if you prepared the people enough, then you could control the panic. Mel said as much to her uncle.

He smiled and answered, "You will have to ask Charterhouse that question. I can't help you there."

They both went silent, until Granville leant forward and said in a low, intense voice, "Look, Mel, we both know that London is in trouble. There are several things that can happen. One, we can turn off the Barrier and see how many people survive the onset of acute agoraphobia. Two, we can leave the Barrier on and slowly suffocate inside. Three, we can prepare the people as best we can, and then rejoin the rest of the country. Four, we can make the transition easier by eliminating any possible dangers outside. That way, we won't have any trouble expanding."

"Eliminate any possible dangers outside. How can that be done?"

"You could engineer a poison and put it into the water supply. Remember one of the first things that had to be done when the Barrier was energised was to eradicate as many illnesses as possible. Living in such close quarters made it much easier for diseases to go from person to person. Every child is now inoculated against all the old killers.

"A plague could be manufactured and introduced outside, and drop the population down to pre-Barrier levels. The people of London would be immune, and so the Republic could expand without problems."

"That's horrible." Mel's face wore a stunned expression. "The president would never sanction such a move."

Granville sighed. "It's no secret that I have never liked Charterhouse. That was one of the reasons I fell out with your father. But shortly before he was killed, Melville contacted me about the exact thing you and I have been talking about. He said he had some information for me, but we were never able to meet before he died. I still feel that his death was a bit convenient."

This was too much for Mel. Now her uncle was saying that her father's death might not have been an accident.

"You think that Daddy might have been killed by the government?" Her voice quavered as she spoke, her head buzzing with all the information she had learnt in such a short time. "Then . . . ," she was loathe to ask this question, "do you think that Uncle Terry had anything to do with it?"

"I think," Granville chose his words carefully, he knew of his niece's affection for the president, "that Terrence Charterhouse is a politician who has always had his finger on the pulse of government. I can't say that he definitely knew what was going on, but I would be surprised if he didn't."

Mel felt numb all over. Terrence Charterhouse was the one person she thought she could trust with anything. Now she was learning that even he could be involved in a conspiracy against the outsiders.

"What shall I do?" She looked at Granville, desperately hoping for guidance.

"Well," he said, "I think the first thing we should do is get your story out to as many people as possible. Do you have a copy of your report?"

Mel fetched it from the bedroom and Granville downloaded it into his own reader. "As I said, this other report will be on the news channels in the next couple of days. I suggest you talk to Charterhouse, carefully, to see if you can find out what he knows about all this. Be careful, Mel. I don't know how Charterhouse will react if he knows you have suspicions. It could be dangerous."

"I have to talk to him first. I will be as careful as I can. I won't accuse him outright. But I have to talk to him."

Granville got up and reached for his jacket. "Good girl. I think I've given you enough to think about for one evening. I'll contact you in a couple of days, to see how you got on with Charterhouse." He pulled her in close and kissed her cheek, opened the door, and said, "Take care."

When Cord arrived home that evening, he found Mel very quiet and uncommunicative. After spending dinner receiving only monosyllabic answers to his innocuous small talk, he finally asked her what was wrong.

Mel looked at him and realised that, if all Granville had told her was true, discussing it with Cord might put him in an awkward position. He was an officer in the Protector forces and charged with the security of London. But she knew she had to talk to someone.

Mel knew that she trusted no one more than Cord. So, taking a deep breath, she told him every thing that Granville had told her earlier. After she had finished, she watched as he silently read the report that was to be broadcast by the media.

Finally, he spoke. "Mel, this is big stuff." He took one of her hands in his. "Over the last week, there have been indications of a panic building. Security has been tightened and troops have been placed on alert. We thought it was just a drill, but this puts a different light on the exercises. What do you plan to do?"

Mel shrugged her shoulders. "I have to see Uncle Terry. I have to talk to him to see if he knows what's going on."

"If you do go to see the president tomorrow, don't tip your hand that you know what's going on. Be reluctant, but ultimately agree with this course of action."

"Agree with it!" Mel exploded. "But it's all bare faced lies. The people must know the truth."

"The last thing the people want to know is the truth. What they want is to do is carry on with their lives as they've all ways done, without any extra complications. The government can't keep up this charade forever; they have to turn the Barrier off eventually. By taking a stand, now you may put yourself in danger."

"Uncle Terry would never hurt me." Mel hated the quaver

that appeared in her voice. Maybe she wasn't so sure, now.

"Maybe not, but other people might." Cord lowered his voice, as if afraid of being overheard. "For all his power, the president can't know everything that goes on in his government. Others might think that, where you are concerned, the president might be blinkered to the best course of action for London, and might act on their own."

Mel gave a deep sigh and leaned closer to Cord, resting her head on his chest. "It was all going to be so simple," she said in a small voice. "When I got back to London, I would tell everyone how safe, how amazing, it was on the outside. We would turn off the Barrier and rebuild England with London's technology. Working together, we could build a paradise."

She sat up and looked up at Cord with an embarrassed smile on her face. "I've been a bit naïve, haven't I?"

Cord smiled back. "Yes, but in a positive way. You believe in people, in their basic common sense. Maybe you're right, that if we turned the Barrier off right now, in the morning people would wake up to find it missing and accept it. Maybe many wouldn't die from shock, maybe they would just adapt. The experts may be overestimating the amount of people who would be affected, or then again, they may have underestimated the amount. It would take a brave person to give the order, and the point is that we won't know until we actually turn the Barrier off."

They sat silently until Cord urged Mel to bed, where she lay for a long time in his arms, trying to work out what she was going to do.

CHAPTER 7

Eventually, she decided that she would take a positive attitude. When she met with the president tomorrow, she would tell him that she was sorry that they couldn't agree, and that she could not let this report go out with her name attached to it. Then, she would tell him that she wanted to leave London and travel to Exeter and talk to the people there.

Feeling sure that she was making the right decision, and optimistic as to what the morning would bring, she slipped into a deep, refreshing sleep.

The next morning, Mel awoke early still determined to face the president. She felt sure she could argue a good case for her to return to the outside. She contacted his office and announced that she would be there at 9 a.m., then cut them off before they could offer any reasons why not.

She left Cord getting ready for his day and walked to the Palace, her spirits high.

An obviously disapproving Laura met her at the door and escorted her to the president's private apartments. Charterhouse was still eating breakfast and, waving her to a chair, dismissed the still glowering Laura. After offering toast and coffee, he pushed his plate away and began to pour himself a cup of coffee, saying, "Well, Lina, what's so important that you have to disturb my breakfast and upset my secretary?"

"My problem is simple, Uncle Terry. When is my report going to be published? I've waited patiently for over a month now. I want to go back, back outside. I want to be the one to make contact with the people in Exeter."

The president leaned back in his chair and raised one

eyebrow. Her returning to the outside obviously hadn't occurred to him. He sipped coffee for a moment before he replied, "That doesn't sound like a good idea, Lina. The outside needs a lot more research before we make a commitment like that."

"And my report, when will that be published?"

"I've arranged for you to meet Dr. Marks tomorrow afternoon. He will tell you what conclusions the committee have come to and you can discuss their findings with him, okay?"

Mel smiled dutifully and thanked him. She still wasn't quite sure if he was a friend or enemy, but she could not bring herself to believe that he would do her harm.

She would go to Dr. Marks' lab tomorrow and see what report they presented to her. If, as she suspected, they offered her the same report that Granville had shown her, she would denounce it, then and there. Then she would publish her own report and, as the saying went, be damned.

She walked home slowly through the park. A class from the school was there, gathered around their teacher who was showing them different types of vegetation, pointing out the shapes of leaves.

The children were about four years old. *It would be nice*, she thought, *if they were to be the last children to be born in the confines of London*. There were only ten children, probably a complete year from the only school in London. She remembered doing the same trip with her schoolmates, except that there were over fifteen of them. It was confirmation to her of what her father and her Uncle Granville had told her.

London was slowly dying.

CHAPTER 7

She sat for a while and watched the teacher show the children several bushes and different types of leaves. Outside, they could have seen giant trees and the animals that lived in them. Here, there were only stunted bushes and insects.

Despondent, she made her way to the South Gate and watched the Barrier shimmer for awhile. But it didn't have the uplifting effect on her that it used to have. Once she had thought it a thing of beauty; now it was just in the way. What had once saved London and enabled it to become so technologically advanced was now going to kill it.

Mel went back to her apartment and waited for Cord to return home.

She told him what she was going to do over dinner that evening. He tried, half-heartedly, to talk her out of it, but he knew how upset she was by the government's attempt to distort her experiences to their own ends.

But he watched with concern as she paced the room, agitatedly telling him what she was going to do. Eventually, he stood up and took her by the shoulders, giving her a small shake. "I will back you on whatever you think is right, Mel. But make sure you know what the consequences of what you do now will be. Okay?"

Mel looked up into his eyes and smiled. "I have thought it through, Cord. But my choices are limited. Go with them and condemn all my friends outside to being forever known as savages, or make sure that the truth is known. I now realise that I am more like my father than I knew. I think that this is what he would have done."

Cord kissed her and pulled her close. "I wish I had known him better."

"So do I, Cord, so do I."

Mel spent the next morning digitising her paintings and sketches and downloading them onto a hand reader. She then mailed them to her uncle's address before setting off for the doctor's lab.

The doctor himself met her at reception and escorted her to his impressively messy office. Sitting her down, he handed her a reader and remained quiet while she read the same report her uncle had given her.

Mel laid the pad down on the desk and looked up into the eyes of the old scientist seated across from her. He had a concerned look on his face, and when he attempted to smile, the try was only half-hearted.

"So, please, Miss Wilson, your opinion."

"My opinion," Mel stopped a moment to gain some control. "I think that this is one of the best pieces of fiction that I have read in a long time."

The old man said nothing and, for a moment, there was a deep silence between them, until Mel continued.

"The people outside have been made out to be savages, by YOUR report. Little better than Stone Age savages. The people outside, and that's what they are, Doctor, people, human beings like you and me, are, for the most part, kind and helpful. Any disadvantage they suffer is because of us. They are primitive because they don't have the technology that we enjoy in London. But they can learn, and we can teach them. The Barrier must come down. Not instantly; that would be reckless and dangerous. We must find willing people and take them outside to educate the rest of the country. We must make official contact with Scotland and persuade them to help us. There is a whole country out there waiting for us to help them and we have a moral duty to do so."

Mel watched the doctor as she made her impassioned speech. His faded brown eyes seemed to get sadder as she spoke. Her hopes rose and she wondered if she was getting through to him.

She was mistaken.

"It's so sad. So very sad," he said in a soft voice.

Mel smiled encouragingly. "Yes it is sad. But we can help them."

"No. Not the barbarians outside. They can never be like us. Maybe with some intensive work they may get to the level of children, to be used as servants, maybe. No, what's so sad is your condition."

"My condition? What condition?"

"As we dissected your report, it became obvious that you have been brainwashed into believing that the outsiders can be our friends. Then you were returned to us to convince us to turn off our Barrier." A visible shudder went through his frail frame. "Once our only protection was gone, the savages would attack, steal our technology, and murder us in our beds."

Mel was speechless. The whole idea that she had been brainwashed and returned as some sort of Trojan Horse was ridiculous.

It suddenly struck her what went hand in hand with

agoraphobia and xenophobia.

Paranoia.

Dr. Marks shook his head slowly. "My colleagues and I discussed this possibility with some eminent psychologists, and they suggested that we let you read this report before it was released, in the hope that it would trigger your true memories."

"My true memories? Please, do tell me what my true memories are, Doctor." Mel's voice was deep with anger and laced with sarcasm. There was no way she would ever accept this report or the ridiculous brainwashing story, but part of her was curious as to how far this subterfuge went.

"We believe that you have been the victim of a complex plan. Someone entered London and destroyed the train your father was on. It was, as we know, a suicide mission. They knew a search would be made outside the Barrier, so they created the campsite for us, hoping we would send out a ground patrol to examine it. Once there, they attacked again and kidnapped you. I don't suppose they knew you were going to accompany the patrol. That was kept very quiet. They probably just intended to take the most senior officer; you were probably recognised by one of the spies and were taken instead of their original target, most likely Captain Taylor. You were then taken away and brainwashed into believing all that you put into your report. A particularly cunning ruse was to include an obvious danger like the Druids. The way you were rescued in the nick of time gave us our first clue that all was not right with your recollections."

"Tell me, Doctor," Mel sat stiff-backed in her chair, her voice tight with the control she was exercising, "if outsiders are so primitive, how exactly did they manage to brainwash me so completely?"

"Yes, this worried me as well, until I looked back into our history. People have been using brainwashing; laying false memories over true ones, for hundreds of years. Of course, they don't have access to the technology we have in London. But, evidently, their methods are very effective. I hope once we regain your true memories, you will be able to tell us what they did exactly."

Mel sat and studied the old scientist for a moment. He had an anxious look on his weathered face. She gave a small laugh and relaxed in her chair. "This ridiculous cock and bull story your paranoid minds have concocted will never be believed by any reasonable person. As soon as I leave here, I will release the true story of events, even if I have to give everybody in London a copy personally."

The doctor looked at her and shook his head sadly. "Of course, this reaction to this news was anticipated." One hand disappeared briefly under the desk and then came back. He leaned forward and took both her hands in his, saying, "But be assured, Miss Wilson, help is at hand. We will restore your memories in no time, and spare no resources to help you come to terms with the ordeal you have undoubtedly suffered."

Mel heard the door behind her open, and looked round to see a woman enter, carrying an injector gun. She tried to pull away, but the doctor was stronger than he looked. Mel felt the cool touch of the gun against her neck and heard the hiss of the gas as a sedative was fired into a vein.

Then everything went black.

When Mel regained consciousness, she found herself lying in a bed, and when she tried to sit up, she found she was strapped down securely. She lifted her head and looked around her. The room was all white and there was nothing else to be seen but the bed she lay in. Her head fell back and she could see a screen in the wall giving her vital signs.

Mel realised that she had been sedated. The doctor had said something about anticipating her reaction. Cord had been right. She should have been more careful.

The door opened and Dr. Marks entered with another man. There was an anxious expression on the old man's face, which turned into a smile as he saw she was awake. "Miss Wilson, I am so sorry we had to sedate you. But we feared that the conditioning might run deep, and we didn't want a struggle where you might hurt yourself. The president was most insistent about that."

Mel's heart fell, Uncle Terry did know about this. She felt like crying. She had always loved and admired her uncle and he had betrayed her. But she held her composure and tried to reason with her captors. "Doctor, there in no reason for all this. I am not ill; I have not been brainwashed. All I wrote down in my report was true. The outsiders are of no threat to us. No threat at all."

The other man spoke, ignoring Mel completely. He was a younger man, tall and dressed in the same surgical blues as Dr. Marks. "You see, Doctor. I said we should have brought her in earlier. The conditioning has gone deep, very deep. But given time, I believe that we will be able to break it and help the patient regain her proper memories."

Mel's frustration overflowed. "There is no conditioning. You are the ones who are ill. You're suffering from delusions. I don't need help, you do." She began pulling at her restraints, trying to get loose. She needed to escape. Mel knew that her memories were not false and she wouldn't give them up without a fight.

Dr. Marks put a hand on her arm. "Please, Miss Wilson, stop struggling. You will only hurt yourself. This is Dr. Barnard. He is the best on auto-conditioning; you are in good hands."

The other doctor looked down at her and gave her a cold, professional smile. "Dr. Marks is right, Miss Wilson. You have been crudely interfered with and I will fix that. As soon as your body is clear of the sedative, we will begin. I think twelve hours should do it. Until then, try and get some rest."

They turned and left, leaving Mel pulling at the straps and almost crying with frustration.

Shortly after that, a nurse came in with a tray of food. She sat on the bed and began to feed Mel by hand. When Mel asked for the straps to be removed so she could feed herself, the nurse told her there were strict instructions that under no circumstances should her restraints be removed, as she might attempt to harm herself.

No amount of protests or pleading by Mel could get the nurse to change her mind, and when the nurse left, all Mel could do was lay there and wait for the time to tick down until Dr. Barnard returned and ripped away memories of Ma, the Travellers, and the Fergusons.

Three hours had passed before the door opened again, and

another nurse entered carrying a tray. She stopped just inside the door and stood for a moment, then there was a soft bleeping sound and she approached the bed. To Mel's surprise, it was Abbi, the nurse that had cared for her after her father had died. Mel was getting desperate now. Time was running out. "Abbi, it's me, Mel. You have to help me. They want to mess up my brain. Please help me escape."

Abbi looked down on her with a serious expression on her face, which then broke into a wide grin. "That's no problem, Mel. It's what I came to do anyway." She put down the tray and began to unbuckle the straps. "I am a friend of Granville Wilson. We believe in the same course for London. I read your report on the outside; it sounds wonderful."

Abbi helped Mel stand up and handed her a dark jumpsuit. "He's waiting for us at the back of the centre. That bleeping sound was him signalling that he's overridden the security cameras. That should give us some minutes before anybody notices that some thing is up. Follow me."

Relief washed over Mel and she took Abbi into hug and whispered, "Thank you."

Abbi opened the door and looked out into the corridor. The coast was clear and they made it to the elevator and to the back entrance without being seen. Mel later learned that it was three o'clock in the morning and very few staff were on duty. At the back of the centre, Granville emerged from the shadows to meet them. As Mel opened her mouth to speak, he told her, "Save all your questions for later, when you're safe."

She shook her head and thought, *Will I ever be safe*

again?

He took her arm and began to lead her away. "London may be small compared to the outside, but there are many nooks and crannies that most people don't realise are even there. This way."

Mel soon realised that they were heading for the park, then she noticed that Abbi was missing. When she asked where she had gone, she was told that Abbi knew what to do. Keeping his voice low, Granville explained, "Abbi signed in under a false identity. She'll return to her own life and keep a low profile."

When they reached the park, Granville led her into a thicket of bushes and, sweeping away a covering of loose undergrowth, he revealed a steel trap door. It eased up silently and Granville gestured Mel to precede him. A steel ladder led down into a single chamber. It smelt of dampness, but appeared reasonably dry. Granville closed the trapdoor behind them and flicked a switch to provide some lighting.

"We are safe here. Nobody knows about this little hideaway. Your father and I discovered it when we were children. After he died, I cleaned it out, supplied some light and the furniture you see. I thought it might be useful."

Mel looked around her. There was a small bed and a table; there was also a bucket in the corner which brought back memories of her time with the Druids.

Mel sat on the bed and looked up at her uncle. "How did you know where I was?"

"It was Abbi who realised what they were going to do. She saw you being brought in and was concerned about you. But she was told in no uncertain terms that it was none of her business. That alerted her to something wrong, so she bugged Barnard's office and overheard him and Marks talking to Charterhouse about your case. She knew, from what she had heard, that your memories are true but unacceptable to the government. Abbi realised that they planned to replace your memories with false ones so they could terrify the public by having you relate horror stories of the outside. That's when she contacted me. We both belong to a small group of people dedicated to removing the Barrier. Until now, we've just talked about it, but your report from the outside has energised us into action. Copies have been made and are being handed to people we think can handle the truth."

Granville continued to explain. "We got together and set up your rescue. It wasn't overly difficult, as the government wasn't expecting any action to be taken against them. However, now they know that there are people acting against them, I expect security will be beefed up. You'll have to stay here until we can find some way of getting you out of London."

"I need to see Cord."

"What! Under no circumstances. He's a captain in the security forces. He'll turn you in and all this would have been for nothing."

"No, I have to see him. I can convince him that I am telling the truth. He can help me get out of London." Mel stopped when she saw the horrified expression on her uncle's face. Leaning forward, she lowered her voice. "I can convince him, Uncle. When I tell him what they were going to do to me, then he will understand why I have to leave."

"It's too risky, Mel. If you get caught again, they will change your whole personality and you won't think twice about telling them about Abbi and me. Once they have us, then they will get the rest of our organisation."

"I will try not to let that happen. You find out where Cord is and I will go and talk to him. I'm sure once he knows I'm in danger he will help."

Granville went silent for awhile before sighing deeply. "Very well, I will try to fix up a meeting with him, but it will be under my conditions. Okay?"

Mel leaned forward and hugged him. "Thanks, I really need to do this."

Granville left, telling her that he would not be back until the early hours of the next morning.

The next day passed slowly. Mel could hear the noise of people above her, but tried to put it out of her mind and relax. She spent some time working out what she was going to say to Cord. She felt a little guilty at putting Granville and Abbi at risk, but felt she couldn't leave without saying something to Cord. As she thought over her words, she felt sure that he would at least understand. She hoped that he would accompany her. But there was a nagging doubt inside her that left her feeling cold.

Finally, the entrance opened again and Granville came down the ladder carrying food and drink. While Mel ate hungrily, he told what had been going on since her rescue.

Abbi said that all the staff had been questioned, but the authorities were so paranoid that they wouldn't actually tell them why they were being questioned so, consequently, they learned very little. Granville had also been questioned covertly. A man posing as a reporter had asked if he knew where she was so he could do an interview with her.

"I told him to get in touch with the president's office and he said something about not wanting to go through official channels. But I put on my shocked and outraged face, and he left with me picking up the phone to 'warn' the Security forces. They said that they would look into it."

"You told the Security forces!"

"Of course. There's nothing like a bit of misdirection in this game we're playing. I haven't laughed so much for years." Granville sat down on the bed and leaned back against the wall. "They are playing straight into our hands. Your kidnapping was known only to a select few. They can't even put out a general bulletin about you."

"And what about my meeting with Cord?"

Granville took a deep breath. "Let me say again, I am opposed to this meeting. I dislike introducing unknowns into carefully laid plans. But if you still insist on taking this risk . . ."

Mel nodded. "I am. I've grown very close to Cord. I won't just disappear and leave him wondering where I've gone."

Her uncle nodded. "I thought as much. I've left a message on your house computer, supposedly from you, that you will meet him by the statue of Victoria at the edge of the park. You're due there," he looked at his watch, "in thirty minutes."

Mel stood up, ready to leave. But Granville waved her

back down. "Not so fast, young lady. You're not going alone, I'm coming with you."

"It's not necessary. I would prefer not to put anybody else at risk."

"It's too late for that. This whole meeting is a risk, to myself, Abbi, and the rest of our organisation. I have people in place, watching to make sure that Captain Taylor comes alone. If he is not alone, we will then return here, hopefully without any fuss. Do you agree to leave if he has friends with him?"

"I do. But I think that Cord will surprise you. I haven't been home for forty-eight hours and I wonder how they've explained my absence to him. It will have to be a good reason; he's not stupid. He will know if the wool is being pulled over his eyes."

Granville stood up and gestured to the ladder. "Well, I hope you're right. Let's go meet the captain, shall we?"

They worked their way around the edge of the park, keeping in the shadows. It was now the early hours of the morning and the only thing they saw was an automated cleanup cart. Mel looked around for the people that Granville said he had watching Cord, but saw nothing. If they were there, they were well hidden. As they approached the statue, Mel's heart leapt as she saw the tall figure of Cord standing there with his back to her.

Granville stopped behind a large bush and squeezed Mel's upper arm as an indication she should go on alone. She looked back at him and was surprised to see he held a small stun gun in his hand. Mel had a sudden realisation of just how dangerous Granville thought this situation was, and it dampened her spirits.

She stepped out from the bush and cleared her throat. Cord turned quickly, his hand going to his hip as he did. Mel raised her hands. "Don't shoot. I'll come quietly."

"Mel!" Cord came forward and enfolded her in his arms, then, gripping her arms, he pushed her back and said, "Mel! What is going on? When you didn't come back from the medical centre it took me ages to find out where you were. Then I was told some story about how you had an unknown disease and they were going to keep you in isolation for a week.

"Then I get a visit from a so-called reporter asking if I knew where you were and could he set up an interview." Cord paused for a moment and guided Mel to a bench where they both sat down. "Then I was really suspicious. Not that many people know about us and any reporter worth his credits wouldn't bother a security officer when he would go straight to the president's office. So I called in to see Dr. Marks and he told me how you collapsed in his office and the medics took you to the medical centre. Except I knew he was lying. I spent all of yesterday making discreet enquires. Then to top it all, I get a message from you telling me to meet you in the park in the dead of night. What have you been up to?"

"Did you come alone?"

Cord shrugged. "As instructed. I thought about having some friends waiting around, in case of trouble, but I seem to have developed a bad case of paranoia. So here I am."

"Well! You were right. Marks was lying. He was the one who drugged me and, when I woke up, I was in the secure wing of the medical centre. Cord, the government is denying all that I

CHAPTER 7

told them about the outside. They tried to tell me that I had been brainwashed by outsiders so we would lower the Barrier and let them kill us all in our beds. They were going to give me new memories, so that I would tell everybody that the outside was populated by mutants and savages."

"So how did you get away?"

"I had help from some friends, people who believe me."

"Who?"

Before Mel could answer, Granville spoke from his hiding place. "It's better if you don't know, Captain Taylor."

Cord started and his hand drifted towards his stunner again.

"Please keep your hands where I can see them. There are three stunners aimed at you, not lethal, but they'll leave you with a nasty headache."

"Mel?" Cord looked around, trying to spot if he was being told the truth or not.

"Please, Cord, do as they say. I've put them at risk by insisting on meeting you like this. But I couldn't leave without telling why."

"Leave! Where are you going?"

"Back outside again. It's too dangerous here for me. Seventy percent of London and most of the government are xenophobic. They won't turn off the Barrier until they are sure there are no dangers outside. The only way they can be sure of that is if they can subdue and rule the population outside. Until then, they are going to feed stories of mutants and savages to Londoners. I won't be part of that deception."

Cord relaxed, although his eyes kept darting back and forth, looking for Granville's companions. "What about the president. Surely he wouldn't condone these lies?"

"I had hoped he wouldn't, but he seems to be as paranoid as the rest of them. He may even have had my father killed, if he found out that he wasn't for the Isolationists."

Mel's head went down and Cord placed an arm around her shoulders. He could feel that she was deeply disappointed about what she had learned about the man she considered family. "Where will you go?"

"I plan to make my way to Exeter. I told you that there seems to be some sort of government setting up there. I want to warn them of what's going on in London and see what they want to do about it."

Cord fell silent as he mulled over what he had been told. Finally, when he spoke, Mel's heart leapt, as he said the words she had hoped he would say. "I want to come with you."

She moved in closer and kissed him. "Thanks, I hoped you would say that. But you should know that it will be hard going at first. We will have to go on foot until we can get to the Ferguson place, where, hopefully, we can borrow some horses."

"Horses! Well, I was a great fan of westerns when I was a child. It didn't look that hard to ride."

Granville interrupted from his hiding place. "I think it would be best for all concerned if Captain Taylor left with you, Mel. If he stays here, I think he could be in some danger. I have got some equipment together for you and you can leave tonight, through one of the old sewers we have reopened."

CHAPTER 7

Cord stood up, holding Mel's hand tightly. "If you can give me twenty-four hours, I think I should be able to get a ground car. It will make travelling much easier."

"Won't it be missed?" Granville asked.

"Of course, but then, so shall I."

Mel squeezed Cord's hand. "Cord has a point; I'm not sure how much rough ground we will have to cover, or if the car will be up to it. How far will they go on one tank of fuel?"

"The new fuel cells last ten hours before they need refuelling."

Granville remained silent as he thought over this change in his plans. "Will you be able to open a gate?" he asked.

"If there are no patrols due to leave, then there is only a minimum guard of two. It's a boring duty, so it's normally assigned to new recruits. They won't be surprised to see an officer dropping in unannounced. If I tell the officer on the night shift that I want to do the first check, he won't complain about having a late start. If we secure them at the start of the shift, then we'll have four hours before they are checked again."

"Do you think that security forces will follow you?"

"They will send out a patrol, but it will take time to organise, at least another two hours. I don't know how far they will be willing to go; either way, we will have a big head start."

"I must admit I like this idea," Granville stated. "With a ground car and a security captain missing, it will throw even more confusion into the Isolationists. If you are sure you can pull it off." Cord said he was.

"Then, which gate and what time?"

"The South Gate at just after midnight. I'll be in the gate control booth. If I've been successful then the lights will be off. You'll be able to see that."

"Very well, then. Tomorrow night. Mel, you come back with me for now. Captain Taylor, I suggest you carry out your duties as normal. Don't forget to contact the medical centre for an update on Mel's condition. We will meet you at the South Gate at midnight."

Mel moved into Cord's arms and kissed him soundly. "I knew you wouldn't be fooled by the government's lies. I can't wait to show you the real outside; you'll soon see that it's nothing like the paranoids would have everyone believe."

Cord returned her kiss and backed away towards the statue. Mel went back to her uncle and began to follow him back to her hideout.

Mel spent the next day with her excitement rising. She was going back on the road again, this time prepared and with a man she loved.

Finally, the clock ticked away and Granville returned to escort her to the South Gate. They arrived just after midnight, and the lights in the control booth were off. Mel approached the control area on her own, and Cord came out to meet her. Inside, two troopers lay on the floor. Cord kissed her and sat down at a computer terminal and began to type in his access code and the command for the gate to open.

Mel watched as a section of Barrier dissolved in front of her eyes.

Cord swivelled around in his chair and looked at her.

CHAPTER 7

"Ready to go?"

Mel nodded and Cord led her to the ground car waiting nearby. With its lights blazing, they slowly moved out of the gate and towards the open area. Moving slowly and carefully, they reached the hill at Richmond after a couple of hours driving. Mel directed Cord to the old mansion house and they stopped to await the dawn. Cord was concerned that running with the lights on would exhaust the fuel cell too quickly and, as it was dangerous to move without light, he thought that it would be better to wait for daybreak.

Mel sat on the ground watching as dawn broke over London. A feeling of sadness washed over her as she wondered how long it would be before she saw her home again.

Cord called to her and, as she climbed into the ground car, her spirits lifted as she thought of seeing more of the country she had only recently found out existed. Mel wondered what awaited them in Exeter. Would they be welcomed with open arms, or, as she was now developing a healthy streak of cynicism, would they be viewed with suspicion?

Cord looked at her and smiled as if he sensed her worries. "Let's just take each place as we come to it. We'll be fine."

As Cord began to drive away from London, Mel gripped his hand and smiled back. Into the unknown, with Cord, that was want she wanted. That was what she had.

End Book One

Lightning Source UK Ltd.
Milton Keynes UK
16 December 2009

147425UK00001BA/21/P